HAVOC

ROGUES OF THE ZATHARI
BOOK 1

STELLA FROST

ISBN: *978-1-944142-46-9*

Cover Design by Natasha Snow Designs

Editing by Hart to Heart Edits

Formatting by Stella Frost

READER NOTE

Dearest readers—I believe that reading should be enlightening, exciting, but above all else, fun. If you would like a detailed list of tropes and topics in this book, please visit my website at stel lafrost.me and visit the Books menu.

Take care and enjoy!

PROLOGUE

HUMANITY ONCE GAZED UP AT THE STARS WITH WONDER AND curiosity. But in the year 2107, we looked to the stars in terror and anguish. When the great gleaming warships of the Aengra Dominion arrived in our galaxy, we assumed the worst. And when their first ships arrived on Earth's surface, their diplomats laid claim to the Earth as property of the mighty Aengra Dominion.

Humanity did not take kindly to being claimed, and they made a brief and ill-advised attempt at rousting the Dominion. Armed with superior weaponry and numbers, the Dominion fought back to protect their ships. A short, but brutal war left much of the Earth in ruins, with most of the damage wrought by humanity's inelegant and cataclysmic weapons. The planet was already in a downward spiral due to escalating temperatures and disease, and the arrival of the Aengra only hastened along its slow demise.

As an act of peace, the Dominion spent another ten years on

the Earth's surface, using their advanced technology to rebuild several large cities. They also established the colony of New Terra in the distant Imrathi Belt, the galaxy at the center of their mighty empire. Millions of settlers accepted the rule of the Dominion and left Earth for a better life, leaving their home planet to those who were deemed unfit to settle the new colony.

Now, in the year 2198, Earth is a backwater planet in a distant galaxy. The intergalactic corporation Ilmarinen Interstellar constructed an interstellar jump gate near Mars, making Earth an occasional stop for travelers in search of fuel or a visit to the quaint, decaying planet. The Dominion maintains a loose grip on Earth through their embassy that sends fewer and fewer colonists each year to New Terra. Much of Earth belongs to the lawless criminals and corrupt politicians scrambling for the scraps that remain. It is a place where dirty deals are made and the law is little more than words on paper.

Many unfortunate enough to be born on Earth since the great migration still look to the stars, dreaming of what lies beyond those great gleaming gates.

Some are fortunate enough to find out.

CHAPTER 1

Vani

HERE IN THE DUSTY RUIN OF THE PROSPECTS—AN IRONIC NAME given that there were none for girls like me—every day was an echo of the one before. Show up for work. Let a bunch of big men with little boy's brains and short tempers grab my ass. Smile, like I didn't fantasize about killing them every day of my life. Pour drinks, keep the tips coming, and hope that Dinesso and his boys got too drunk to get it up before I escape to my apartment.

But today was different. Today, I had my sights on an alien smuggler, and if he was lucky, I was going to fuck his brains out. I hadn't decided yet if that made today a great day or an exceptionally bad one, but either way, it was something different.

My employer, Robehr Allid Dinesso, was one of the reigning crime bosses of the Prospects. He had been the thundercloud looming over my life since I was old enough to look up and wonder where the sun had gone. And he never let me forget who paid the bills, who kept me safe, or who put food in my mouth—when he wasn't putting a cock in it.

On Dinesso's dime, I had a tiny apartment just across the alley from the Dahlia, the club where I spent most of my waking hours. My roommate and adopted sister, Naela, was hard at work already. I'd put in an early shift to prep the bar, then headed home to freshen up for my special assignment. A lukewarm shower and a good scrub had me nice and clean. I took a little extra care with my nether regions considering they were about to be wielded like an illegal firearm.

I dressed in the criminally skimpy uniform of the Dahlia, then headed back to work. There, in the windowless club, it was eternally five past midnight. At four thirty in the afternoon, the drunks of the Prospects were turning up to buy watered-down booze and watch a barely eighteen-year-old girl writhe on stage. Amira was already up, her petite body covered only in a thin lattice of silver strands and a whole heap of glitter that was going to be showing up in every nook and cranny she had for months.

Amira had joined our happy little family a few months ago, fresh-faced and completely oblivious. I'd tried to persuade her to leave before she got in too deep. Like Naela, she'd come off the streets after aging out of the church's charity home. Nesso sure knew how to pick them. Pretty, hungry, and desperate enough to not ask too many questions. The Prospects were a hard place to live, especially for a cute little blonde with big eyes and a sugary sweet voice. I'd tried to convince her to go back to the church to join the sisterhood, but she'd said praying all day wasn't for her. Her baby face went sheet-white when I asked her if getting gang-banged was more to her liking, but she'd stuck her chin out and said she was tough.

No one was that tough. They were going to destroy her, and it was just a matter of *when*, not *if*. The protection of wolves came with its own bloody cost. The only reason they hadn't touched her yet was because Dinesso was working out how to make the most money off of her. She'd already had a rude awakening when she came off the stage for the first time, delighted with that wrinkled fistful of cash. It was probably more money than she'd ever seen, and every bit of it disappeared into Luka's sweaty fist. The look of shock on her face would have been funny if it wasn't so predictably heartbreaking. No one could say I didn't try to warn her.

I headed for the back of the club and up the stairs to Dinesso's office. The dim lights and dark wooden paneling made it feel like a descent into purgatory. Though I tried to keep calm, my legs were rubbery. There was no telling what awaited me. Sometimes there was a glass of wine and a halfway civilized conversation before he glanced down at his crotch in silent command. And sometimes, he'd been wronged by some asshole amongst this city of assholes, and he vented his anger on me as if I was the one who'd crossed him. It was a coin toss, but I always lost.

That's just how it is, angel, my mother used to say. *Could be worse.*

Could be a whole lot better, too. Theoretically, at least. The few times I'd tried to make it better for myself had only sent me further into the muck. At this point, I had just accepted my lot.

Rico stood at the door, big arms bulging through his too-small shirt. Judging by the way his honey-brown eyes raked over me, I'd done a decent job with my alien trap. Then again, he would probably fuck a dish of chili in a curved bowl, so that wasn't saying much. He rapped on the door, then pushed it open. "Boss is waitin' for you."

Great.

I took a few tentative steps into the well-furnished office. Not a single speck of dust dared invade his impeccably polished space. Dinesso sat at his desk, swiping idly at a dizzying expanse of spreadsheets on his computer. His salt-and-pepper hair was neatly combed back from his smooth, tanned skin. A single signet ring gleamed on his left hand. As I entered, he swiped and closed the file.

His dark, sharklike eyes swept over me. "Take your hair down," he ordered. It had taken me half an hour to braid the little headband over my brow and tame the rest into a high ponytail. It was pretty, and I liked it. Maintaining a neutral expression, I carefully removed the elastic and shook out my ponytail.

"Braid, too?" I asked.

He seemed to ponder and then shook his head. "It's fine. You're prettier with it down."

Then he rose and crooked his finger. I approached, remaining still as he flipped up my short skirt and stuck his warm, dry hand into my panties, with as much ceremony as I would check the water temperature to wash dishes. His fingers brushed over my smooth mound. "Nice and smooth," he murmured. "Very nice."

"Just like you asked," I said quietly.

He glanced down. "Get the tits up. Make them look bigger."

I frowned at my breasts, which were already strapped in like they were being launched into orbit. "Much further, and they're going to be on my chin."

He looked unamused, and I calmly adjusted my bra, tightening it within an inch of its life until my small breasts were absolutely spitting in the face of gravity. If the wind blew wrong, there would be nipples everywhere.

"You look good," he said. It wasn't a compliment but a simple assessment of my usefulness for a task. He gestured to his lips. "Get something on there."

His hungry eyes followed the motion of my hand as I painted my lips crimson. He chose the color because he liked the way it looked when it was smeared on his dick. When I was done, he tilted his head slightly toward the dark leather chair. As I sat, he leaned against the desk, looming over me. I sat ramrod straight, nerves still fluttering through me. "The Zathari just left Henri Agalov's place. Henri says he's alone, packing at least one gun."

My stomach twisted in a knot. "And you're sure he's coming here?"

"I paid good money to have our specials advertised at the Anchor Drop, and Henri's crew talked up sweet little Amira," Dinesso said. "He's been before. If he doesn't bite, we'll go to Plan B."

"And what if he's not interested in what I'm selling?" I asked.

"Then I'll push Naela his way and see if she can do better," he said calmly. "And then Amira. Maybe two for one if he's stubborn." His eyes narrowed. "Convince him. I know you wouldn't insult me by doing any less than your best, would you?"

My mouth was dry. I had no idea what sort of man the mysterious Havoc was, nor what he would do to me or my sisters. About eight months ago, he'd come to the Dahlia after making another trade with Henri Agalov, an arms dealer who supplied half the guns to the city. Henri's boys had big mouths and tiny brains, and they'd talked all about Havoc's pretty little jump ship for days.

But I was more interested in the man himself. Earth was hardly a hotspot for the civilized races of the universe, and the Prospects were not on anyone's list of must-see tourist locations. The people who passed through, particularly in the Dahlia, were here to do illegal business without being bothered by the authorities.

Now and again, I saw Vaera officials passing through on a perfunctory sweep of the area, as if to remind us that Earth was still technically under Dominion rule. Their berry-red skin and gracefully pointed ears were enchanting. Henri Agalov even had a couple of Proxilar on his crew, with that strange alligator skin stretched over massive frames.

But Havoc was something altogether different. When he walked into the bar, I was so entranced that I confused my gin and vodka and made one of my regulars throw a glass at me.

At six and a half feet tall, he was significantly bigger than Dinesso's biggest enforcer, Rico. Curled horns framed his face, sculpted from dark gray that reminded me of stone. And his eyes were like nothing I'd ever seen, a shade of violet that I thought existed only in pictures of flowers that were long dead on this desolate rock. Those eyes had swept the bar, landed on me for a split second and then moved on like he hadn't seen me. He took a private booth in the corner, ignored the half-naked woman on stage, and drank alone for an hour. Eventually, he joined a card game, won a little, and lost a little more.

For two hours, I'd poured his drinks, even sending him a few freebies, and then goddamned Luka grabbed me for a handy in his office. When I came back from washing my hands with sandpaper and battery acid, the Zathari was gone, and there was a generous tip for me at the bar.

That was the last of him, I'd thought. That beautiful glimpse that came and went, and I'd missed my chance.

Until today, at least. I never should have told Dinesso about him, but it slipped right out when he told me about Henri's unusual customer with the jump ship.

He was here.

That greedy look had flicked through Dinesso's eyes, and I knew I'd made a terrible mistake even then.

I wanted to meet Havoc, but not like this. I wanted to find out what those beautiful eyes had seen. I wanted to know where he went when he wasn't on this dusty rock. Even if it was only for a minute, I wanted to brush up against something new and exciting, to imagine what life could be like anywhere but here.

I fiddled with the hem of my skirt. "Why don't you just jump him at the hangar?"

"He's docked at the Anchor Drop," Dinesso said. "And Tima won't take a bribe to drop her security. I'm not risking my men ending up like the Limbo Boys."

"But you'll risk me," I said, before I could stop myself. As if I was going to fare better than a violent gang. My neck would snap just as easily as theirs did.

His large hand closed around my jaw, squeezing tight. The cold band of his ring bit into my jaw as he glared down at me. Time crawled by as I contemplated whether I was going to do this job with a broken nose. "If you don't feel up to it, I'll offer him Amira. Would you prefer that?"

I shook my head rapidly.

"You have plenty of practice to handle him. With you on your knees, he'll be more concerned with his cock than his ship," he said. Then he released me, and with a frighteningly delicate touch, he gently fixed my hair around my face.

Could have been worse.

No one told Nesso no. Or rather, no one told Nesso no more than once. I'd learned that very young, although it took some painful lessons for it to sink in. I'd given up on telling him no, since he would take what he wanted anyway. And once Naela came along, I'd started saying *yes* even when I wanted to scream *no*. Over the years, Nesso had scraped me out and taken whatever tiny seeds of good were once in me, but Naela was still kind and generous. Standing in her way meant that maybe she'd stand a chance, that maybe she could pull together a life if she ever got out of here.

Dinesso took a slip of paper from his desk and handed it to me. "I'll have a crew waiting out in the desert to deal with him. You drug him and override the ship. Do you need a review?"

I shook my head. "I got it." Most small civilian ships were entirely run by artificial intelligence, so we'd acquired manuals for the most popular AI models to learn the commands. I didn't have to know how to fly; I just had to know the magic word to get the ship to fly herself.

"That's right," he said, sparing an indulgent smile. "You're my clever girl, aren't you?"

My stomach was a roiling knot. "Yes," I said, smiling a little. I looked down at the slip of paper. The string of numbers had to be coordinates. "Are you going to kill him?"

"Depends on him," Dinesso said. His eyes drifted down. "Convince him to play nice, and I might let him live. I can find a use for a horned brute around here. We've got the big fights coming up. A Zathari savage would fill the seats and rake in bets."

I didn't want Havoc here any more than I wanted Naela or Amira here. They had gotten snared and dragged slowly into this pit. I was born here, and I was where I belonged. But not him. Fucking Dinesso ruined everything he touched.

And it didn't matter, because I was going to do it, because no one told Nesso no. I wished it could be another way, but if it came down to protecting my sisters or protecting a Zathari man I'd never met, it was no question at all.

Dinesso slid his hand up my thigh, cupping my pussy. "Good work gets rewarded, Vani," he said in my ear. His reward would be thirty seconds of half-assed foreplay and a glass of wine to dull the edges of reality. Not the motivation he thought it was. "I know you'll make me proud. Won't you?"

I stared up at him, hoping he couldn't hear the abject hatred roaring in my skull. "I will."

CHAPTER 2

Havoc

Earth was a shithole, and considering I spent a good chunk of my life on a desolate planet nicknamed the Devil's Asshole by its denizens, that was saying something. Thankfully, my brief stay was nearly over. Soon I'd be on my way to better places where civilization wasn't actively regressing.

It was hardly the fault of the Terrans. Sure, they'd plundered and ravaged their planet of resources until it was a dry, scorched rock, but far more advanced civilizations had done the same before fucking off to the next untouched planet. Unfortunately for Earth, they hadn't figured out interstellar travel before the Aengra Dominion made it to their sleepy little galaxy. The arrival of a far more powerful force had hastened along Earth's decline, leaving it in ruins.

Typical fucking Aengra.

Sweat trickled down my back as I hauled the last of the

refrigerated cases into the cargo hold. The weaselly arms dealer in the ill-fitting suit had offered to loan me his crew for a modest fee, but there was no way in hell I was letting them anywhere near my beloved Nomad. Hustling crates of liquor and handguns was easy compared to mining amidst caustic fumes in trembling tunnels a mile deep.

Once I strapped in the last case, I showered quickly and changed into a clean shirt. On my way down the boarding ramp, I ordered the ship's AI, Diana, to enact her tightest protocols. If someone came within twenty feet of the Nomad, I'd get an alert, and they'd get a single warning shot before the ship electrocuted them.

If I was a machine like some of my brothers, I would have climbed right back into the cockpit and launched into orbit. But my scheduled jump wasn't for another eighteen hours. What was the point of floating through space alone for half a day, with nothing other than my hand and a polite but disembodied AI to keep me company? Diana was infinitely helpful, but I was more interested in an eager and willing Terran girl who wanted to walk on the wild side.

From previous trips to Terra, I knew I'd fill most of my appetites at the Dahlia, a halfway decent club near the hangar. By Earth standards, the Prospects was a bustling hub that had grown up around an ancient spaceport. Here, the drug lords, pimps, and mobsters fancied themselves big men with bigger reputations, but this was a playground compared to some of the nastier places I'd been. I knew men—and women—who would have crushed them on their way to breakfast and forgotten about them by lunch.

The Nomad was parked safely at the Anchor Drop, one of

the only reputable hangars in the Prospects. My ship had her own private room with a top-of-the-line security system. Upon arrival, I'd chosen an eight-digit code to lock her in. Even the hangar's owners couldn't get in to ogle her and make plans for her parts. Only the best for my best girl.

Outside the hangar, I caught an auto-shuttle headed into the city. Inside the open-top hovercraft, the cracked leather seats were stained with decades of wear and tear. Ghosts of graffiti crawled over the scratched metal surfaces.

Following its electric track laid into the concrete, the shuttle swung wide to turn onto a wider main road lined with bars and crowded storefronts. Shuttles trundled along the other side, while passenger vehicles and motorbikes streamed down the center of the street. Sputtering engines and shouting street hawkers filled the evening with noise. The Prospects smelled of exhaust, with an ever-present dust cloud that obscured visibility.

Deeper into the entertainment district, things were marginally cleaner, as if someone made an effort, once in a fortnight, to clean the windows and sweep the sidewalks.

As I rode, I slid a thin puck of glass with a burner chip over the surface of my watch. Most places here in the Prospects still operated on cash instead of Dominion Crescents, but I kept a shell account at the ready, just in case.

Amidst skyscrapers bristling with broken glass and graffiti, the Dahlia was a wilted flower in a barren junkyard. Its strange, curved roof reminded me a bit of the temples on Zaalbara, though there were certainly no holy women inside. Neon red lights spelled out *Dahlia* in looping Aengran script on the roof.

This place paled in comparison to the lush decadence of Niraj, but by Earth standards, this was high-brow.

Two scantily-clad human women flanked the tinted glass doors, red lips wide and smiling as I approached. "Good evening, sir," they said in unison. "Welcome to the Dahlia."

I raised an eyebrow. "Ladies." The one on the right gaped at me, her lips parting as her gaze drifted up. It was the horns. In every galaxy, women loved the horns. Call it the one gift our gods had ever given us.

A vidscreen next to the door advertised an upcoming fight series, featuring a Proxilar champion and a slew of human fighters. The tickets were cheap, but I'd bet that the showrunner was raking in cash on bets.

Walking into the Dahlia was an all-out assault on the senses. Cheap booze and cigar smoke filled the air, while distorted music boomed through over-stressed speakers. Tantalizing red lights swirled over a long stage, where a petite woman writhed for a crowd of leering men. Eyes followed me as I slid through the crowd, headed for a table in a corner. I planted myself there, back pressed into the wood where I could see the door.

Wearing only an ensemble of thin silver ribbons, the blonde girl dancing on stage had a great body. Her glossed-pink smile looked real enough, but when she spun around to give her audience a view of her barely covered ass, she let the expression drop for a split second, her chest heaving in a soft sigh of exhaustion.

But when she tossed her golden hair and looked over her shoulder, her game face was back on. She strutted down the narrow stage to a chorus of raucous shouts. Despite their leers and overstated promises of what they had in their pants, I'd bet my ship that not one of them could have pleased the girl if she came down off the stage and offered herself to them.

I raised my hand to flag a waitress and caught a thin blonde staring at me with obvious hunger in her glassy eyes. Even in the low light, I could see the wormy blue veins on her arms, a sure sign that she was using Blitz, the drug of choice in this part of Terra. She'd probably suck my dick here in front of the entire bar, but she might just as easily bite it off. No thanks.

When I tore my gaze from the predator, I caught a glimpse of a dark-haired beauty behind the bar. She grabbed a bottle from the top shelf, deftly balanced two glasses in one hand, and headed for me.

Her long legs were tan and muscular like the trained dancers of Al D'Omethe. I liked the thought of them wrapped around me. I followed the legs up to a black skirt that was so short it was somehow more revealing than if she'd foregone the garment entirely. Narrow waist, nice chest, and an absolutely wicked smirk that said she knew I'd just inspected her and didn't particularly mind.

The spicy, floral scent of her perfume hit me before she got to the table. It was a little heavy for my tastes, but an improvement over the ever-present stink of the Prospects. She plunked the glasses onto the nicked wood table in front of me. Her breasts nearly spilled onto the table as she poured a finger of whiskey into one glass and said, "Someone bought you a drink."

She spoke Modern Aengran, so I raised one hand to my ear and turned off my translator. I much preferred a conversation without the translators.

"Who's that?" I asked. When I responded in the same language, she smiled and turned off her own translator.

"Me," she replied, pouring one for herself as she sat across from me. She clinked the glass against mine and sipped it. Up close, I could see a constellation of dark freckles across her nose and cheeks. Her thick dark hair was neatly braided across her head like a crown, leaving long waves loose over her shoulders.

I was intrigued. Her outfit matched the girls outside, so she was an employee. But that didn't mean she wasn't up for a little fun off the clock. "Who says I want a drink?" I said, ignoring the drink.

"You came into the Dahlia for one of three things. Booze, entertainment, or pussy," she said. "And you haven't looked at the stage, so that narrows things down."

"And which of the three are you providing?"

She nudged the glass toward me. "I think that's obvious. The real question is, which one you want next," she said, a wicked smile on her red-painted lips. Gods of the void, what a mouth.

I smirked and took a drink of the whiskey, savoring the fiery burn. It wasn't the battery acid I expected from this place. It certainly wasn't as good as the Xhaarosian whiskey I'd smuggled a few months back, but considering it was free and being poured by a gorgeous woman, I couldn't complain. "Haven't decided yet."

She was probably one of their working girls trying to get me on the hook for some easy cash. A little liquor to loosen my wallet was a shrewd business move. But her boldness was refreshing. And with those full round lips, I was already imagining what she could do with my cock. No harm in playing along.

"What's your name?" she asked.

"I don't have one," I replied.

Her red lips pursed. "Everyone has a name."

I had more than a few names, but none of them belonged in the mouth of someone I didn't know or trust. I glanced at the bottle of whiskey, which had a hand-written label with *07* on it. On Earth, it could have meant anything from *bottled seven years ago* to *seven percent goat piss.* "Seven."

"That's not a name, it's a number," she said with a derisive laugh.

"I'm Zathari," I said. "In my language, it means one of great honor."

"Bullshit."

"Do you speak old Zathari?" I said. "It's an insult to mock someone's name."

There was a split second of panic on her face. I maintained a stony expression long enough to make her back away just an inch. Then I grinned. Her fearful expression melted into a magnetic smile that lit up her entire face, glowing across her cheeks and creasing around her eyes. "You're screwing with me."

"Maybe," I replied. "Pour me another."

She tipped up the bottle, filling the small glass nearly to the top. "I've never met a Zathari before."

"Now you have. Lucky you," I said, draining half the glass. "What's your name?"

"Vani," she said.

"Pretty name," I said. "Like you. What does it mean?"

"I don't know," she said. "I didn't pick it out."

I laughed. Sexy and witty. There were worse ways to kill a few hours on Terra. "Vani, so far, you're two for three. You're entertaining me, and the booze isn't the worst I've ever had. Do you want to make it three?"

"Are you paying?" she said.

"I don't pay for sex," I said.

She didn't get up immediately. Instead, she folded her arms and leaned forward, pushing up her breasts. It was a calculated move, one she'd probably done a thousand times. Her breasts were perfectly nice, but I'd seen enough of them that I wasn't going to lose my senses at a couple inches of cleavage. "What's in it for me?"

"Me," I replied. "If you've never met a Zathari, then you've never fucked one either, have you?" Without breaking her gaze, I slid my foot between her calves, hooked the bar stool, and pulled her closer to me. I reached under the table and ran one hand up her thigh. She was either going to storm off or lean in. Her cocky bluster dissolved into a flicker of fear, and then a subtle shift into curiosity as I slid my hand higher. Gods, she felt good, all warm and pliable under my fingers. Holding her bright green gaze, I inched upward until I felt the soft lace of her panties at my fingertips. I let one finger graze there, just barely feathering across her lower lips. Her lashes fluttered, and her thighs clamped tight on my hand. Now I had her. "I'm off this rock in a few hours. Want to see if I can make you forget your own name before then? Might be six months before another Zathari comes your way, and most of them aren't as charming as me."

Her eyebrow arched in a delightful expression. "Meet me outside in ten while I pay your bill, Mr. Seven."

CHAPTER 3

Vani

MY MISSION WAS A GO. I FLASHED MY SWEETEST SMILE AT THE huge Zathari male as he grabbed his coat and headed for the door of the Dahlia. His eyes glinted, flicking over me one last time before he walked out. My heart was already pounding, and I could still feel the echo of him touching my thigh, fingers grazing my sex. Plenty of men had groped me, but I'd never wanted one of them to grab on and never let go, until this one.

"Focus," I muttered.

When the tinted glass doors closed behind him, I grabbed the glasses and returned the whiskey to the bar. With adrenaline coursing through me, I entered my code to the back hallway. In one of the back offices, Dinesso's meat-slab of a flunky was watching the security feeds. A half-empty bottle of vodka stood sentry at the corner of his desk.

"Luka," I snapped. His glassy eyes drifted to me. "I've got the Zathari on the hook. I need the stuff."

Rolling his chair across the office, he opened a stainless steel cooler and took out three syringes already loaded with a clear amber liquid. I stuffed two into the tiny purse over my shoulder, and tucked the other between my breasts.

As I turned to leave, Luka grabbed a handful of my ass with his warm, sweaty hands. He pulled me back and rubbed his crotch against me. "Want me to warm you up for him?"

I would rather fuck a cactus. "Wouldn't want to keep him waiting," I said sweetly, trying not to shudder at the slug trail of Luka's filth on my skin.

When I emerged from Luka's office, I stopped dead in my tracks. Dinesso was making a rare appearance out of his office, dark eyes fixed on me. "It's time?" he asked.

"Yes," I said. "He's buying what I'm selling."

He smiled, but it was the unsettling grin of a predator on the hunt. "Bring me that ship, Vani. Don't disappoint me. You know what happens when you let me down."

For just a moment, I considered opening one of those syringes and stabbing him the throat. I could pull the gun from under his arm, blow his head off, and go on a rampage through this whole fucking place. The syringe in my bra felt like it was pulsing against my skin, screaming *do it do it do it.*

But I couldn't bring myself to move. Part of it was sheer terror of crossing Dinesso, and part of it was the aftermath if I failed. This place had a delicate and dangerous equilibrium, and the safest thing for everyone was to let it be.

When I hurried back to the bar, my friend Naela emerged,

wiping her hands on a dingy towel. Her brown eyes were wide and concerned. "Please be careful," she said. She rose on her toes to kiss my cheek. "Promise."

"I will," I replied, giving her a little hug. As she embraced me, I whispered into her ear. "Stay away from Luka tonight. He's drunk and handsy."

She sighed. "What else is new?"

"Get him an order of those greasy potatoes from across the street," I said. "The spice makes him drink more, and—"

"Whiskey dick," Naela finished. She smiled, a sad expression that didn't reach her warm eyes. "I'll put in the order. Maybe a slice of pie, to be safe."

"And make sure Amira goes the other way back to the apartment. If she gets in front of him..."

Naela glanced at our younger companion on the stage and frowned. "I got it."

My heart thumped as I headed for the doors. The plan was simple enough. Get in. Drop the Zathari. Take his ship. Hope he didn't kill me.

When I emerged from the Dahlia into the dusty twilight of the Prospects, a big hand fell on the small of my back. I glanced up and put on my dumbest *fuck me now* smile. Havoc didn't say a word as he hailed an auto-shuttle that glided down the main road. He occasionally glanced down at his watch, but the language was set to a flowing script that I couldn't read. Smart man.

It was a short ride from the Dahlia to the Anchor Drop, the biggest hangar in the Prospects. There inside hangar number eight, I saw her, all sleek curves covered in dark metal plating. The Nomad was the prettiest little ship I'd ever seen on this dust heap, complete with a momentum drive, messenger capabilities, and most importantly, completely clean papers. This ship could go anywhere that Ilmarinen Interstellar had planted one of those beautiful gleaming gates, like keyholes to another world.

You could escape on a ship like that. You could go anywhere in the universe and never look back.

A blue light on the ship's hull flicked on, casting a bright glow on the concrete below. For a moment, I had the insane fear that the ship sensed my dark intentions. But a door on the underside opened, lowering a boarding ramp with a quiet mechanical whir.

"Welcome back, Captain," a pleasant female voice greeted.

"Thank you, Diana," he replied cordially. "Switch languages to primary."

When he spoke again, he spoke in an oddly melodic language that seemed counter to his big, rough appearance. Like most of Dinesso's staff, I had a Babel implant hooked over my ear, loaded with most of the commonly spoken languages in Dominion space. I reached up to check the implant, even turning up the volume, but there was only dull static.

Clever bastard. He had a signal jammer. Dinesso had one for delicate business deals, making sure no one could listen in. My translator was nothing but an ugly earring until he turned it off.

All I could do was watch him while he talked to his ship in what I assumed was his native language. The towering Zathari male looked like a statue come to life. His pale gray tailored coat was simple, but I recognized the fine fabric and precise fit over his big shoulders and narrow waist; it had cost good money, and it looked damned good on him.

For twenty-eight years, I'd lived on Earth, which was scorched red and dust brown as far as the eye could see. Everything here was broken glass and splintered wood, but Havoc was one of the most beautiful things I'd ever seen. I really didn't want to kill him.

I pretended to look around in awestruck wonder as he led me onto the ship, looking for the cockpit. The Nomad's interior was sleek silver and gray all over, with brushed steel panels and a light blue glow on its displays. Just a glimpse of the ship made me wonder what it would be like to soar into the stars and never look back at this trash pile. I couldn't even dream of the things he'd seen from this ship.

The boarding ramp ended in a narrow hall. To my right, I saw at least three doors, one marked with *Caution: Engine Access* in bold red letters.

Before I could venture down the hall for a closer look at the other doors, a muscular arm looped around my waist and dragged me into a big, central area. With two big, semi-circular couches, it was the closest thing the spartan little ship had to a lounge. Between the two couches was an odd, spindly table with silver legs. On the opposite side from where we'd entered, I could see the lighted control panels of the cockpit.

"Is that the—" I gasped as he scooped me into his lap. There was no conversation, just a hungry mouth on mine. His big hands slid over my breasts, and I nearly froze in panic. If he got too eager, I'd lose my needle.

I let out a breathy moan and grabbed his broad wrists, sliding his hands down until he grabbed my ass instead. He didn't seem to mind the redirection, squeezing hard as he pulled me closer. His tongue speared into my mouth, and I opened for him, shocked at how my body flared to life. I didn't have to tap into my limited acting skills to pretend I was enjoying myself.

My body molded to his, and he slid one hand under my skirt to cup my pussy, the pads of his fingers stroking in tiny circles. I gasped, widening my legs for him as he smiled against my mouth. "Not wasting any time," I teased.

"Told you I only had a few hours," he growled. Without breaking eye contact, he ripped my lace panties in half and tossed them aside.

"Hey," I complained. "Those were nice."

He held my chin firmly, giving me a dangerous look. "I was going to keep them anyway." He caressed me slowly, that big hand just pressing and circling lightly. The warmth of his touch was intoxicating, and I was soaked already. One finger curled slightly to tease through my lips.

Focus, I thought. If he kept doing that, I was going to forget why I was here. I grabbed his jaw, and he gave me a startled look. "Will you take me out of the city a little bit? I've never been in a ship like this."

His violet eyes narrowed. "Awfully trusting of you," he said. "I could be a bad man."

"I really hope you are," I teased, rolling my hips against him. "Please? I'd love to see the view from up high. If you're willing." I leaned in and whispered in his ear. "Then I could say I fucked a Zathari a mile above the ground. Two novel experiences for the price of one."

He smirked at me. "Efficient. Diana, take us five miles south of the city."

It was amazing how I could be proud of my own cleverness

and hate myself for manipulating him at the same time. This wouldn't be the first time I'd stolen from someone, but this was the first time I felt like shit for it.

"Yes, Captain. Alerting the hangar system," the AI answered.

There was a shuddering lurch, and the ship rose. I held Havoc's shoulders tight as gravity grabbed onto me. "First launch?" he said.

The rising sensation faded, and then I got the feeling that we were flying. The subtle thrumming reminded me of being in an auto-shuttle, nice and smooth. Then I glanced down at him. "Where were we?" I gently touched the hard, ridged surface of one horn, following the curve to the smooth tip.

He grabbed my wrist and plucked it away. "Don't touch," he said firmly.

I bit my lip. He didn't look angry, but this was clearly not up for debate. "Then where can I touch you?"

"Anywhere else you like," he said. One big hand tangled into my hair, bringing me in for another hungry kiss.

I couldn't remember the last time I'd kissed someone and enjoyed it. Most of the time, Dinesso and his men didn't bother, which was good, because I hated their faces. But this, I liked. I liked the decadent aggression of it, the way I could never quite get my balance and had to break away gasping before he dove in for more. Every stroke of his tongue ignited a little firebloom of heat between my legs, until my whole body was hot and tingling, desperate for more.

I pressed my hand to his chest, finding the firm outline of a holster over his shoulder. The feel of it startled me out of my daze, and I remembered why I was here. Still tangled in his kiss, I touched his cheeks, then traced down his throat.

Where was the weakness?

His skin didn't just look like smooth stone; it was nearly as tough. The Limbo Boys had learned that the hard way when they tried to shoot him and ended up with a bunch of useless slugs and broken spines. Dinesso said the only way to take him down was electricity or drugs, and drugs were easy to come by in the Dahlia. But I had to be clever about where I placed the needle. I'd only get one chance.

In his mouth? It was as warm and soft as any human's, but I'd never get a needle in there fast enough.

As I considered it, I slowly unbuttoned his shirt and found a deliciously chiseled chest. His skin looked like cold stone, but it was wonderfully warm. I kissed the center of his chest, then slid down slowly until I was on my knees in front of him.

"Not wasting any time," he teased, unbuckling his pants to unleash his cock.

"If I only have a few hours, I'm getting down to business," I replied. Hunger and fear twisted through me all at once at the sight of his thick shaft jutting up from a neatly groomed patch of dark hair. I could smell soap on him; so he was hot and thoughtful.

And gods, his cock was just as gorgeous as he was. There was a graceful curve to its crested head, which was darker gray than the rest of his skin. A thick vein curved over a bulge in his shaft, which tapered again before swelling to a larger bulge. The mere thought of what that would feel like inside me sent a nervous flutter through me. I wanted to know so badly I nearly forgot why I was there.

"You know, where I come from, we believe in taking care of our women first," he said, propping one hand behind his head.

It was tempting as hell to let him have his way. A little cultural exchange, as it were. But I was afraid if I went down that route, I'd forget why I was here, and Dinesso would make me regret it if I botched this job because I wanted to get off on the alien's absolutely stunning cock.

"You're on Earth, now," I said. "Do you mind?"

"Can't argue with the locals," he said. "Just this once."

He gazed down at me, heavy-lidded and smiling as I darted my tongue out and flicked it against his head. There was a strange sweetness to him that made me want more. I slid closer, running my hands up his thighs to meet at his root as I took him into my mouth. Relaxing my jaw, I braced myself for him to ram himself down my throat.

Back when she was still new and naive, Naela had fretted that Dinesso's men were rough, that they pulled her hair and made her gag. Sweet as she was, she'd politely asked Luka to be more careful. In return, he'd been so vicious that she could barely talk for two days. She didn't understand that suffering and humiliation was the point for them.

"Fuck, that's good. Just like that," he groaned. His fingers combed through my hair, but he didn't grab a handful and yank me onto him like I expected. His fingers curled and released along my temple, almost like he was petting me. The sensation sent a shiver down my spine and made me want to please him even more.

I did my best to occupy him with my mouth while my hands explored, cupping his heavy sack, then gripping him at the root. That lovely bulge pulsed in my grasp, like he was wearing his heart on his cock. It was delightfully warm, with a velvety soft texture.

Aha.

It seemed unsporting, but it seemed that the great stone statue had soft bits just like human males. I prepared to draw the needle from between my breasts, but he let out a soft sigh that was oddly sweet. I stole a look up and saw him smiling, head laid back on the couch with his eyes closed.

It was bad enough that I was going to steal his ship. The least I could do was let him go out happy. And to tell the truth, I was starting to enjoy myself. His powerful thighs clenched and shifted under my hand, his hips rising and falling ever so slightly to meet my mouth.

My jaw ached with the effort of taking him in, but I closed my eyes and gave him my best. Something ignited between my thighs. Like a lovesick idiot, I was thinking about what it would be like if this was real. I wondered what it would be like to climb onto him and ride him into sweet oblivion. A throaty growl escaped me as I withdrew, catching my breath as I stroked him intently.

"Vani, look at me," he said sharply. I looked up at him, breathing hard. He was alert now, brilliant eyes fixed on me. "I'm sorry for what I'm going to do to you."

I froze. "What?" Had he read my thoughts somehow?

"When you're done with me, I'm going to show you what Zathari men do with their tongues," he said. "And you'll never be satisfied with a human man again." I just gaped at him as heat twisted through me, slicking my thighs.

Then his violet eyes flicked down in a silent command, and I practically choked myself in my effort to swallow him down again. His big hand rested atop my head, fingers idly circling as I worked him. That was one hell of a promise.

But I wasn't here to get laid, no matter how good it sounded. The regret of missing out on a good fuck with Havoc was more tolerable than the threat of what Dinesso would do to me if I failed.

With the needle concealed in my free hand, I withdrew slightly to finish him off. He let out a noisy groan as he came, spurting sweet warmth over my tongue. The feeling of it sent a surge of heat prickling down my spine. I swallowed, still gently caressing him as I slid the needle into the bulge at his root. He let out a clipped cry and shoved me away, staring in horror at me, then down at his crotch. "What the fuck did you do?"

The drugs were as fast-acting as Luka promised, and his violet eyes were already going heavy. "I'm sorry," I murmured.

"Bitch," he groaned. He tried to lunge for me, but his feet tangled, and he hit the ground face first.

Despite the heavy fall, he managed to crawl toward me. I fumbled another syringe out of my purse and straddled him. As his mouth opened to swear at me, I stuck the other needle into the soft gray-purple inside his cheek and emptied the syringe. He didn't even manage to smack my hand away before his head hit the floor with a thump.

I waited. "Havoc?"

No answer. I nudged him, then put my fingers to his throat. Steady pulse. Good.

"Diana?" I said.

"Please identify," the ship said.

"I'm the captain's guest," I said. "He has a medical emergency and cannot command the ship. Please override commands temporarily."

Please work.

"Temporary override granted for thirty minutes. Activate medical probe immediately for first aid administration." I let out a sigh of relief.

"Will do, Diana," I said. Then I kicked off my shoes and got to work at ruining Havoc's life.

CHAPTER 4

Havoc

I OPENED MY SANDPAPER-DRY EYES TO FIND MYSELF LYING ON MY side, hands bound tight behind me. Cold, textured metal pressed into my cheek.

What the...

I squeezed my eyes shut, then opened them again. Still bound. My shoulders hurt like hell. Not a dream. Usually, I preferred to do the tying, and considering there was no scantily clad woman nearby, something was very wrong.

Where the hell was I? What did I do? There was a stinging ache in my cock and a foul taste in my mouth. My head pounded, reminding me of the trash liquor we used to brew in buckets on Kilaak. Good for a night, but hell for the day after.

Then it slammed into me like a fist to the gut. Vani, the little dust rat from Terra with those innocent eyes and the absolutely wicked mouth.

Red pulsed in my vision. I was going to fucking kill her. That little rat had—

She'd outplayed me. If Viper saw me like this, he'd laugh his ass off. Playing sweet and innocent, she'd asked me to launch and take her out of the city, getting the Nomad out of the secure hangar. So she could check off two fantasies at once and fuck me in the air, and in all my sex-starved brilliance, I was all too eager to comply.

And then the conniving little Terran sucked every functioning brain cell right out of my dick and drugged me while I was still coming up from the sweet haze. Two weeks of travel with no company but Diana had made me horny and stupid. I was lucky she hadn't just shot me in the face.

As the haze cleared, I felt a faint thrum beneath me. The Nomad was moving. All at once, my annoyance and begrudging respect turned to searing fury. I nearly shouted, to let her know that the wrath of the Zathari was coming for her, but I held my tongue. Let her think she'd won.

Craning my neck, I realized quickly I was in the galley with the door closed. My arms were bound to the metal leg of the dining table, which was bolted to the floor. Clever girl.

The motion of the ship was lateral, with none of the surging sensation of the thrusters driving us into the upper atmosphere. If I had to guess, Vani was moving the Nomad away from town. She was either meeting a buyer or finding a place to dump my body.

Fury surged through me in a hot wave from balls to brainstem, heating my skin. My brothers and I had climbed out of hell itself when we fought our way off of Kilaak. It took me years of dirty work and dirtier deals to get my hands on the

Nomad. This ship was mine, and I would kill her before I let her take it.

With a snarl, I looked around the small galley. Like most quick transport ships, the Nomad was streamlined and efficient. Everything was stored in neat drawers and latched boxes. Before heading to the Dahlia, I'd secured everything so I could make a quick jump, because I was a good captain and took care of my ship.

That meant everything sharp was safely put away where it belonged. Knives, guns, and more were stowed all over the ship, but I hadn't planned for being bound on the floor of the fucking kitchen. I always carried a stun gun, but she'd taken it away, leaving me with an empty holster.

Cunning and clever.

I twisted my wrists, sliding my tough skin against it enough to feel the wide wrappings. The bite of it felt like the strong nylon straps I used to secure my cargo. She'd been thorough and wrapped it several times up my forearms. I could appreciate her attention to detail while still pondering how I was going to exact vengeance.

Pushing off the cold floor, then the wall, I walked myself around the table. I nudged off one of my shoes and used my bare foot to pry open the latch on the bottom drawer of the cooking station. My foot cramped, but I gritted my teeth and finally got it open. Hooking the lip of the drawer, I maneuvered it open and pulled it out completely. The drawer tumbled out with a metallic clatter, spilling its contents onto the floor.

A few small jars of spices rolled across the floor, along with a stirring spoon and a small paring knife. I managed to grab the knife's handle with my toes and worked it closer. Over what felt like an hour, I slid it closer, then turned around the table again so I could grab it.

"Fucking dust rat," I muttered. The blade pricked against my skin, but good Zathari genes kept it from piercing. As I sawed through the nylon strap, I entertained myself by imagining my revenge. Maybe I wouldn't kill her right away. Maybe I'd strip her down and leave her in the front of the Dahlia to send a message.

The thought of tossing her out into the street was amusing enough, but I knew damn well that someone had probably put her up to it. Maybe Henri, the prick who'd sold me the cargo. He'd eye-fucked the Nomad up and down the last time I was here, which was why I had paid extra to store her safely at the Anchor Drop. Maybe one of the squirrelly little bastards watching the hangar had taken a bribe and alerted Henri, or one of any number of small-time scumbags on Terra. Why spend millions of credits to buy a ship when you could just steal one?

The strap finally split, and I grinned in victory. It took another minute of twisting to get myself untied, but I surged to my feet and dug through one of the overhead storage cabinets for a gun. I tucked it into my holster and listened at the door.

No voices, and we were still moving. Then it was just her and me. Good.

I quietly pressed a button to open the galley door. As soon as I did, Diana chirped, "Galley door opened."

Fuck.

There was a yelp and a clatter from the lounge. Centuries of primitive instinct took over, and I sprang into action, clearing the narrow hallway in one lunging stride. A blur of black and tan darted into the cockpit, while Vani's frantic voice yelled, "Diana, close cockpit door."

"Diana, override," I yelled. I barreled into the closed door hard enough to rattle my teeth. "Stop engines."

"Yes, Captain," Diana said politely. The subtle vibrations faded, and then there was a slight lurch and thump as the ship landed.

With adrenaline coursing through me, it took three attempts to enter my override code for the cockpit door. When I yanked it open, I found Vani pressed into the corner, emerald eyes wide and terrified. "What the fuck do you think you're doing?"

"I'm sorry," she pleaded, backing into the console. "They made me."

Over her shoulder, the dust-streaked cockpit windows were unshielded. The deep purple-black of night filled the sky. I'd been out for hours. I took another step toward her, and she shrank back. "Who put you up to this? Tell me, and I might let you live."

She lunged for me. As her arm swung around, I saw my own gun clutched in her small hand. Her expression faltered, and I could see her battling with the instinct to pull the trigger. That hesitation cost her dearly. I caught her arm easily and twisted it, forcing her to drop the gun.

Given her obvious disadvantage, I expected her to beg and grovel, but there was pure primal fury in her eyes as she launched herself off my chair. Strong legs hooked around my waist as she swiped at my face. I caught her other wrist just as her thumbnail scraped over my brow.

Squeezing hard, I brought both of her useless hands

together in front of her. Her pretty green eyes went wide with terror. "You fucking hellion," I marveled. "You were going to gouge my eye out."

"Let me go!" she screamed in my face, trying to pull away. If she wasn't aiming for my nose, I'd have been impressed when she swung her head back and tried to headbutt me. Too bad she broadcast the move, and I caught her ponytail as she wound up.

I twisted that thick sheaf of hair around my hand until her neck arched back to spare herself. She yelped and stared up at me in shock. Then I smiled, and her face went slack with horror. "Turnabout is fair play, Vani."

CHAPTER 5

Vani

THIS WAS LUKA'S FAULT. HE'D SWORN THAT THE SEDATIVES WERE enough to keep the Zathari down for at least a day, and they hadn't lasted even four hours. And now, I was pinned against a wall while he yanked off his belt and bound my wrists with it. I struggled fiercely, but it was like wrestling with a mountain.

With my hair still twisted around his fist, he hauled me back into the lounge and pinned me against the couch with one knee pressed against my legs. It was then, with what was probably three hundred pounds of pissed-off Zathari male holding me down, that I realized Luka was not the only one who had miscalculated.

"Let me go," I bellowed. Little hot needles pricked my scalp as he twisted my hair and shoved my face into the dense cushion.

"Stop shouting," he growled in my ear. "It's over. You lose, Vani."

My stomach twisted with dread. "Let me go," I said. "Please."

"I'm going to give you a choice," he said. I threw my head back, but I only managed to hit his shoulder. At that, he chuckled and looped one big arm around my shoulders, almost crushing me against him. "Do you feel better now?"

"Diana, the captain is—"

His big hand clapped over my mouth. "Stop that," he said sharply. "Under different circumstances, this feisty act would be a real turn-on. Too bad you had to try to steal from me."

I let out a muffled protest and tried to bite him, but his long fingers curled around my face and kept my mouth sealed. One firm yank and he'd snap my neck. Maybe that would be better than what Dinesso had in store if I failed.

"As I was saying, I'm going to give you a choice about what happens to you now," he said. "One, I dump you here in the desert to fend for yourself. I'll even give you some water. But I'm thinking you don't want to go back to your boss empty-handed, do you?"

I shook my head. He removed his hand. "I can't," I said quietly. "Just kill me." If I went back empty-handed, Dinesso would break me, and then he'd turn to Naela and Amira. But if they found my body, maybe that would make Havoc the target of his fury instead. And it was selfish, but I'd finally be free.

He laughed. "I'm not going to kill you. What a waste."

"Then just leave me," I said. My chest heaved. "Rough me up first. Make it look like I tried."

He was quiet for a while. "I've got a third option."

I remained silent.

"You want to get off of Earth?"

"Not with you," I said.

"Liar," he said with a laugh that rumbled against my spine. Despite everything, that sound sent a warm thrill through me. "You don't even believe that, so how the fuck do you expect me to?"

"You don't know me well enough to know I'm lying," I said.

In a split second, he spun me around, hands secured around my wrists. He loomed, those violet eyes just inches from mine. "Say it again. Tell me you don't want to leave here."

I stared at him, my lip trembling. His beautiful gaze demanded the truth, but I managed to whisper, "I don't want to."

"You're a bad fuckin' liar, Vani," he said, shaking his head. "Who put you up to stealing my ship?"

"Me," I lied. "I did it because I wanted to. I'm going to sell it."

He just grinned. "Was it the Limbo Boys?"

I shook my head.

"Henri Agalov? Tell me," he said, a dark edge in his voice. I just stared at him defiantly. Maybe in another universe, there was a version of me that would have snapped to attention at that firm command, but it didn't come close to sinking through the scar tissue Dinesso had left on every inch of my soul. "And if I send you back empty-handed, how bad are they going to hurt you for failing?" I tried to maintain my poker face, but I must have flinched, judging by his soft sigh. "You want to hear my third option?"

"Sure," I said.

"Terra is the asshole of this galaxy," he said. "I'll take you somewhere nicer and let you take your chances. Whatever you're afraid of won't find you there."

My heart thumped as something threatened to burst open in my chest. He couldn't be serious. "What's the catch?"

"I make things even," he said. "I punish you to clean the slate, and then I forget about all this mess."

My stomach twisted in a knot. "Punish me how?"

"However I see fit," he said. He smirked. "I'm not going to fuck you, if that's what you're worried about. You haven't earned it."

My mind was spinning at terminal velocity. If I stayed on his ship, I had a chance to steal it out from under him. I could still salvage this and maybe keep all of us alive. "Option three," I said meekly. "Take me with you."

He smiled faintly and roughly turned me over, pressing my chest to the couch. "You count," he said inexplicably. His big hand smacked my ass, jolting all the way up my spine.

I gasped in shock. "Stop!"

"You told me you accepted the third choice. I told you I was going to punish you," he said.

"This isn't fair," I protested. He was treating me like a toddler having a fit. The fact that his chosen punishment was so childish made it doubly humiliating.

He chuckled. "Vani, you put a needle in my balls, tied me to a table, and attempted to sell my ship to gods only know who. I can only assume they would have killed me and left me to rot in the desert. If you want fair, this is going to get ugly. Otherwise, tell me you accept my terms."

I held my tongue, swallowing back a yelp when his hand landed hard on my ass. The sound of it was almost deafening.

"Do you want me to dump you in the desert?" he asked.

"No," I murmured. I was confused and overwhelmed. There were consequences for everything. I'd learned that a long time ago, but I'd never been given a choice. I didn't like any of my current options, but simply having them was a revelation. "Can you at least untie my hands?"

"No," he said calmly. "I don't trust you. This happens on my terms or not at all."

I pressed my face into the cushion and sighed. Then I drew a deep breath. "Fine."

His big hand skimmed up my thighs to flip up my skirt. The absence of his touch filled me with dread. Then he gave me another firm blow. "Tell me you accept my terms, and we begin."

"We begin? What do you call this?"

"I call this you drawing things out unnecessarily," he said. "When you accept my offer, I'll get this over with."

I looked over my shoulder and found him staring evenly at me, those violet eyes calm and cold. "I accept your terms," I said, biting back the profanity threatening to spill over my trembling lip.

He nodded. "You count." He delivered two sharp smacks to my thighs, sending searing pain through my legs.

"Fuck," I swore into the cushion. He was strong, and he wasn't holding back.

"That's not a number," he said calmly. The next one drifted lower, and his fingers grazed my pussy on the way back. And in the wake of that sparkling pain that threatened to overwhelm me, there was a curious warmth. I hated him for doing this to me, and I hated myself even more for the twisting knot of heat gathering in my core. "The sooner you count, the sooner it's over. This is your choice. You take my punishment, or you go back to your boss and take his. Make up your mind."

My chest heaved. He wasn't just going to let me lay here and take it. He was making me participate in my own punishment, which made it somehow worse. I couldn't drift away and pretend this was happening to someone else, that I hadn't agreed to his devilish deal. "How many?"

"I'll tell you when to stop," he replied calmly. He gave me another sharp blow that echoed in the small cabin. After a pause, he matched it on the other side.

The pain was nothing compared to the heat in my face as I realized that my body was responding in a most unexpected way. A bolt of pure heat sizzled down into my clit and I knew it was only a matter of time until he noticed the wetness on my bare thighs. And then I would die of embarrassment and save Dinesso the trouble of killing me.

"Any day now, Vani," he said in a teasing voice. "Or don't. I can do this all day."

With a heaving sigh, I whispered, "One."

"I didn't hear that," he said, following it with another sharp smack that echoed through the chamber. My ass had to be on fire.

"One," I said loudly. Each blow was hard enough to sting, sending lightning radiating through me, only to race back into that pulsing knot between my legs. And he didn't ease up in the slightest because I complied.

As it continued, I felt my throat tightening, my eyes burning with tears I didn't dare release. It wasn't the pain; Dinesso and his men had hurt and humiliated me far worse than this. I was furious at Havoc for doing this to me, but I was becoming over-whelmed by a deep ache. With each second, I was genuinely sorry, and I wished I could just blurt it out instead of holding it in. I was sorry for who I was, that I was the kind of person who could hurt a man who'd done nothing but walk into the wrong fucking bar. If he had to spank me a thousand times to make things right, then so be it.

His calm voice broke through the swirling emotions in my head. "You're not counting. Start again, or we go back to one," he said.

"Five," I said hesitantly.

"That's it," he said. "That's your only warning before I start again. You don't want me to count, Vani, I assure you."

I couldn't hold back the tiny yelps and whimpers as he continued. We passed ten, and I felt like I was staring into the abyss. How long was he going to do this? I was going to cry if he kept it up, and I would rather die than let him see me cry.

But at thirteen, he paused and rested his hand on my hip. His huge palm stroked instead of striking, but there was no relief. His callused hands were rough as sandpaper on my tender skin. "Step one is done."

"Step one?" I blurted. "What the fuck?"

"Well, you tied me to a table," he said. "It's your turn."

Without warning, he hauled me to my feet and spun me around. "Diana, prepare prison apparatus for Resting Prayer position."

The strange silver table suddenly spun around, and the flat metal surface disappeared as spindly, claw-like limbs spun around and repositioned themselves like a cage.

"What the hell?" I muttered. I dug my heels in, but he simply picked me up and set me on my knees in the middle of it. A silvery cushion inflated beneath my bony knees. He roughly removed the belt from my wrists, still holding me firm, as one of the limbs emitted a blue light over me.

"Calibration complete," Diana said politely. The limbs whirled around again. Before I could even try to move, cold metal bands encircled my ankles and wrists. Havoc released me, and the metallic arms pulled my wrists behind me, forcing my chest forward.

"This is a Malzek torture device," he said, tilting his head as it whirred into place. "I bought it on a whim. I figured I might use it for its intended purpose someday, but this is much more interesting."

"Good for you," I snapped, pulling in vain against the metal cuffs. I stared at him defiantly, keeping my knees pressed together. He could stare at my angry face all he wanted.

He smirked at me. "Diana, activate pelvic access modifications." Two more limbs pushed my knees apart, spreading me wide. His violet eyes gleamed as he looked down, where my tiny skirt barely covered me. "Lovely."

My chest heaved as I stared up at him. Three guesses why he had this monstrous thing spreading my legs.

He smirked.

I bowed my head to regain my composure and throw him off. I shouted, "Diana! Release prisoner control apparatus."

"Passenger commands are not authorized," Diana replied.

"Goddammit, Diana!" I shouted.

"Don't be rude to my ship," he said, almost teasing. "You accepted my terms. I have to prepare for launch, and I don't trust you to roam my ship while I do so. By my calculations, I was tied to that table for approximately three hours and forty-two minutes. Your time starts now."

I gaped at him. "You can't be serious."

"I'm deadly fucking serious," he replied. "If you think I'm going to leave you unattended while I try to get this ship in orbit, you're a fool. And I don't think you're a fool at all, Vani."

I sighed and hung my head. Staring at the smooth silver floor, I was already onto my next plan. Letting my shoulders slump as much as I could in my bound position, I nodded slowly. "Okay," I said meekly. "I'm sorry."

"Duly noted," he said. He glanced at his watch and then strode to the cockpit. I could hear him speaking quietly to the computer, a muttered curse. There was a thrum as the ship changed directions.

Think, Vani. My last syringe was still in my little purse in the cockpit, along with the gun he'd knocked from my hand. His belt lay on the couch behind me. I hated the thought of it, but if I could get behind him, I'd have enough leverage to choke him out.

I didn't want this. I wanted to accept his terms and clear the slate.

But there was far too much at stake. And the longer I waited, the worse my chances were. I swept my eyes over the cabin again. My high heels were still in the corner where I'd kicked them off to drag him into the galley. Between the belt and the sharp point of the heel, I had a couple of decent weapons.

My heart thrummed as I raised my voice.

"Diana, safety override. The captain has a medical emergency. He is non-responsive and in cardiac arrest. Medical intervention is needed."

"Emergency status activated," Diana replied. "Shall I shut down non-essential hardware?"

"Yes!" Thank God for good programming.

The arms started to move. "Now deactivating non-essential hardware. Diverting power to defibrillation device. Please listen to directions." The bands on my wrists loosened. The blunt edge of the cuffs scraped against my skin as I pulled free.

"What the fuck?" he said from the other room.

"Come on, come on," I said, trying to extricate my ankles. "Diana, close cockpit door!"

"Closing cockpit door," she said helpfully.

"Oh, you little shit," he swore.

I was free.

My freedom lasted all of three seconds before a big hand twisted into my ponytail and hauled me backwards. I screamed in frustration and lunged away, sending a rippling pain burning through my scalp.

"For fuck's sake," he protested. Without warning, he gave me another firm smack on the ass that startled me so much I froze. He took advantage of my distraction and forced me to my knees. Within seconds, I was trapped again.

"Diana, ignore safety override," Havoc said loudly. "The captain is safe. Resume detention and ignore commands from non-authorized personnel."

"Please confirm with the captain's access code," Diana said.

He spoke in Zathari, and Diana responded, "Thank you, Captain." The bands locked again and tugged my wrists back. I strained against them and let out a scream of frustration. I threw my body to the side, but I could barely get any leverage with this thing holding all my limbs.

Havoc rose and crossed the room to rifle through a drawer. When he turned, I shook my head vigorously. "No, no," I protested, staring with dread at the tangle of straps in his hand. I frantically tried to recall the manuals I'd read, thinking of how else to shut Diana down. "Diana, I—*mmph!*"

The contraption of straps went over my head, and my mouth was suddenly filled with a hard black ball with holes in it. Havoc tightened the straps until I let out a quiet whimper. He slid one warm finger along my cheek, then tightened a buckle at the back of my head. I tried to push the ball out with my tongue, but there was no budging it.

He sighed and stared down at me. My jaw stretched awkwardly around the hard ball, and I knew I had to look beyond ridiculous. My feeble protests were muffled against the hard surface, only emphasizing how helpless I was in front of him. He tapped on the ball, sending an echo into my mouth, almost taunting me. "There are nicer things you can do with that mouth than lie, or try to take control of my ship."

I let out a quiet growl and cursed at him in an unintelligible mumble.

"I'm sure that was thoroughly impolite. You only have yourself to blame," he said. He raised his head and ordered, "Diana, please monitor vitals for subject." One of the bands tightened around my wrist with a strange pulsing sensation.

A few seconds later, Diana announced, "Vitals are currently within healthy range, Captain. Would you like more details?"

"No, thank you, Diana. Establish baseline and stand by," he

said. He knelt in front of me, his head tilted. Despite what I'd tried to do to him, he didn't look terribly angry. Almost disappointed. "Are you in pain? Actual pain. Don't lie to me, or I'll know."

I considered it. Considering I was half naked with my ass burning, immobilized by some weird torture device, and gagged, I was not at my peak.

"Vani. Answer me. Are you in pain?"

I shook my head slowly.

"Good," he said. "Then you can stay here for a while and think about what you've done, and more importantly, what you're going to do next. I'm disappointed in you. Right now, you're proving that your word is worthless."

I averted my gaze and stared at the ground.

"Look at me," he said sharply. I reluctantly raised my eyes. "My word is not worthless. I will not touch you without consent. Your punishment is to remain here until it's time to launch. When it's time, I'll release you, and this nasty business is done. Understand?"

I nodded slowly. I wanted to hate him and blame him, but this was on me.

He patted my shoulder lightly. "Diana, turn up central cabin temperature five degrees. Check circulation at five-minute intervals and notify me of signs of distress." He got up then, leaving me alone in the room.

As he left, there was a quiet sound of vents opening and a whirring fan that blew warm air over me. Held there by the inescapable device, I was utterly helpless. My heart pounded, and with a shameful heat in my cheeks, I realized my clit was throbbing in time with it.

A shrill beep filled the room, jolting me. Havoc returned and gave me a quizzical look. "Explain alert, Diana," he said sharply.

"Subject shows signs of distress," Diana said. "Elevated heart rate and body temperature."

Havoc raised an eyebrow, then knelt in front of me. He tipped up my chin, hooking his fingers under one of the leather straps. "What's wrong with you?"

I let out a muffled complaint against the gag.

He slid his fingers beneath the binding on my wrist, then squeezed one of my fingers. "Diana, is the subject's circulation sufficient?"

"Yes, Captain," the computer said.

I clenched my fist to get away from him, trying to regain my composure. I was certainly not going to think filthy thoughts about what he could do to me while I was bound tight.

He held my chin firmly, staring into my eyes with a devious smile. "Vani, what would you say if I offered to bend you over and fuck you until you scream?"

It was like his words struck a match, sending liquid fire through my body. I squirmed, as if that would somehow douse the raging lust burning in my core. The alarm sounded again, and I groaned with embarrassment. His violet eyes drifted up as a satisfied smile crossed his lips.

"And if I took this gag out and fucked your pretty mouth instead? Do you want to taste me again? Maybe ask for forgiveness?"

Another sizzling bolt of heat. Another alarm.

He patted my cheek lightly. "Oh, this is going to be fun."

CHAPTER 6

Havoc

WITH THE THOUGHT OF VANI BOUND AND GAGGED IN THE central cabin, it took all my willpower to focus on the task at hand. I ran a series of diagnostics on the Nomad, pacing as I waited for the final report. Even with the cutting-edge computer systems, it took fifteen minutes for Diana to finish checking the engine and the shielding system.

Fifteen minutes to consider how my stupidity—and her absolute gall—could cost me this deal. If she'd sabotaged my ship, I wouldn't make it to Vakarios. What the fuck was I going to tell Mistral and Storm if I blew this deal? We'd outrun the bounty hunters of Deeprun for more than ten years, successfully completed hundreds of lucrative smuggling runs, and I was going to ruin my reputation because I let a Terran girl get in my pants. Not only would I burn a dozen bridges with well-connected clients, I'd never be able to look my brothers in the eye again.

While I waited for the grim verdict, I brewed a cup of coffee with a triple dose of caffeine supplements in the galley, hoping it would burn off the narcotic haze. I returned in time to find the final tests completed. The large monitor in the cockpit flashed green as the readings scrolled across the display.

"All systems are operational," Diana said. I let out a heavy sigh of relief. She hadn't touched the hardware, thank the gods. She had, however, cost me nearly four hours. Between our little dalliance, my unplanned nap, and delivering her much-deserved punishment, it was now past midnight on Ilmarinen Universal Time.

Just under twelve hours until jump time. I ran the calculations in my head quickly. Barring any other interruptions, I might still make it to the Gate. I ran my flight plan through the computer again, only to receive the harsh sound that signaled bad news. My fists tightened as Diana reported, "Captain, your current flight plan is no longer viable."

"Explain, Diana."

"Insufficient fuel stores to reach Ilmarinen Gate MW A-1. Refueling advised prior to launch," she said.

"Fuck," I swore, my mind already spinning ahead of her explanation. "Plot a course to the nearest fueling station outside of the Prospects." I wasn't heading back to the city for Vani's employers to grab my ship. I had no doubt I could outfly them, but that didn't mean they wouldn't shoot at the Nomad and damage her hull.

"One hundred forty-eight miles," Diana said.

"Can I refuel and make a launch to the Gate before twelve hundred IUT?"

"No, Captain," Diana said. "According to the most optimistic calculations, you will still miss your jump. The next scheduled jump with vacancies is at zero hundred."

Another twelve hours. "Are you certain?"

"Yes, Captain," she said. "Would you like me to reschedule your jump?"

"Yes," I seethed. What I wanted her to do was rewind time and shock some sense into me before I let that fucking dust rat onto my ship. What was a supercomputer good for if she couldn't override my dick's poor decisions?

As I was fuming over my disrupted schedule, there was another alarm. "Subject is in distress," Diana said.

Let her be in distress. I was tempted to go in there, but taking out my anger on soft little Terran women was hardly sporting. And I suspected that whoever had put her up to this wouldn't care one bit.

Another alarm from Diana. "Subject is in distress."

"Understood, Diana," I snapped. "Plot a course to the fueling station. Get us to top speed. Ignore efficiency protocols. Burn everything."

"Yes, Captain," she said politely. There was a stomach-twisting lurch as the Nomad made a wide turn and accelerated dramatically. Another beep. "Subject—"

"I got it, Diana," I said archly. "Thank you."

I stormed into the cabin and found Vani breathing hard through her nose, eyes squeezed shut. I knelt in front of her, tipping up her chin. Her emerald green eyes flew open, and her cheeks went bright red. "What's the matter?"

She was frozen, eyes locked on me like she couldn't break away. With one finger, I lifted the bottom of her skirt. She tried to twist away, but there was no hiding the gleaming streaks of desire on her thighs. Her chest heaved, and she squeezed her eyes shut.

"Are you hurt or horny?" I asked. For someone who'd been so bold in swallowing my cock like a shot of whiskey, she was awfully embarrassed. "Well, well. You like being tied up and helpless."

Her head bowed, and there was a ripple in her beautiful legs as they tensed. It was tempting to take the gag out of her mouth and slip my cock past those plush pink lips. I knew she wouldn't fight it. Maybe in her head, but her body was all but screaming for me.

Something dark and hungry in me wanted to conquer her. Even without the wicked Malzek cage, I could have easily over-powered her and fucked her into sweet oblivion. But there was no victory or pride in such a thing. I wanted her mind to be so consumed with desire for me that she begged for it. That was true victory.

"You know, I could fuck you right now," I teased. A low groan vibrated in her chest. I tilted her chin up. The sight of her pretty pink lips stretched around the gag was enough to whittle away my resolve. "You like the thought of it."

She shook her head and made a sound of protest. Her eyes found mine.

"Liar," I said with a laugh. "And just think, if you'd been sweet, I was going to eat your pussy like it was my last meal." Raising my hands to my shoulders, I gave her a lascivious smile and rolled my tongue at her. "Thighs up here. Licking you until you screamed."

Another shrill alarm sounded as her head tilted, like she was contemplating her mistake.

"Captain—"

"Thank you, Diana," I said.

I knew I was taking a stupid, unnecessary risk. I shouldn't have given her a choice. I should have killed her and left her in the desert. But the thought of it made me nauseous. For one, if someone made her do this, they'd probably torture or kill her for fucking it up. Despite everything, I liked her, and she deserved a second chance.

There was still a glint of fury and defiance in her eyes, which told me I'd been gentler than she probably needed. I didn't normally like causing pain, but she'd needed the lesson in humility. If she was a man, I'd have killed him where he stood. But fighting her off had awakened something in me that had slept for a long time.

Some Zathari men, like my brother Razor, liked their lovers soft and gentle. They didn't want a challenge, when so much of our lives were filled with blood and violence. But I liked friction, the scrape of sandpaper on my skin, the electric spark of two dangerous forces facing one another. I liked the bite and the burn of it, and Vani had that in spades. I liked that she was fighting me tooth and nail.

I grabbed a tablet to monitor the ship's progress while I sat on the couch and watched her. Her eyes followed me as I reclined and propped my feet up. I pretended not to notice as I tweaked tiny details on the flight plan. Based on the new plan, I could reach Vakarios on time, but I would be cutting it close.

Any further delays could jeopardize the deal, and by the time I made the jump, it would be too late to notify my buyer. That would kill my connection, and there was too much riding on our continued business relationship.

Out of the corner of my eye, I caught Vani squirming again. "Diana, report on subject's oxygen saturation," I said calmly.

Fifteen seconds later, Diana reported, "Ninety-nine percent, Captain. Would you like a full report?"

"No, thank you, Diana," I said. What filthy things was she thinking about now? I'd have paid a pretty penny for a peek inside her head. If she played her cards right, I might give her exactly what she wanted.

I'd bought the Malzek cage from a dealer on Vakarios, mostly on a whim. I'd wanted to show it to Wraith, who had colorful ideas of how to use it on his enemies. And then there was Viper, who had far more colorful ideas of how to use it with a willing partner who was both flexible and adventurous. I'd been on the lookout for another one as a gift for Viper but hadn't had any luck so far. And after seeing Vani in it, I had to give him credit. He wasn't wrong.

It was much too quiet.

"Vani, what do you think of coming up here and riding my cock? How do you think it would feel with me in that sweet little pussy?" I asked her without looking away from the screen.

She groaned, and Diana alerted me, "Captain, subject is in distress."

"Thank you, Diana," I said. "You're welcome, Vani."

CHAPTER 7

Vani

As time passed, my shame ate away what remained of my defiance. It wasn't enough for him to spank me, gag me, and tie me up. He teased me relentlessly with increasingly lewd—and irresistible—suggestions. And with my treacherous body responding to everything he said, there was no hiding.

He had taken my freedom, my dignity, and my voice. Or perhaps more accurately, I had handed them all over for a chance to survive. All I had left now was my mind, and my mind was shitty company.

The Nomad slowed, then ground to a halt. There were no windows in the lounge, but I knew we hadn't left Earth yet. Havoc rose from the couch and patted my ass, awakening the burning sting again. "Don't go anywhere," he said in a mocking tone.

I growled against the gag, trying to rattle my way free. He'd set an alert to make sure I didn't die, but Diana clearly didn't know the difference between a heart attack and being a horny idiot.

I drew a deep breath through my nose and held it until my chest ached and my head pounded with desperation. Diana shrilled an alarm. "Subject is in distress." Desperation clawed at me, but I squeezed my eyes shut and tried to shut out the panic. Another ten seconds passed. The next alarm was almost deafening, like a fire alarm. "Subject is in significant distress, Captain Havoc. Medical intervention is necessary."

Come on. Let me go.

Surely she had a protocol to release someone on the verge of death.

The ship rattled as footsteps thundered down the hall. He gaped at me. "Are you holding your fucking breath?"

I could barely see him through my darkening vision. So close.

"Captain, shall I raise oxygen levels in the cabin?"

"No, Diana," he said. Without missing a beat, he flipped up my skirt and gave me a hard smack on the ass. I gasped. Tears pricked at my eyes as I tried to regain my composure. He grabbed my ponytail and glared at me. "You can do that all you want. She's not going to release you without my permission. But keep trying. I'll be impressed if you can make yourself pass out."

I let out another growl of frustration and twisted my head away from him. "Asshole," I mumbled around the constricting gag.

"You are really something," he said, though it sounded like a compliment rather than a complaint. Shaking his head, he left me behind again.

Metal clanked outside the ship, and then there was a metallic whirring sound. If I had to guess, he was refueling. When Havoc was unconscious, Diana had given me a bunch of warnings about low fuel efficiency, recommending that I either speed up or take the ship higher. Our slow trip out to meet Dinesso's guys in the desert must have burned up his fuel.

I didn't have to go slow. The crew had been out there for hours, so I should have hauled ass like an obedient little pet. But I didn't want to give Dinesso the Nomad, and I sure didn't want to give him Havoc. Even though I knew I was screwed either way, with a vicious crime lord on one side and a furious Zathari smuggler on the other, I couldn't do it.

Just this one fucking time, it was my choice. If I'd just punched it, I could have dropped the ship off within an hour. Havoc would be in Dinesso's hands, and I'd be back in the Dahlia. Our little interlude would have been a memory, and this would have been just another day in the Prospects. Instead, I'd taken the ship in the opposite direction and flew slow circles out in the desert, wondering what my decision was going to cost me even as I held tight to that tiny shred of power.

Even now that I was paying the price, I wasn't sure I would have done things differently. And I had to wonder if Havoc would really make good on his offer to take me somewhere else. I'd never met a man like him.

The way he'd handled me made me feel like we were a bizarre, dysfunctional little team. Even though he'd clearly been in control, he'd made me part of my own punishment. This was something we were handling together, in a twisted but logical sort of way. If he released me as he'd promised, then maybe I could trust him. And that was a whole new world of experience.

Finally, Havoc returned with streaks of black on his white shirt. Reddish dust streaked his face. Brushing past me, he headed down the narrow hall. When he returned a minute later, he had shed his shirt and was wiping his hands clean on a towel. I couldn't help admiring the broad expanse of his bare chest. Muscle shifted and rippled as he wiped his face clean.

He knelt in front of me. "Technically, you've still got quite a lot of time left," he said. "But I need to launch soon, and I can't leave you there."

I raised my eyebrows, trying to plead with my eyes. He reached for the buckle at the back of my head. His fingers laced through the straps, giving me no room to move. I had no choice but to look at him. "If I release you, you're going to be polite, and you are not going to speak to my ship. If you do, I will put the gag back in and I'll find something to plug up the rest of your holes for good measure." I shivered. Diana let out another alarm, and he smirked. "Maybe that's not the threat I thought it was. Nod if you understand my expectations."

I nodded, and he released the buckle to remove the gag. He gently smoothed my hair and untangled it from the straps. I let out a sigh of relief as I stretched my jaw. My voice sounded tiny and meek as I said, "Thank you."

He was quiet for a while, watching me warily. I deserved that. His eyes drifted up, then back to me. "No sneaky plans?"

I shook my head. "No. I just…I can't leave."

"Why?" he asked. "Be honest. I'm Zathari, and honesty is sacred to me."

"Because there are people who depend on me. People I care

about," I said. "If I don't go back, they could get hurt. That's the truth."

His brow furrowed, and I caught a glimpse of something vulnerable. "Really?"

"Really," I said.

"So, if you don't go back they get hurt. And if you do go back, without my ship, you get hurt," he said quietly. "Either way, you lose."

"I don't suppose you want to let me have it," I said, failing to sound light-hearted.

"Not in a million years." He glanced at his watch and shook his head. "What if we came back for them later?"

I raised my eyebrows. "Why would you do that?"

"Are they decent people?"

"Better than me," I said quietly.

He cupped my jaw and tilted my face up, forcing me to look at him. "I don't like that," he said. "When my job is done, I'll come back and get them, if it's that important."

"Why not now?"

"One, I can't trust that you don't have a crew waiting to shoot the Nomad out of the sky," he said. Before I could protest, he put a finger on my lips. "You haven't earned that trust from me. Two, I'm on a tight schedule because of you. I've got to get in the air as soon as possible or everything falls apart. Understand?"

I nodded solemnly. Despite being on display for him for hours, it was his hard, unblinking gaze that made me feel vulnerable and exposed. I didn't know the first thing about him, but I desperately wanted to go with him. I wanted to see the things those amethyst eyes had seen. I wanted to go anywhere that wasn't caked in dust and filled with vile men.

His fingers skimmed my brow, smoothing my hair back. Despite everything, I tilted my head into his touch. "You like me touching you," he said softly.

"Yes," I admitted.

"And you like submitting to me," he said. "Don't you?"

I shook my head, but I could feel the entirety of my body ready to scream *yes*.

"So, if I put my hand up your skirt, you'll be dry as a bone," he teased.

"Fuck," I muttered.

He lightly stroked my jaw, keeping one finger just beneath my chin. "There's nothing wrong with it. Admit it. There's no one else here but you and me."

"And Diana," I said weakly. "She and I got fairly intimate today."

He chuckled, but I got the sense that he was genuinely amused, not mocking me. His smile was hypnotic, exposing a sliver of straight white teeth. "Say it."

"I didn't hate it," I finally said. "And I wouldn't hate going with you. You promise you'll bring me back?"

"I promise," he said. His thumb skimmed my lip. "Do you want me to touch you now?"

My defiance was gone. I simply nodded.

His hand slid up my leg and finally to that burning heat between my thighs. With deft, practiced fingers, he slid a finger inside me, never losing his smug smile. "I'm tempted to deny you, but since we're being honest, you should know how much I enjoyed watching you," he said, stretching me further with a second finger. His fingers curled just so, finding a mysterious place inside me. It felt like something radiated from my pussy all the way to my brain and wrapped it in a hazy cloud. I shuddered, then let out a moan of protest when he withdrew. "What's wrong, Vani?"

I wiggled against the bindings. Somehow, I would have preferred it if he just took what he wanted. "Please," I whispered. *Don't make me say it.*

"Please what?"

"Please touch me," I said, raising my gaze to meet his.

There was a faint flicker of something lovely on his face; satisfaction, pride, maybe hunger. Then he was inside me again, fingers working slowly as he teased me. I sighed, but he went still again. "Honesty, Vani. Speak the truth."

"I want your fingers inside me," I said, louder this time. "It feels good."

"Then you will have it," he growled. I squirmed against his hand, desperate for more, and he gave it. He fucked better with one hand than human men did with their cocks. As he dragged me toward a fiery peak, he buried his face in my neck and nipped at my skin.

This was happening. I was getting a glimpse of something strange and forbidden and I wanted more. I wanted to drown in it and forget that anything else existed.

Another alarm sounded. "Captain, subject is in significant distress. Medical intervention is recommended."

He chuckled against my throat. "Thank you, Diana," he said as calmly as if he was combing his hair, not dominating every inch of my body. His voice rumbled against my throat. "Deactivate notifications."

"Yes, captain," Diana said.

"Prepare launch sequence," he said. "Thirty minutes."

"Beginning engine checks and fuel preparation," Diana said. The ship vibrated suddenly, and there was a distant whirring noise. As he gave orders to the ship, he never stopped stroking and caressing me.

I was losing my mind in that grasp. He grasped my chin and forced me to look up at him. "Vani?" His thumb joined his fingers, strumming hard across my clit. I squealed and twisted violently against the bindings, but there was no escape. He was so much, so good, so overwhelming. "Vani, are you listening to me?"

"Yes," I panted. I wasn't even sure what language he was speaking anymore.

"After you come for me, I'm going to fuck you," he said, like he was telling me the sky was blue. "Bound and bent over, ass up in the air. How does that sound? Do you want my cock inside you?"

"Yes," I moaned. "Yes, please, yes."

"One of my favorite words," he said. Then he kissed me, tongue plundering my mouth as his skilled fingers drew me over the edge. Orgasm clawed through me, rising from a fiery chasm and bursting through me in a brilliant, searing explosion. My whole body shook so hard that the metal cage rattled. I made wordless noises of desperation as he smiled against my lips. His big hand finally withdrew, tracing small circles on my quivering inner thigh. "Wasn't that much more fun than killing me?"

I could only whimper against him, going limp with my head on his shoulder. I'd been with plenty of men, but I could count on one hand the number of times I'd even come close to orgasm. It was a revelation, that someone could want me to feel pleasure.

He leaned in, nipping at my earlobe. "The slate is clean, Vani," he murmured in my ear. I just gazed at him in wonder as he pulled away and licked his index finger like he'd caught a drop of chocolate.

He was tasting me. And he fucking liked it.

"Diana, adjust subject to Position 21," he ordered, backing away as the machine whirred to life again. Suddenly, several of the limbs twined together, extending smooth metal plates to form a curved base that lifted my stomach and chest to push me up at an angle. "Fuck, that's a beautiful sight," he murmured, flipping up my skirt to expose me. "Do you want me to fuck you now, Vani? Be honest."

"Yes," I said. Every fiber of my body wanted it, and I didn't have the energy to pretend otherwise. For just a moment, I felt like I'd side-slipped into another world, a place where I was just a primitive creature with a desire for one thing and the perfect opportunity to get it. No shame, no inhibition, just raw need and desperate hunger. There was a clean slate in front of me, and this Vani could have what she wanted before the universe caught up and claimed its share.

He chuckled as he slid his pants down, stroking himself. "Say it," he said. "You can have it if you ask."

His cock was a masterpiece, with that dusky gray skin and a bead of pre-cum like a gemstone glistening at the head. "I want you to fuck me," I said boldly. "Right in the—" I gasped as he stepped behind me in a single powerful stride and thrust himself so deep I thought he might split me in two. There was a hint of pain as that pulsing bulge breached me, and another when he withdrew.

"Fuck," he groaned, grabbing my waist as he thrust harder into me. His hips awakened the fire on my ass again. The spark bloomed into a searing inferno as he fucked me with deep, pounding strokes. I was practically seeing stars as he awakened something monstrous and primal in me.

Every cell in my body vibrated with need and want. I didn't care what I should want or enjoy. *Should* couldn't touch me here. There was nothing in all the galaxies that I wanted as much as I wanted this. It was simple. He demanded. I bowed. I needed. He gave.

His fingers drummed lightly against my clit as he drove deep, and I spiraled over the edge again. My entire body tensed, my back arching into him as I let out an animal scream that echoed off the walls. In the shimmering aftermath, I went limp and boneless, but still he drove into me.

Then he swelled, stretching me until I thought I would burst, and his hips slammed home. Heat radiated from him as his warm seed filled me. My body fluttered with the echoes of orgasm, squeezing him tight. His broad chest lay against my back, lips resting against my spine. There was a distinct pulse where our bodies met, steady and quick.

"Fuck me," he murmured.

"I think I just did," I said weakly. The weight of him was a pleasant anchor, keeping me from floating into uncharted space.

He laughed, and the delightful rumble passed into my chest. "I'm quite sure I fucked you."

"Yeah," I murmured. "You did."

In that hazy afterglow, part of me was screaming. *How could you ask for this? How could you let him do this?*

But there was another part of me that curled up and purred like a little kitten. That part was sated and well-fucked and completely unashamed. That part told my defiance to shut the fuck up and go back to the Prospects and let Dinesso tear her to shreds.

"Diana, release subject," he said. The arms started to shift, but he caught me around the waist before the devilish contraption dropped me flat on my face. He scooped me into his arms and glanced down at me. "Shower?"

CHAPTER 8

Havoc

GODS, I DIDN'T KNOW IF I WAS A GENIUS OR A COMPLETE FUCKING moron. But with Vani leaning against me under the hot spray of the shower, I knew I couldn't have made another choice if my life depended on it.

Maybe it did. I wasn't so stupid that I trusted her. There was a solid chance she was still working on another attempt to kill me and take the Nomad, but I was enjoying myself.

Her head rested against my chest as she caught her breath. My ship was utilitarian, but one of my few soft touches was a good soap from an artisan back in Ir-Nassa. The mix of herbs and flowers smelled good on Vani, and I took my time scrubbing her warm, golden skin. She clearly took care of herself, but I wanted the scent of Terra gone. I wanted her to smell like me.

While I scrubbed her clean, I found dozens of faded scars. Some were thin cuts that could have been accidental, but the distinct round burns certainly weren't. Several dotted her back, the insides of her thighs, and there was a large one under the curve of her breast. The sight of those precise marks sent fury coursing through me.

I knelt in front of her, taking my time to wash between her legs. Her body still answered me, a shiver rippling through her as my fingers grazed her. The smell of her was intoxicating, and I was tempted to pin her to the wall and make good on my promise of fucking her with my tongue until she forgot her own name. But there were boundaries to be etched in stone, and I would have a hard time of it if I gave in to temptation.

The water recycler made my decision for me, as the spray started to cool. I placed a light kiss on her hip and rose to wash myself quickly. When I was done, I said, "Diana, activate dryer."

Vani startled as the spray faded and gave way to the warm air dryer. Then she laughed, a wonderfully rich, throaty sound. "I love this ship." When we were both dry, I picked her up again and carried her out to the small sleeping cabin. She pushed gently against my chest. "I can walk, you know."

"I'm aware," I responded sharply. "The question is whether I need to tie you up or if you can sleep with me like a civilized person. Are you going to try to drug me or kill me again?"

"I'm out of needles," she joked.

I squeezed her just hard enough to get her attention. Her brow furrowed as her smile evaporated. "I'm serious. I gave you a clean slate. Are you going to throw it in my face?"

Her chest heaved, and for a moment, I thought she might call my bluff. But there was something here on Terra that scared her more than I did. I was inclined to do something about it when this run was over. Someone needed to learn a lesson about leaving scars on pretty things like her. She nodded, averting her eyes. "I'll be good."

"Honesty. Look at me when you answer me."

Her eyes lifted to meet mine. "I'll behave."

"Good girl," I said, depositing her on my bed. Though the bedroom was sparse and utilitarian, like the rest of my ship, the bed was big enough for both of us.

As her ass hit the covers, she winced and eased onto her side. "Can I have some clothes? You tore my only pair of panties to shreds, and my uniform is dirty."

"I like you naked," I replied, rooting through one of my drawers.

"I'll get cold."

"Then I'll keep you warm," I replied. I set out a tube of numbing ointment, then left to retrieve a bottle of water from the galley. My heart thumped, and I grabbed a stun gun from the cockpit before I headed back. I hesitated at the door, peeking in before I stepped into the room. She was still sitting where I'd left her. Her hands were splayed casually on the bed; no sharp objects in sight. I poured her a glass of water and handed it over. "Drink."

She frowned at me. "I'm not thirsty."

"There are battles worth fighting," I said. "This isn't one of them. It's just water." I took a long sip from the bottle and then handed it over. She watched me warily, then drained it. I refilled it, and she sipped it slowly. Despite her protests, relief washed over her pretty face. "Are you hungry?"

She shook her head. "Not right now." I raised my eyebrows, and she smiled softly. "I'm really not."

I nodded and pointed. "Lie on your belly."

Her eyes widened as she shrank back. I just gave her a stern look, and she slowly rolled onto her belly, giving me a fine view of her lovely, golden body. There was a beautiful curve from her shoulder to her hip, as perfect as it had been carved by a master sculptor.

The stinging red of my hand was still on her skin, and I could see the distinct imprint of my fingers on her bottom. It would probably bruise by tomorrow. A hint of guilt panged through me, though she had tried to gouge my eyes out. I sprayed a fine, cool mist of ointment on her skin. She tensed, then let out a happy sigh as I rubbed it in.

I spread her legs and sprayed the soft pink of her sex. Her thighs squeezed my hand as I rubbed it in slowly. The way her body whispered to me filled me with pride. "I was rough with you. You may be sore later."

"It's all right," she said.

"I didn't apologize," I said archly. Her shocked stare made me laugh. Normally, I would have given her more time to adjust to my cock, but she had awakened something desperate and hungry that smashed through my self-control. When her sweet voice said *I want you to fuck me*, I almost lost my mind, burying myself balls deep before I could even consider going slowly.

"I appreciate it, but why are you making me feel better after you spanked the shit out of me?" she asked.

"Have you forgotten the sting of punishment already? Should I do it again and gag you for a few more hours?"

She flipped over and rolled directly into the wall on the other side of the bed with a noisy *thump*. "No!" she protested, rubbing her head.

I pulled her back to me, forcing her onto her belly again.

Flattened under my strong hand, she stared at me with fear-filled eyes. The fear evaporated as I simply stroked her back, savoring the softness of her skin. There were not enough soft, beautiful things in my life. "What did you learn today?"

"That you like it rough?"

"So do you," I said. "Should I have Diana replay a recording of you screaming in ecstasy?"

Her cheeks flushed, and I watched her toes curl slightly. "And you're a lot stronger than me."

"Do you understand that I can deal with you if you try to kill me again?" I asked.

"Yes," she said.

"Do you understand that I am a man of my word?"

She was quiet for a while, but I let her ponder it. Then she nodded. "I understand."

"Then you learned a valuable lesson," I said, lightly patting her ass. "And if not, I'll explain again. I'm persistent."

"You don't have to," she said quietly. "I get it."

Suddenly, the Nomad rumbled. Vani sat up abruptly. Shit, I'd nearly forgotten. I'd been buried to the hilt in her, drifting in another dimension entirely while the countdown commenced.

I tossed her one of my loose jackets, then yanked up a pair of pants. She followed close on my heels as I hurried to the galley and stowed the loose items I'd knocked down in my escape. Grabbing her hand, I headed into the cockpit. "Diana, update on launch status, please," I said.

"All systems are launch ready," Diana replied. "Prepare for launch in three minutes, Captain. Please ensure that you are in a seated and safe position."

I pointed to the second chair. "Sit," I said. She plopped into it, eyes wide as I buckled her into the harness. Then I settled into the captain's chair, buckling myself in.

Most of the procedures aboard the Nomad were automated, as they were on most small ships. Diana had programming to check for air traffic, wind conditions, and a thousand other things that I'd never remember. I'd done dozens of trips without ever putting my hands on the controls. I reached out and grasped Vani's hand. "It's going to feel strange, but it's all right. It'll be over fast."

Her chest heaved as she stared at me, looking infinitely more afraid than she had when I'd pinned her down. "Please don't let me go."

Something I couldn't even put a name to twisted through me. If I could have done it safely, I'd have held her in my arms the whole way. "I won't."

"Launch sequence in thirty seconds, Captain," Diana announced.

Vani's hand tightened on mine, and I squeezed it back. Then the engines fired up, rumbling the ship. It went eerily still for a moment, then surged upward with a crushing rush of gravity. "Oh shit," she gasped, squeezing my hand so tight I thought my fingers were going to snap.

Even as the powerful force pressed us back, threatening to turn my stomach out and crush us both to paste, I savored every miserable second. This was the feeling of freedom, of flying free of this shit heap and every other one like it. This feeling meant I was a free man. Nothing could trap us. Not the Dominion, not the dust heap of Earth, not even fucking gravity.

The ship vibrated violently, and Vani let out a tiny gasp. "It's okay," I shouted over the noise. "Everything's fine."

It probably felt like an eternity to her, but it took under ten minutes from launch to break out of the Earth's atmosphere. The tug of gravity lessened, and I felt myself lifting from the seat. There was a mechanical thrum as Diana activated the artificial gravity generator, and I settled back into the seat.

"Diana, please open cockpit viewing windows," I said.

The louvred shields retracted, giving us a nearly unbroken view of an endless field of stars. Looming large on Vani's side of the cockpit was the pocked gray surface of Earth's moon. Beyond that was the huge steel construct of Ilmarinen Gate MW A-1, the only such gate in their galaxy. Concentric rings of steel gleamed, with the bustle of dozens of ships moving all around it. This was nothing compared to the gates in more developed systems, where hundreds of ships glided through the dark sea of space.

Vani's eyes were wide and filled with a mix of terror and wonder. "I can't believe it."

"It's beautiful, isn't it?"

"It's so big," she whispered. Then she writhed against the harness and unbuckled herself. "I don't feel right. I think I need to lie down."

When she rose, her legs were shaky, but she waved off my help and inched back to the cabin. Her head hung as she sat on the edge of my bed, breathing hard. I let her sit in silence for a while before I finally asked, "Are you all right?"

Her face was pale when she looked up. She nodded. "Sorry, I just feel like my body turned inside out. It's overwhelming."

"I know the feeling," I said. I yawned and shucked off my loose pants, then beckoned to her. "Jacket."

Without protest, she handed me my jacket, and I hung both

garments neatly in the tiny closet. After tugging on a pair of snug briefs, which would hopefully give me some bit of warning if Vani tried to stick a needle in my dick again, I slid into bed. It would have been smarter to lock her up somewhere, but I was looking forward to a warm body in my bed. "Are you going to sleep with me or not?" I asked.

"Do you mean you want to fuck again?" she asked.

"Do *you* want to fuck again?"

Her lips quirked into a smile. "I'm really tired. I mean, it was great." Her cheeks reddened. "Really great. But I don't think I could do much more than lay here and stare at you."

"Vani, if I want to fuck you, I won't be coy. I'll say it outright." Her smile widened. "Unless you're desperate for a ride, I really do need to sleep." Then I hesitated. "My name is Havoc."

Her head tilted. "I know."

"I never told you."

She chuckled. "Henri Agalov told my boss, and my boss told me. But I know that's not your real name." Her eyebrows lifted in an unspoken question.

"Zathari don't give their real names to anyone but *shanharah*."

"What's that?"

"People we trust intimately. Family. Friends. Lovers," I said. "No offense, but you're none of those things. Havoc will do."

A flinch rippled across her face, as if I'd threatened to strike her. "Fair enough," she said. When she reached for the soft blanket, I held it back to admire her. With one hand, I traced a line from her ankle, up to her hip, then over her bare breasts. I sketched a spiral around one rosy pink nipple, watching with pride as it tightened into a pretty little peak. Her glimmering green eyes followed me.

"Your body is very beautiful." I traced a pair of long, twisted scars on her flat belly. The raised texture and straight lines intersected at a nearly perfect corner. No accident. "Who did this to you?"

"A stupid little boy in a big man's body," she said absently. Her golden fingers traced my arm idly. "At least your punishments are a bit more pleasant."

Despite everything that had transpired between us, the thought of someone hurting her infuriated me. It wasn't even so much the physical scars, but the fact that someone had made her afraid. And I felt slimy at the thought of being in the category of men who would punish her. My actions were justified, considering she'd been about to shoot me, but I vowed it would never happen again. My touch would be for her pleasure, or she would not have it at all.

She sat up suddenly and covered her mouth. "Where's the toilet?"

I lurched out of bed and shoved the narrow door open, and she barreled inside just in time to eject the contents of her stomach. Her shoulders heaved, and I turned away to give her some privacy. When she emerged, her face was drawn, and I handed her another cup of water.

"Your first launch can be rough," I told her. "You're not the first to lose your breakfast."

She laughed weakly, then sat on the edge of the bed. "Can I sleep on this side just in case?" Her green gaze shifted away from mine. Was she embarrassed or hiding an ulterior motive?

I decided to give her the benefit of the doubt and hoped it wasn't my second huge mistake in twenty-four hours.

"I suppose," I said, sinking into bed. "Diana, lights off. Night mode."

"Goodnight, Captain," Diana said cheerfully. The lights dimmed. Vani settled next to me, and I rolled onto my side, cupping her breast gently. She let out a soft sigh, closing her eyes as she began to breathe evenly. I waited. I wasn't sure if I wanted to be right or wrong in my suspicions.

Sure enough, it didn't take long before she groaned again and bolted for the head. But the dramatic noises were almost certainly fake, and she was in there far longer than was necessary. Something rattled inside. Then she lingered at the door, nearly silent as she watched me. I kept breathing evenly even as I peered at her through one slitted eye.

After a long stretch, she crept across the room and reached into the open closet. When she returned, she slid one hand under her pillow. I pretended not to notice and simply rolled over as she laid down. To my surprise, she lifted my hand and put it back on her breast, resting her smaller one atop it. If it was a game, it was one I didn't mind playing for the moment.

The question was whether she was going to cut my throat in the night, and what I would do to her if she crossed me again.

CHAPTER 9

Vani

DESPITE MY UTTER EXHAUSTION, I LAY AWAKE FOR HOURS. I wanted to just roll into Havoc's warm body, let him wrap me in his powerful arms, and pretend we weren't in a tiny metal box floating through the horrifying expanse of space with stars above and below and no solid ground.

This was insane.

He forced me to make a ridiculous choice, and now I was thousands of miles above Earth, zooming toward a gate that would launch me into another galaxy entirely. It seemed like the right choice at the time, given the alternative of being dumped into the slums of Atalia and crawling back to Dinesso empty-handed, but now we were in the void. The entirety of my life experience was gone. Not even gravity functioned properly here. Everything was too big and terrifying, including Havoc himself.

What was to stop him from killing me? Sure, he'd fucked me up one side and down the other, and it was as good as he'd promised. Maybe he'd do it again, and I could disappear into that other world where nothing mattered except how good I felt. But that dream had to end. There was nothing to stop him from killing me when he grew tired of me. Or dumping me on some forsaken planet. Or simply throwing me out into space like trash.

I would be an idiot to think that he actually liked me. Just because he made me come and held my hand while we launched into space.... If my life on Earth had taught me anything, it was that powerful men were not to be trusted. And even if he did mean what he said, my sisters still needed me. How long would Dinesso wait before taking out his anger on them?

I had to get home. If I could take control of the ship and turn it around, Dinesso might take me back. At least he was the monster I knew. And if I told him about that devious little torture device, he might forget about my indiscretion. Dinesso thought all men were like him, so he'd believe it if I said the Zathari tortured me before I made a daring escape. He might even praise me for it. Maybe that goodwill would give some weight to my voice when I gently steered Dinesso and his men away from my sisters.

As if he sensed my impending deception, the Zathari rolled over and slung his muscular arm over my stomach. Sleep cast a veil of gentle peace on his face, entirely unlike the cocky veneer when he was conscious. I hesitated, then reached up to touch one of those lovely, gleaming horns. There were flecks of dark gray and deepest blue in the deep black ridges. Along the curve of the left one, there was a pronounced nick the size of my pinky fingernail. I wondered how he'd gotten it. The edges were soft and smooth, like it had been worn over years.

My fingers stopped short of the dark surface. I could still see his frown when I first came onto the Nomad, even before I'd betrayed his trust. *Don't touch.* Though he hadn't said as much, his reaction made me think there was something special about it, something too intimate to be shared with someone like me, as if I would get them dirty.

I wanted to touch so badly, but I resisted. Instead, I gently stroked his arm. His dark lips pulled into a faint smile as his fingers curled into my side. It should have made me feel warm and fuzzy, but I just felt nauseous. Turning this thing around meant I had to cross him again and delaying was only making it harder.

The slate is clean, Vani.

I believed him, but I was still going to destroy it. I had no choice.

I coughed, then rolled out of bed and into the small bathroom. Staring at myself in the small mirror, I made a loud retching noise.

You can do it. It'll just knock him out.

I'd get him locked up in that silver monstrosity, gag him so he couldn't take control of Diana, and turn this thing around. Hell, with this ship and all the guns onboard, I could finally get Naela and Amira to safety. I'd take out Dinesso, leave the Dahlia a pile of rubble, and never look back. And if Havoc decided to put up a fight, I'd give him his own choice: come along or get dumped in the desert.

Turnabout would be fair play.

When I emerged, he was lying on his back again. I crept closer and slid my hand under the pillow for the gun I'd stolen from his closet.

Nothing there.

His violet eyes opened, and his hand rose with the gun. "Looking for something?"

I bolted. My mind was laser-focused on escape as I careened through the door, bounced off the opposite wall, and stumbled down the hall.

"Diana, close sleeping quarters!" he bellowed, but I was way too fast. He only locked himself in, and there was a shudder as he banged the door with his fist.

"Galley," I muttered. Why couldn't he have an armory like a proper scoundrel?

"Vani!" Havoc roared. His voice was monstrous and terrible as it echoed throughout the small ship. Heavy steps thundered down the narrow hall.

I tore into the galley where I'd bound him yesterday and yanked open the storage bins. Sure enough, I found a paring knife, gleaming sharp and silver. I backed into the cold storage unit, holding my tiny blade at the ready as he burst into the galley.

His violet eyes went wide. "What the fuck?" he snarled.

"Just back up," I said. "I don't want to kill you."

"I know," he said. "But holding that kind of undermines your point, don't you think?"

He took a tentative step closer, and I backed against the wall. I hated this feeling, pressed into a corner, nowhere to go. How many times had Luka and Rico backed me into a corner, toying with me until they decided violence was more fun? It always ended the same.

"I thought we had an agreement," he said gently, taking another small step toward me. "I trusted you."

"No, you didn't," I said. "You're not that stupid."

He laughed. "No, I'm not. But you gave me your word. Now I know that doesn't mean shit."

"Take me back," I said.

In a blur, he lunged for me. I slashed wildly at him. The blade dragged over his forearm without so much as a scratch. He let out a snarl, grabbed my wrist, and twisted me around until I was trapped against his body. I braced myself for another round of his perverse punishment, but instead he backed into the dinette with his big arms wrapped around me.

"Let go!"

"No," he said. "Stop fighting me. We can chase each other around this ship all day long, but we're in fucking space. There's nowhere to go, Vani."

I let out a scream of frustration, fighting in vain against him.

"Calm down," he said, squeezing me tighter. At his height, my head was pinned against his chest. I couldn't even get enough room to smack him in the face again. With one hand, he pried the knife from my grasp like I was a toddler. He tossed it across the room, leaving me unarmed.

"Are you going to tie me down and spank me again?"

He laughed, and I hated him for it. "Is that what you want?"

"No!" I said. I mean, I didn't *not* want it, judging by the fire that exploded to life in my core. "I don't want to hurt you. I just want to go home, but—"

"I know you don't want to kill me," he said. His voice was curiously calm, considering I'd just attacked him again.

I stilled. "How do you know that?"

"I was awake the whole time you were creeping around and going through my closet," he said. "And you were awake the whole time pretending to be asleep."

"So?"

"So if you wanted to kill me, you'd have tried it when you thought I was sleeping," he said. Despite everything, he lightly kissed the back of my neck, then rested his chin on my shoulder. He was so dangerously close. The tenderness was even scarier than the aggression. "Why did you put my gun under your pillow?'

"To make you take me back," I said.

"Why do you want to go back so badly? You don't want to go back to your boss."

"I was afraid you would kill me," I said weakly.

"Vani," he said flatly. "Yesterday I had you helpless and bound for hours." My cheeks flushed as a bolt of heat shot between my legs. "If I wanted to kill you, I'd have slit your throat instead of fucking you senseless. And I'd have done it before launching. You think I want to fly for three days with your corpse stinking up my ship?"

"Things change," I said. He released me, then lifted me easily to turn me around to face him. I didn't want to meet his eyes, but he lightly grasped my chin and tilted it up.

"Look at me. I don't want to hurt you," he said. "And I'm not biding my time before I get rid of you, if that's what you're thinking." His brow furrowed. "You told me yesterday you'd rather I just finished you off, so this isn't really about me hurting you. What's bothering you?"

I sat in silence for a long time, my heart pounding. Finally, I whispered, "There are people back on Earth that I care about. If I'm gone, they'll suffer."

His brow furrowed. "Why are you still stuck on that? I told you that I'd go back for them. That's a promise."

My chest heaved. "Really? Just like that?"

"Just like that. My word means something, Vani," he said. "But it has to wait."

"You can't just take me back now?" I asked softly.

"I can't," he said. "You fucked up my timeline. If I miss another jump, I miss my meeting, and I can't have that. Do you understand?"

"I guess," I said.

He gently brushed a curl out of my face, tucking it behind my ear. "Can you stop trying to stab me now?"

I hesitated, then slid my hand deftly beneath his briefs, finding that warm length easily. Years of dealing with ill-tempered sadists had taught me that men were easy to cheer up. His eyelashes fluttered as I purred, "Let me make it up to you."

He grabbed my wrist. "I cannot believe I'm saying this, but no."

"No?" My cheeks heated as I released his cock. "I thought—"

"I'd love nothing more than to watch you swallow me whole. But I know what you're doing." He gently extricated my hand and clasped it between his. "I told you that I value honesty. I very much enjoyed fucking you, but you're not going to use sex to control me. I'm much smarter than you give me credit for."

Well, that wasn't entirely true. I'd almost managed to steal his ship with nothing more than a blowjob and a couple of syringes, but pointing that out wasn't going to help my cause. I frowned. "How do I make it up to you?"

"Make what up?"

I gestured broadly. "This. Being a pain in your ass. Trying to stab you."

His lips tugged up in a smile. "I'm hungry. And since I'm not sure I can sleep without you stabbing me, coffee would be a good start."

CHAPTER 10

Havoc

I<small>T TOOK ONE RECONSTITUTED MEAL OF BLAND</small> S<small>AHEMNAR CURRY</small> and two cups of terrible instant coffee, but Vani finally relaxed. I was on edge every time I turned my back, and I could practically hear Wraith telling me to tie her down or lock her in a storage container until I could get rid of her.

I wasn't completely stupid. When she finally slept for real, I was going to lock the cabin behind me and sweep the whole ship for weapons.

But goddamn if I didn't like her. There weren't many people, human or otherwise, who'd have put up that much of a fight with a man like me, especially bare-assed naked in the middle of space.

The small dining area was a tight fit for the two of us, but I liked having her close. The firm, warm press of her legs around mine was a delight. Definitely an upgrade from eating alone and listening to Diana read the news from whatever galaxy we were in.

I wrinkled my nose and dug into the mushy rice. "So, little dust rat, how old are you?"

"Twenty-eight," she said.

"Family?"

She shrugged. "No parents. Two sisters. Not by blood, but we're still family."

I nodded appreciatively. "And do you regularly steal ships from your paying customers?"

Her cheeks flushed. "This was a big job," she said. "Usually I just get information. Occasionally cash."

"And who uses your pussy like a weapon?" I asked. "It's a powerful weapon, but it's a cowardly man who puts a human woman in front of a Zathari male to steal from him. He had to know that there was a good chance I'd kill you."

"Maybe I'm the boss," she said.

"If you were the boss, you wouldn't have tried to strongarm me into taking you back," I said. "And I'm guessing you didn't leave those cigar burns on your own back." Her cocky smile evaporated abruptly. "What's his name?" I wanted to know who I needed to kill.

She sighed and stared into her coffee. "Dinesso."

"Is he one of the Limbo Boys?" One of the gangs in the Prospects had sent a crew to grab me a while back. I'd left one alive to deliver a message, just in case the corpses of the other five didn't make it clear.

She shook her head. "He owns the Dahlia and a couple other clubs in town. He controls all the Blitz in the city. And he's wanted your ship since you were last on Earth."

My head tilted. "When I was last on Earth? What do you know about that?"

Her lips pursed as she looked up at me. "Eight months ago, you traded with Henri Agalov, and when you were done, you came to the Dahlia. You played a few rounds of cards, lost some money, ignored the half-naked girl dancing on stage, and left a big tip for the bartender who poured your drinks." Her eyebrow arched. "For me."

I scoffed. "I'd have remembered you."

"Clearly you didn't," she said.

"Shame on me," I said.

I was rewarded with a flash of a smile, but her face went serious again. "Dinesso's been after a ship like this for years. Someone sold him one last year but the shielding fell apart on its first launch. They figure someone stripped the working parts, replaced them with junk, and he was too ignorant to know the difference. He wants to get into the courier business."

"Communications or cargo?" Plenty of people didn't want their communications filtered through official Ilmarinen channels, and I could charge a pretty penny just to carry data on the Nomad's heavily encrypted communication drive.

She shrugged. "I don't know. I assume he wants to move Blitz off the planet."

I scoffed. "He's a little fly in a world of spiders," I said. "There are better drugs sold by far worse men. No one beyond the Milky Way wants that poisonous shit."

"Someone told him that, but it just made him mad," Vani said. She shrugged. "It's not worth arguing with him. Either way, once he heard about your ship from Henri Agalov, he decided he wanted it. And he put me on it."

"Why you?"

"Because he thinks every man will turn stupid for pussy," she said. Her head cocked. "And he's not entirely wrong."

I groaned. "To be fair, I was very horny, and you're very good with your mouth."

Her eyebrows just perked. "I know I am," she said. "If I hadn't come, he'd have sent someone else. And I figured if I pulled it off, he might ease up on me for a while."

"Does he hurt you?" I asked.

"Sometimes," she said. I hated the casual tone in her voice, that some pathetic excuse of a man abusing her was so normal that it didn't faze her. That she would risk unknown dangers at my hands to avoid certain suffering at his. "Sometimes it's his goons. Sometimes men he wants to con." Her eyes were haunted. "Fucking you was supposed to just be another day on the job."

"Was supposed to be?"

"A lot of men have flopped around on top of me with their dicks," she said. "No one's ever made me feel what you did."

It was tempting to gloat about it. I did warn her that I'd be that good, but she wasn't teasing. There was a pit of ugliness yawning behind that compliment; something I wasn't ready to contemplate. Instead, I leaned in. "There's no reason you have to go back to that. You don't have to stay with me, but there's a million places you could go."

"My sisters need me," she said. "Dinesso's not going to quit hurting his girls because I'm gone. I can't run away and pretend like they're not still there."

"And if they were safe? Is there anything else tying you to Terra?"

Her eyes held mine for a long time, asking for something that she didn't dare speak aloud. "If they were safe, I'd leave and never look back." She sighed and rose from the table, giving me a fine view of her naked backside. "More coffee?"

"Storage container to your right. Make two," I said, guiding her through the process of using the compact drink machine. A minute later, she put another cup in front of me and one at her place.

"Where are we going?" she asked.

I was startled at how much I liked the sound of *we* on her tongue. "Vakarios."

"And what's in Vakarios?" she asked.

"Men a thousand times worse than your Dinesso," I said.

She scoffed. "I doubt that."

I scowled at her. "Imagine men with my strength and a taste for your pain. There are men there who would break you for looking at them sideways, to say nothing of stealing from them. They would fuck you raw in every hole until you begged for mercy. The only uncertainty is whether they'd kill you afterward or sell you to the Proxilar, who would certainly make you beg for death."

Her face went pale. "Then why are you going there?"

"I have a business deal," I said. "And when a man wishes to do big business under the radar, he goes to Vakarios." I raised my eyebrows. "You'll have to come with me."

Her eyes widened. "Why?"

"Because I can't leave you unattended there," I said. I might be able to lock her in a cabin, but if anyone caught wind that I had a pretty little Terran girl, they might kill me and grab her from the ship. If she was on my arm, at least I'd see them coming.

"What kind of deal do you have? Selling guns?"

"And how do you know that, little dust rat?"

Her brow furrowed. "Because that's what Henri sold you."

"It's a trade, but yes, that's my side of it," I said. "And some Atalian moonshine. There are buyers who have a strange taste for bad Terran booze. It's a novelty to them."

"And what are you buying?" I didn't like the sharp gleam in her eyes.

"None of your business," I said sharply.

"Captain," Diana interrupted. "We are entering the airspace of Ilmarinen Gate MW A-1. Shall I open frequencies?"

"Go ahead, Diana," I said. "Thank you."

"You're very polite to your ship," she said, the lightest hint of a tease there.

"My ship is the most important woman in my life," I replied. "She deserves politeness." There was a hint of sadness on her face, and I wondered if anyone had ever made Vani feel important, that she deserved the same respect and affection that I gave to a sophisticated computer program. I grabbed her arm and tugged her into my lap. Her chest pressed to mine, and I could feel the thumping of her heart. I rested my hand on her bare thigh, prompting a smile. "Imagine being a voice on a computer. No orgasms. Diana doesn't know what it feels like to have a good, hard fuck."

She laughed and slid my hand further up her thigh. Her fingers traced tiny circles on my chest. "I'm surprised you haven't tried."

"Oh, I've offered," I said. I raised my chin and spoke. "Diana, would you like me to go down on you?"

"Captain, your offer is very generous, but I am a computer and lack appropriate equipment for you to perform oral sex," Diana said. "Would you like for me to play a recording of an erotic literary work instead?"

"No, thank you," I said. "See? Diana has a hard life."

Vani laughed and shook her head. "You are ridiculous."

"Captain, our jump code has been confirmed," Diana said. "Expected time is ninety minutes."

Vani's eyes drifted up. "What does that mean?"

"Ships this small can't make jumps," I said. "In order to make an interstellar—"

She rolled her eyes. "I'm not stupid, Havoc. I may be from Earth, but I can read. I just don't know what the procedure is.
"

I smirked at her. "My apologies. The Nomad has a momentum drive. We're going to get thrown through the gate, which we call a slingshot. The Ilmarinen gate will open and connect to another gate at our destination, then release a huge of burst of energy to our ship. That causes a reaction in the Nomad's momentum drive, which will fire up and shoot us through the gates. The jump gates have to be powered up for hours, and frequently refueled, so they're on a tight schedule. Jump windows open only twice a day here in your galaxy because there's not much traffic. You have to be here on time, no exceptions, or you lose your spot and your money," I explained. "That's why I was so furious with you yesterday. Other than the fact that you stabbed me in the dick."

She winced. "You missed your jump."

"Yes," I said. "And I had to wait twelve more hours for another one."

She hesitated, then glanced up at me. "I'm sorry."

"For stabbing me in the dick?"

"All of it. I didn't want to hurt you," she said. Her eyes were solemn. "I thought you were so beautiful the first time I saw you. I didn't want Dinesso to have you, but I just didn't see any other way out."

"And now he doesn't have either of us," I said, my voice rough. I didn't know what to do with the strange, warm feeling my chest. It wasn't just lust, although I was already considering how I was going to fuck her in this tiny galley. There was something that made me want to shield her and protect her from harm.

Her eyes drifted. "What will it be like to go through the gate?"

"Like the launch from Terra, but much more intense," I said. "But it'll also be over faster. Then we fly nice and steady all the way to Vakarios."

She nodded, then rose to clean up our dishes. "Do you need anything else?"

"You don't have to earn a tip," I teased.

Her lips pursed. "Lifetime of habit. Let me do something to be helpful."

"Container E," I said, pointing to the drawer next to her left knee. She was quiet as she pondered the small sink. I watched her appreciatively, enjoying the subtle dance of muscle in her back as she worked to clean and dry our dishes. When she turned with a questioning look, I pointed overhead. "Dishes go in Container B."

She rose on her toes and stowed them, then leaned against the counter with her arms folded under her gorgeous breasts. "Can I borrow some clothes?"

"Not right now," I said.

"Why?"

"Because I said so," I said. "And because now that I've had coffee, I'm debating whether I'm going to fuck you on this table or in the lounge. And I'm not giving you one of my shirts just so I can rip it off you."

Her cheeks went bright red. "You know, you could take clothes off like a civilized person."

"Where's the fun in that?" I tugged at the waist of my briefs and let them snap against my skin. "You can try it if you want. It's a lot of fun."

A little giggle erupted from her lips. "Maybe I will." Then she gave me a stern look. "We're not doing it in here."

"Says who?"

"Me," she said defiantly. "I just cleaned up, and I'm not doing it again if you make a mess. Besides, if we stay in here, your handy little drawer of sex toys is out of reach."

"What?"

Her head cocked. "Do all ships keep a gag on hand or just yours?"

With a growl, I lifted her around my waist and carried her down the narrow hall. Her ass bounced against my cock, which stiffened beneath her. "Why, would you like to play with it again?"

She shook her head rapidly. "If my mouth is full during sex, I'd rather it was with your cock."

I froze, and she flashed that charming little grin at me. She-devil. Her mouth was as wicked as mine, and I liked it. I set her on top of the cabinet in the lounge and pulled out one of the latched drawers to reveal an assortment of toys. Vani's eyes widened. "See something you like?"

Her hand drifted toward one of the silver plugs with a glittering pink gem in it. "What's that?"

"I'll give you one guess where it goes," I said, raising an eyebrow. Her eyes widened, but I saw the twitch of a smile on her lips. I slid her off the cabinet and turned her back to me, nipping at her shoulder. Her legs buckled, and her head rolled back. I gave her a light smack on the ass, then grabbed her cheeks and spread them. She jolted, but I didn't release her. "A little secret between us. Right here."

"I don't know about that," she murmured.

"Have you ever had anyone here?"

She shook her head, then frowned at me. "There's no way you'll fit."

"Not right now," I said. "I can't help but notice that your protest is about logistics. Not that you wouldn't like it."

"You're huge," she said. Her eyes were filled with a mix of curiosity and fear. "Like, really huge."

"Again, logistics. That's why we take our time." I stroked her there, lightly pressing my finger to the tight channel. She shivered, her whole body undulating in a beautiful wave. "You'd be amazed at how it feels." She didn't speak, but her hips pushed back into me. I took the hint and took a bottle of lube from the drawer. After spilling a generous amount over her hole and my hand, I teased and stroked before gently sliding one finger into her. She gasped, fingers curling around the counter. "Just relax. Tell me if it hurts."

She took a deep breath and nodded. As I teased at her with one finger, I slid my other hand around and teased at her nipple, tweaking it until it was a perfect little bud. Her channel tightened around my finger, and she rose on her toes. Gods, the thought of sliding my cock into her was unbelievable. So tight and hot and perfect. I needed to be inside her again.

I switched to my thumb, and she let out a tiny gasp. I waited, kissing her neck gently. "Are you all right?"

"Yes," she whispered. "But it feels wrong."

"Wrong painful? Or wrong shameful?" I already knew the answer. Her face was flushed, and her breathing told me that she was riding a wave of arousal. Her body pulsed around me, demanding loud and clear.

"Shameful," she said.

"Who is here to make you ashamed?" I kissed her shoulder, then tilted her head toward me. "There's only you and me and Diana, and she's busy. Besides, she's heard way worse." Vani rolled her eyes. "And I certainly won't shame you. Do you want me to continue?"

Her chest heaved as she stared back at me. Shame was a hard burden to shake.

I narrowed my eyes and withdrew my fingers from her. She flinched, but didn't look away. "Vani, you're allowed to tell me no," I said firmly. "Maybe the men on Terra didn't let you say it, but you can say it to me. Speak the truth to me, always, whether the answer is yes or no. On my honor, I will always respect it."

Something was unfurling, rising from the shadows within those gorgeous green eyes. Then she nodded. "I want you to continue."

CHAPTER 11

Vani

THE WAY HE TOUCHED ME WAS SO DEMANDING, AND AT THE SAME time, more fulfilling than anything I'd ever felt. Dinesso and his men had used my body for years, but not once had they cared what made me feel good. And they had ignored my *no* so many times that I had quit saying it. Pretending I wanted it made me feel less helpless than having my protests ignored.

But Havoc delighted in wrapping every nerve ending in my body around his finger, wringing pleasure out of me like precious rainwater. He wanted a *yes*, and I wanted to tell him *yes* a thousand times over.

And for that reason, I was bent over a table while this strange alien male finger-fucked my ass. It sent little warm shivers of pleasure through me, as much for the excitement of it as the strange new sensation. Eventually, his fingers left me, and I let out a little questioning noise of protest.

Then something hard and metallic pressed to my hole. I froze, but his hand massaged my lower back gently. "Push back against it," he said. "I'll go slow."

Despite the hard, unfamiliar feeling, I liked the sensation. I liked doing something forbidden. It felt like a dirty little secret between us. I pushed back and gasped as the plug breached me.

"Just relax. Tell me when to go," he said.

When I looked back, he was smiling, not angry. With another deep breath, I nodded. "Okay." He was gentle as he pushed again, and there was just the tiniest flicker of pain and a spark of heat as the plug pushed past the tight ring of muscle. I felt an odd popping sensation, and then he tapped the end of it, sending little bolts of electricity through my body.

"Fuck," he muttered.

I glanced over my shoulder and wiggled my hips. "Well?"

"Well, I didn't think your body could look any better. But that's a nice touch." He grabbed my wrist and led me back into his quarters, then pointed to the bed. "When I come out, I want you on your back."

My heart thumped as he headed into the small bathroom. While the water ran, I shifted awkwardly on my feet, tentatively clenching around the plug. It was impossible to ignore the sense of fullness, of there being *something* where there was usually nothing. In a weird way, it was like he'd never taken his hands off me, like he was inside me instead of this little piece of metal.

He emerged from the head, wiping his hands on a towel. "I thought I said I wanted you on your back."

I propped my hands on my hips. "Or what?"

There was only a split second for me to brace myself before

he growled and tackled me onto the bed. I yelped in surprise, but he wrapped his hands around me, careful not to hurt me. His broad legs straddled me, his erect cock laying on my belly. His strong hands pinned my wrists. "Or I'll do it for you."

"Oh no. I should definitely follow your orders so I don't end up here again," I said in mock horror. His serious expression melted into a wicked grin, and I was suddenly concerned about what else he might find to stick inside me. There had been much bigger and more inexplicable things in that drawer. "You still didn't answer my question."

"Which was?"

"Why in the world you have these things," I said. "I'm sure none of that is standard equipment for a passenger ship. I read the manuals."

He chuckled and rolled off me. He fluffed the pillows and settled me on them like a throne. "I have a few clients who work as courtesans on Niraj," he explained. "Very expensive and exotic brothels."

"Oh," I murmured. "Did you fuck them, too?"

"One of them," he said.

"I thought you didn't pay for sex," I said.

"I don't," he replied. "She'd never had a Zathari in her bed, and she was curious."

"Did she enjoy it?"

He gave me a look like I'd asked if the sun was hot. "Obviously." I laughed as he continued, "The last time I took her back to Niraj, she sent me a bag of gifts and told me to try them on my next conquest."

"You're so good that she paid you?"

"Lucky you," he said.

"Lucky me," I murmured. Then he grabbed my wrists and spread them wide, pinning my hands to either side of the headboard. I tensed, waiting for him to call for Diana to strap me down somehow. My pussy clenched at the thought of it.

But instead, he stared intently at me, amethyst eyes burning a hole through me. "You're going to keep those hands up there. No touching, dust rat."

"I am?"

"You are," he said. "Because we have seventy-five minutes until we jump. Which means I have approximately seventy minutes to devour you."

My breath caught in my chest, and I hoped I wasn't about to destroy his lovely, tempting plan. "Havoc?"

"Hm?"

"Can I ask you a favor?"

"I'm going to eat your pussy, Vani," he said dryly. "You don't have to ask, although I like to hear you say it."

My hips surged, and a surge of wet warmth slid over my thighs. "Not that."

His head tilted. "What?"

I trembled, my throat clenching with emotion. "Please don't call me dust rat anymore," I said. I didn't know what to expect. The cynical part of me thought he'd sneer and say *I'll call you whatever the fuck I want*. And I would laugh it off, but it would hurt far worse than when he'd spanked me.

But his expression was unusually solemn. He nodded and said, "I understand. Never again." He kissed my lips gently, then lowered his head to my chest. I fidgeted, and I realized it was impossible to ignore the plug filling my back hole, especially as my body clenched down tight on it.

His lips closed on my nipple, teeth grazing ever so slightly as he swirled his tongue and licked and sucked until I was panting. I lowered one hand to cup his head, but he made a sharp, growling sound against me.

The quick but unquestionable display of dominance made me melt. I shuddered and put my hand back up, gripping the edge of the bed as he returned his attention to my nipple.

If Havoc was a human man on Earth, he'd probably have given each of my breasts a perfunctory pass, counted himself a rousing success on the foreplay front, and rammed in his cock to thrust for a few disappointing minutes.

Havoc was not a human man, and we were far from Earth and all its disappointments.

I didn't know if all Zathari were excellent in bed, but he was certainly setting a fine example for his kin. With more than an hour until we were launched across the universe, he was in no particular hurry. He lavished attention on my breasts as if he was being paid by the minute. His tongue circled and flicked, and when he drew me in tight, it felt like a wire connected straight to my core. He occasionally took a breath to suckle at my throat, letting the cool air kiss my tight peaks.

And just when I thought I might explode from the blazing warmth of his tongue rasping against my nipples, he moved down. He was torturously slow, hands splayed over my ribs as he kissed, a millimeter a time. Then to my hipbones, then my thighs, and finally—

"Holy shit," I wheezed, arching sharply. The tiniest flick of his tongue, and I was on fire. I forgot myself and grabbed his shoulders, digging in my fingers.

He laughed and pried my hands loose. "I'm going to stop if you can't behave."

"Please don't," I blurted. I threw my hands back. "It feels so good, I couldn't help it."

"I suppose I can let that one slide," he teased. "I did warn you that I'd ruin you for Terran men."

I was already ruined.

I gripped the headboard tight as he lowered himself again. His powerful arms slid under my thighs, lifting my pussy up to his face like he was holding a platter of the finest desserts in the universe. His deft tongue lashed over me, in and out, teasing across my clit, flicking my thighs.

And gods, the sounds he made. He sounded like a man dying of hunger, finally given relief with the sweetness between my thighs.

My whole body jerked as his tongue struck a spark that sizzled from my clit and zipped up my spine. I let out a sharp gasp and gripped the bedframe so hard it rattled against the wall. His big hands clasped over my belly, holding me tight against him as he devoured me.

"I'm coming," I said breathlessly. "Oh, fuck."

He lifted his head. The sight of his lips, glistening with my juices, almost finished me right there. It was filthy and messy and so beautiful I couldn't believe it. One dark eyebrow arched. "I am well aware," he said drily. He flicked his tongue over my clit, and my whole body arched against him. His muscles strained with the effort of holding me still. "Vani, I need you to do something."

"What?" I said breathlessly, wiggling my hips. He touched the tip of his tongue to me, and I nearly bent in half.

"Don't even think of holding back," he said. "Do not deprive me of one second of this orgasm. Do you understand?"

"Yes," I blurted. "You can have it."

His glistening lips split to reveal that dazzling grin. Then he sealed that wicked mouth to me and drove all coherent thoughts out of my head.

Fireworks exploded in my pussy. Every inch of my body tensed, squeezing tight, then fire rolled through me like a shockwave. I clamped my hands together, pressing back into the wall as my body convulsed in his grasp. And I let out a joyous cry that echoed off the walls, without shape or language, just sheer joy and disbelief that my body could feel this way.

He made his way up my body, then kissed my lips. I could taste myself on him, and I kissed him hungrily. His tongue plundered my mouth, just as deftly as it had claimed my pussy. I broke away breathlessly. "I want to touch you. Please."

"You may," he said. I grabbed his shoulders, wrapping my arms around him as I kissed him. Still drawing his tongue into my mouth, I reached down to stroke his cock. He was already hard, and his hips slid forward in my grasp. He broke away. "You sound like music when you come. I want to hear it again."

Lifting my hips, he slid his cock against my entrance and guided himself in. I was still sore and tender from yesterday, but I didn't care. I just needed more of him, as much as I could take, and then more beyond.

And I wanted to see that pleasure in his eyes. I wanted to be the reason he was breathless and sated.

His powerful arms hooked under my legs, spreading me wider and letting him go deeper. With the plug in my back hole, he felt huge, almost overwhelming. I clenched myself around him and watched the sensation ripple up his body. His voice caught as he said, "Do you want me to fuck you, Vani?"

I gasped sharply as he withdrew, nearly pulling out entirely. "I think we're past that." Staring down at where our bodies joined, the soft pink wrapped around that stone gray, I was stunned at how good he felt. This felt primal and natural and unquestionably good. I wanted him in my body, wanted him to mark me and claim me like I had never wanted it before. I wanted him to burn and scrape away every filthy thing Dinesso and his men had ever done, so that the only memory my body could hold was him.

He grinned and slid in an inch. I tried to push my hips toward him, but he held my legs so tight I couldn't move. "Say it. Honesty, Vani."

"Havoc, I want you to fuck me," I said, staring at him intently. A satisfied smile spread on his face. "I have never wanted anything like I want you fucking me right now."

"Now that's honesty," he said. His voice lowered to a growl as he slid deeper and deeper until he was fully seated inside me. My body shuddered around him. I could feel the firm, insistent pulse in the base of his cock, each beat a little flicker of sensation that tickled through me. He took me in long, deep strokes. Each time jolted the plug, and I couldn't help wondering what it would feel like for him to take me there.

Watching his face was a revelation. He was not drifting in another world while he used my body to make himself come. He was watching me, intent on seeing the results of his efforts. "I want to hold you," I said. A curious smile spread on his face, and he released my legs, lowering himself to me. I kissed him hungrily, running my hands over his broad, muscular back as he drove deep into me.

How strange, that I could want something and have it.

I had never wanted a man close to me like this, to feel his body slide and twine with mine as he fucked me. Small, soft grunts escaped his throat, and I swallowed them hungrily, trying to draw every bit of him into me.

Sweat dripped from his brow, and he sat back on his heels suddenly, withdrawing from my embrace. I grasped at him with a desperate, needy whine, but he held my hands in one of his, still thrusting in small, undulating gestures.

"Come back," I pleaded, trying to hook my leg around him to pull him back in.

"After," he said, his tone almost a threat. With a decadent, lewd gesture, he licked his fingers and stroked my clit. My back arched violently, and he laughed. "After this." He was so controlled as he wound me tighter and tighter. "Remember. This is mine. Do not deny me what is mine."

My brain was already shutting down, black pressing in and my hearing fading. The world was nothing but the fire where our bodies met, where his fingers twisted me into a knot, a singularity of wildness and pleasure. But I kept my eyes on his until I simply couldn't, when I fell into the abyss. I couldn't breathe, couldn't think, could only let him carry me along like a current, like gravity.

Then his huge, warm body was close again as he hiked my legs over his shoulders and drove deep. It was so tight and full with the plug that I could barely take it. His lips sealed to mine as I panted and whined the echoes of my climax. "Give that to me," he growled against my mouth. "All mine."

CHAPTER 12

Havoc

"All yours," she whispered. Her eyes were wide as she stared up at me, still panting and whimpering. Her walls fluttered and clenched around me, so tight that I was going to explode any second. Her voice was breaking as she said *yes, yes, please*, as I lost myself inside her.

You are mine.

In my world, you kept what you found. I had stolen and killed to make my way from the hellscape of Kilaak up to the endless stars.

And now I had found her.

I wanted to claim every inch of her, so that she would always know she was mine. Let the entire universe know that she was all mine.

My roar echoed off the walls as I finished, driving deep into her as I spilled my seed. When my eyes refocused, I lowered my head and covered her face and neck in rough, hungry kisses, tasting the salty warmth of her skin. I started to withdraw, but she grabbed my hips hard. "No," she ordered. Then she looked startled at her own sharp tone. "Please don't."

"Why?" I asked. I was shocked at how much I needed her to say it. That I needed her to want me. There was no doubt that she desired me, that her body responded to me. But I wanted to hear it, so that it would echo into the void and reach the distant Wayfarers who'd long turned away from me.

"Because you feel good," she said. "I like having you inside me."

"You're getting good at this honesty thing," I told her.

She gazed up at me, green eyes full of wonder. She suddenly put her fingers to the side of her throat, then touched mine. After sitting in silence for a few seconds, her smile widened. "I can feel your pulse inside me," she marveled. With each insistent pulse of the *dzirian*, the rounded knob at the base of my cock, her body fluttered around me in response. It was a lovely, quiet conversation between our bodies.

I nodded. "Another perk of the Zathari." It might have been the horns that caught their eye, but it was Zathari dick that kept them coming for more. Literally.

"I really won't ever be able to touch a human man after this," she replied.

"Oh no. I'm heartbroken, really," I said. Holding her hips close to me, I rolled onto my back and resituated her on top of me. And what a sight she was, with that golden skin all aglow. I admired her body, raising my hands to trace the subtle curve of her waist. "We have to jump soon."

"I'll let you go before then," she said. She gripped my wrists and lightly pinned them on either side of my head. "Maybe one day I'll tie you up." She leaned in and kissed my forehead, long waves of hair tickling over my shoulders. "What would you do?"

"Oh no, please don't," I drawled. I raised my head and caught one rosy nipple, sucking hard enough to prompt a gasping little giggle. "You're sitting on my cock with a perfect pair of tits in my face. Whatever shall I do, you monster?"

She threw her head back and laughed. "I'm serious."

"Maybe one day I'll let you," I said. If she kept smiling at me like that, I was going to be addicted. She was better than any drug the cartel pushers were selling.

"I'll bribe Diana," she said.

"She likes me better," I told her. I broke her grasp and reached back to cup her ass, drumming my fingers against the sparkling gem. "What did you think?"

Her smile broadened. I could feel her clenching around me, like she was testing out the pretty little jeweled plug. "I never thought I'd say so, but I kind of liked it."

"I'm glad," I said. "One day, I'll fuck you there, and you'll beg me for more."

"You seem awfully confident," she said.

"I have every reason to be," I said. I jolted my hips up into her and relished the ripple of muscle down her flat stomach. "I've made good on my promises thus far, haven't I?"

"Yeah, you have," she said quietly. With a little wince, she rose up, releasing me from her body. Her nose wrinkled. "I should clean up."

I grabbed her hips and settled them back against me. "I think not," I said.

With a faint smile, she settled her hands on my chest. "Can I touch?"

I nodded my agreement, and let out a satisfied sigh as she kneaded those small, deft hands into my shoulders. "You can do that as long as you like, angel."

Her hands stopped, and her head tilted to one side. There was a look of utter confusion on her face. "Angel?"

"You don't like it?"

The smile on her face wasn't cocky or flirtatious. It was gentle and soft, something I hadn't yet seen from her. I felt like I'd caught a glimpse of the sun through stormclouds. Her eyes drifted away from mine. "I really like it."

With that, I felt like I had solved the problems of the universe. "Angel," I repeated. *My angel.* Giving her a name made her mine, didn't it?

Her smile widened as she massaged the tight muscles in my shoulders. "Where do you live?"

"Right here," I said. "This ship is my home."

She frowned. "You don't have a house? Or an apartment?"

"I keep a place in another galaxy, on a little planet called Phade. Heard of it?" She shook her head. "I stay busy, so I'm rarely there." My brothers and I threw money into a common pot for the small apartment in Ir-Nassa, the biggest city on Phade. There, the government officials had deep pockets and were easy to distract. We had an agreement to never bring our dirty business there.

"Were you born there?"

My stomach twisted in a knot. "No."

Her head tilted, wavy dark hair spilling over her shoulder. "Is that all?"

My instinct was to flip her over and distract her from her invasive line of questioning. My tongue in the right places would drive those questions right out of her head. But for some reason, I answered. "I was born on Sonides, the home planet of the Zathari. But I spent much of my life on Kilaak. It's a prison planet for the Dominion." From one shithole to another, but that was more than I was ready to explain to her.

"The whole planet is a prison?"

"Cheaper than a building," I said. Why build walls when you could dump off your undesirables on a hellhole like Kilaak? And the real kicker of it was that the Aengra Dominion prided themselves on their merciful treatment of lawbreakers. No confining cells or corporal punishment. They simply dumped you off on a strange planet with a week's worth of food and a handful of basic supplies that would be stolen within a day. And when you put the worst of your society on a planet with no boundaries, they did far worse to each other than the most sadistic prison guard would do.

"What did you do?"

My chest tightened, and I tapped one of my horns. "The Zathari are not well-liked in the Dominion. I crossed the wrong person as a boy, and I paid the price for it." And even with all we'd suffered, I'd have done it again.

"Can I ask what you did?" she said quietly. "Did you hurt someone?"

"I did," I said with a nod. "My mother died when I was very young, and my father..." I sighed. "He wasn't a bad man, but he couldn't raise two children. He took a job off-world working in a factory and sent money for us. For a while he sent messages promising to bring us to him, but they eventually dried up."

"Did something happen to him?" she asked.

I shrugged. "I think he was far enough from us to forget about us. My friend Storm's mother took us in when I was six or so. My sister was a year younger, and I tried to protect her."

She flinched. "Did someone hurt her? Is that what got you in trouble?"

The memory of Nashira wailing still made my stomach twist with fury and shame. Storm had pulled the bastard off her, and I finished the job. It was bad enough that the Dominion officials on Sonides treated us like shit. They were outsiders, and we expected it. But the man who'd attacked my sister was Zathari. He thought his loyalty to the Dominion made him untouchable. In the end, he was.

"Someone tried. They learned that it was a mistake," I said. Her brow lifted. "I broke his back and ruptured his testicles. I'd have killed him with my bare hands if someone hadn't pulled me off. He learned not to put his hands on someone who said no. Unfortunately for me, he claimed that I attempted to kill him for no reason. The Dominion judges sent me away, as I was clearly too violent to be a part of a civil society."

"But they let you go?"

I gripped her wrist. "No, angel, they didn't let me go. My brothers and I cut a bloody fucking path out of there and killed everyone who stood in our way." I sure as hell hadn't been too violent before Kilaak. But after more than a decade in a vicious place, with no hope of freedom, I had become the monster they claimed I was.

I expected her to shrink back in horror, but she leaned in, eyes gleaming. "What was that like? Getting away?"

"Almost as satisfying as fucking you," I said. "But not quite."

At that, she grinned. "Flatterer."

"I've not told you a single lie, Vani," I said, sliding my hands up her thighs.

Her playful expression faded. "Do you ever see her? Your sister?"

I smiled faintly, even though I felt like she'd gutted me. "Not often," I said. "But she's in a good place. She has a family and a good life." She had a peaceful life in a place where I was unwelcome. Even so, I did what I could to take care of her from afar.

"So why aren't you there?"

"Enough about me," I said. I gently brushed my finger over the L-shaped scar on her ribs. "Who did this to you? I want a name."

"Luka," she said absently as she moved my hand back to her thigh. "One of Dinesso's men. I mouthed off to him, so he punished me. He intended to carve his whole name, but Dinesso stopped him." She let out a bitter laugh. "After all, stitches would have kept me out of work for a few days. Good for me, because I'm pretty sure he would have spelled it wrong."

"Why would you allow these men to treat you like this?"

Anger flared in her eyes. "We don't all have your strength, or a band of brothers to back us up. I couldn't break someone's neck because they looked at me wrong. At least with Dinesso, I had a clean place to sleep and regular meals. All it cost was my dignity and my freedom, and I wouldn't have had those anyway if I starved to death on the streets."

"You didn't have a family?" I asked.

She drew a deep breath and sighed. "Sort of. My mother worked for Dinesso, too, so I grew up watching her under his thumb. She used to tell me that an angel brought me to her, but it was probably some random asshole from the Prospects. Hell, I sometimes wonder if it was Dinesso who knocked her up. I wouldn't put it past him." Her nose wrinkled.

"That's fucked up," I said, shuddering with revulsion. And the fact that she was so casual about it made me even angrier. This was her *normal*.

"Tell me about it," she said with a bitter laugh. "When I was young, I saw her getting roughed up by some of his guys and I told them to stop. I thought she'd be happy, but she slapped me and told me that Nesso took good care of us. She had to do her part to be grateful. Things could be worse, she always said. When I was fourteen, she left one day and never came home."

`"She left you there with those pigs?"

She shrugged. "Maybe she left. Maybe someone killed her. Either way, I never saw her again. I used to pretend that she was far away, building a beautiful house for us, like a tower from a fairytale that no one could climb. In the meantime, Dinesso promised he'd take good care of me. I knew what that meant, and I knew why all of his goons looked at me the way they did. I was fifteen when I started serving drinks at the Dahlia. Then I was dancing, and then I was entertaining Dinesso's guys. I thought it was what I had to do."

I barely knew Vani, but I felt a sharp knife of pain through my chest at her casual tone. Her playful spirit hid a tremendous pain. Words of pity would only scrape that festering wound, so I simply nodded. "Did you ever run away?"

"Twice," she said. "The first time wasn't long after Mom disappeared. I didn't get far. One of his boys saw me on the street, picked me up, and took me right back. I told him I'd been running an errand, but Dinesso knew. He let one of his new guys beat me black and blue, then locked me in a filthy basement for a week." Her head hung, her shoulders hunching. "The next time, I was old enough to know better, and old enough for a real punishment. They all—" She just shook her head and laughed bitterly, leaving me to envision exactly what a group of sadistic assholes had done to her. "I don't want to talk about it. I don't want them here."

"Then don't," I said gently. Suddenly, I couldn't be angry at what she'd done to me. I'd done worse things to survive, and worse still to protect my brothers.

Her eyes were haunted. "I know you probably think I'm weak and pathetic, but you can't imagine what it's like to be a woman in that world. I said *yes* to a lot because it made me feel like it was my decision. And when I said *yes,* my sisters didn't have to say anything at all."

"I don't think you're pathetic at all," I said. Her green gaze locked on mine. "But it infuriates me that you had to do those things. Someone failed you. Someone should have protected you and taken care of you."

She shrugged. "Maybe, but they didn't. So I took care of myself. And now, I take care of Naela and Amira the best I can."

Never again.

Nearly a century ago, the Zathari had gone to war when the Aengra Dominion pushed into the Vela Cluster and discovered the lush forests and rich mineral resources on Sonides. Though they were advanced in their own right, our ancestors couldn't withstand the Dominion's far superior war machines. They were slowly driven away from the planet that had been their home for millennia. Refugees eventually settled on the dangerous planet of Irasyne, millions of miles from their homes.

For years on Kilaak, my brothers and I had clung to the hope of finding a home with our people. The colony on Irasyne was a glowing beacon of hope through the dusty murk of the prison planet. I was twenty-nine when we escaped, and thirty-one when we arrived, ragged and hopeful, on the outskirts of the Zathari settlement. Nashira had resettled there when she was twenty, and the thought of a reunion kept me going through some of the worst days. I would have a family again, maybe even a wife if someone could look past what I'd done to gain my freedom.

But our shared heritage was not enough to make us welcome. We were killers and thieves, and worst of all, wanted men by the Dominion. Their warriors surrounded us and made it clear that we had no place there.

The leaders of the refugee settlement would not let us endanger their people. And despite the injustice of our situation, they would not bend in their ways to speak to the gods for us. Nashira came to me, tearfully promising she would do whatever she could, but the leaders of the refuge wouldn't budge.

I'd been imprisoned on Kilaak for much of my life. I'd turned nineteen in a camp full of vicious men, where I had already grown up fast. I never stood beneath a full moon for a naming ceremony. No Elder had given me a proper name, nor whispered it to the Wayfarers of the Void, who would align the stars to guide me to a mate. I would never know the power of a starbound mate. The other half of my soul would wander endlessly, because she would not know where to look for me. She would have no name to call, and I could never answer.

The old ways were fucking stupid, Wraith said. The Wayfarers had let us all rot on Kilaak, until we took fate into our own hands. Furthermore, starbound mates hadn't saved our ancestors from being obliterated, and there was more than enough pussy in the universe to keep us satisfied for the rest of our lives.

But there were times when childish optimism and foolish hope overtook me, and I thought, just for a moment, that I could find my mate. Billions of people across a hundred galaxies, and somehow I'd find her.

Right.

Wraith was right. There was no destined mate for me, but if there was, I'd like someone like Vani, all full of fire that burned brighter with every mile further from Terra. Regardless of what she'd suffered, something brilliant shone in her. I could see it emerging from the dark, like unearthing a diamond far beneath the earth.

No one had taken care of this brilliant little spark, but I would. And if I had my way, no one would hurt her ever again.

CHAPTER 13

Vani

There was something oddly pensive about Havoc as he reluctantly rolled me off of him and started the shower. He kissed my neck gently and took the plug out of me, leaving me oddly empty. Instead of joining me under the hot spray, he watched from the door as I scrubbed myself down. His eyes lingered as I scrubbed between my legs. I raised an eyebrow and asked, "Not going to join me?"

"We're going to miss the jump if I do. Don't take too long. The recycler can't keep up with two people taking hot showers." He disappeared, leaving me alone to finish washing myself.

I sighed. My body was tired and pleasantly achy. He'd been thorough and generous, but no one would make the mistake of calling Havoc gentle. I liked his intensity, but if we kept this up, I'd need an ice pack. And without him there, flooding my senses with desire, I was suddenly ashamed. I could see Luka sneering at me. `

Filthy slut, he'd say. Funny how men like him could demand our bodies and insult us in the same breath. He liked to remind us that us girls, we were good for one thing, so it was fortunate that we had three holes to accomplish it. My stomach twisted in a knot.

I liked the way I felt with Havoc. It made no sense. He was the most dangerous man I'd ever met, but I'd never felt so safe in my life. *Someone should have been taking care of you*, he'd said. What would it be like to feel like this forever? To be with someone so strong and feel comfort, not fear? The thought of it was almost unfathomable.

"Captain, prepare for slingshot in twenty minutes," Diana announced. From down the hall, I heard him politely thank the ship. It made me chuckle every time.

A minute later, he leaned into the tiny bathroom. "Out," he ordered. "If the water's cold, I am going to be very upset."

"And what will you do about it?" I teased.

"You don't want to find out," he said ominously, though there was the tiniest hint of a smile on his lips. I raised my eyebrows and slid out. On my way past him, he handed me a towel and smacked my wet bottom hard enough to make me jump.

"What was that for?"

"Because it was there and I wanted to," he said. "There's clothes on the bed for you."

While he showered, I investigated the neatly folded garments. To call them clothes was a drastic overstatement, and I was tempted to call him out on his supposed policy of honesty. There was a silky black nightgown with thin straps, a matching robe, and a pair of soft, flat slippers. But this was better than my clothes from the Dahlia. Even if I had to be naked for weeks, I never wanted to touch them again.

I dressed in the soft robe and nightgown, which barely skimmed my knees. I'd just slid on the slippers, when he emerged from the shower, gloriously naked. Water still ran down his body, glittering in the hard lines of muscle on his legs. He had no business being so gorgeous. And if he didn't get dressed, I was going to grab something that would distract him. "See something you like?" he asked.

"I see several things I like," I said, averting my gaze. Then I plucked at the thin nightgown. "This hardly qualifies as clothes."

"The second best option was a leather harness with the nipples cut out," he said archly. "I'd have preferred it, but it might run the risk of pinching in rather uncomfortable places when I strap you in. Would you rather—"

"No, no," I said. "More gifts from your courtesans?"

He nodded and dug in his closet. I bit back my pointed comment about why he got pants and a nice snug shirt that covered him from neck to ankles. Crisp white fabric hugged his chest tight, outlining his broad back and defined musculature. I wasn't complaining about the view. "If you're going to be part of my crew, then come help me lock down."

Warmth rolled over me. "I'm part of your crew?"

"Of course," he said, carefully bolting the closet. "I'm just debating your title."

"Well, considering there's just the two of us, I think I'm the first mate," I said.

He froze and stared at me, amethyst eyes wide. "First m-mate?"

"Yeah," I said, startled by his reaction. "On Earth, I think that's what they used to call them on ships. Or maybe a lieutenant."

"Well, Lieutenant..."

"Adros," I said. "But I think I want an exciting name like yours."

"Angel," he mused. "Havoc and Angel. That sounds good to me." He gave me a sidelong glance as he strapped on his watch. I joined him at the bed and helped him make it quickly with fresh sheets, then followed his directions to put the pillows in a big sliding drawer beneath the frame. We worked in quiet concert, leaving the room as neat and sharp as if no one had ever used it.

Where my little room back at Dinesso's compound had loose knick-knacks, a jewelry box here and a stack of books there, everything had a place here. He showed me how to check the latches on each drawer and storage compartment. While he ran diagnostics in the engine room, I straightened the kitchen and stowed everything neatly. Out of habit, I found a cloth and wiped everything down, the way I would have when closing down the Dahlia. When I was done, I did the same in the lounge, after stealing one last peek at his drawer of kinky delights.

I'd done only small tasks, but when he returned to inspect my work, he said, "Looks good." Paired with his smile, those two simple words made me feel like the sun had shone only on me. "Launch time, Lieutenant."

Like for our first jump, he buckled me into the seat, then

kissed my lips gently. "This one will be rough, but it'll be over fast."

I nodded, my heart racing in anticipation. For the first time, it occurred to me that I had nothing with me, not even identification. "Are they going to know I'm with you?"

He shook his head. "They slingshot ships, not people," he said. "Part of my license is a presumption that I'm carrying out legal activities. That's why clean papers are so desirable, and why I'm so fucking careful not to slip up. As long as you stay on board, we can pass easily through Dominion space." He glanced over, his violet eyes full of an unusual softness. "You're with me now."

"I am," I mused. *I am with you.*

Over the next ten minutes, he calmly explained what was happening to the ship. There was a strange jolt, then a subtle vibration as the Nomad was pulled into a magnetic field. The huge silver rings of the Gate disappeared from sight as we got closer and closer, and suddenly, the louvred screens closed. I felt a weird lifting sensation as the artificial gravity was deactivated.

"Captain, we're next in the launch sequence," Diana said.

"Thank you, Diana," he said. He gripped my hand. "When she counts down, take a deep breath and blow it out. It'll feel like forever, but I promise that it will end quickly. I've done this hundreds of times." He tugged on my hand, and I turned to look at him. My chest tightened with fear. "When we come out the other side, you'll be millions of miles from Terra. How does that feel?"

My breath was shaky. "I don't know. Ask me when we get there."

He laughed. "I'll try to remember."

"Thirty seconds, Captain," Diana said.

I closed my eyes, trying to breathe as I listened the pleasant female voice counting down. When this was over, I would be so far from Terra that it might as well not exist. I would be where Dinesso could never touch me again. But my freedom meant abandoning my sisters to his hands. All of our futures hung on nothing more than Havoc's word, which I prayed was as solid as he claimed. Could I risk the dangerous delusion of hope? Could I put my faith in someone other than myself?

"Ten," Diana said.

"Vani, breathe," Havoc ordered. I sucked in a deep breath and held it, holding his hand tight. He squeezed it back.

"Three. Two. One. Launching."

"Exhale," Havoc said as the world crushed in around me. A huge fist pushed me back into the chair while another reached inside me and yanked my stomach out of my body. The ship vibrated violently around me, and I was certain it was going to shatter into a million pieces and toss me out into space.

I promise it will end quickly, he'd said.

Holding tight to his hand, I forced the breath out, focusing on how the air felt over my lips, and more importantly, the warm, strong hand in mine. But I was nearly out of air, and still, the universe was folding in around me. How would I—

"Breathe, Vani," he said gently.

I gasped, and the world came zooming back into sharp focus. As I filled my lungs, the pressure ceased, and I realized that we weren't being crushed into an infinitely tiny little speck of metal. My eyes blinked rapidly as I turned to him. "Is it over?"

"It's over," he said. He raised an eyebrow and unbuckled himself, then opened a panel beneath his seat. With a flick of his wrist, he turned a circle of thin plastic into a small bucket and handed it to me. "No offense, but you should hold that for a while." He unfolded himself from the seat and reached up to flick a switch on a panel.

"Diana, run full diagnostics. Update flight plan, then begin message transmissions," he ordered.

"Yes, Captain," Diana said.

He glanced over his shoulder. "Do you want to see outside? Or is it too much?"

My stomach heaved, but I didn't feel like I was going to lose it this time. "Let me see, please."

He flicked a switch, then unbuckled the harness that held me into the seat. He scooped me up, then sat in the bigger captain's chair with me in his lap. His big hands looped around my waist. Shifting lightly, he tweaked a touchscreen, and the louvred window screens retracted. I gasped in surprise.

Beyond the windows was another sea of stars, but it was like nothing I'd ever seen. Half a dozen ships radiated around us, as if we were little sparks thrown from a firework. A great purple orb blanketed in swirling white clouds loomed to the right. "What's that?" I murmured.

His voice was a pleasant rumble at my back. "That's Rubresan."

"Who lives there?"

"No one," he said. "Well, a handful of miners with more greed than common sense. It's a frozen wasteland." He reached around me and detached a small tablet from the dashboard, then set it in my lap. The bright screen displayed a small map with arrows all around the perimeter. "Touch it and move the view. There are lenses outside the ship so you can see everything."

I swiped at it and gasped when I saw the massive rings of the Gate behind us. Docked on its edge was a ship that had to be as big as the entirety of the Prospects. "Is that a ship or a city?"

"It's an ark ship," he said. He reached around me to zoom in on the blue logo. "That logo is from Outroads Shipping. They move products all across Dominion space. If the Nomad didn't have a momentum drive, I could buy a spot on a ship like that to ferry her to a new galaxy," he explained. He tapped an arrow, then spread his fingers to get a closer look at something beyond the Gate. "And that little yellow blip is Inan Prime. After Vakarios, we'll refuel there."

"How many planets are there?" I asked.

"How many grains of sand are in the deserts of Terra?" His hand slid under the silky nightgown, though he didn't go past my thigh. His fingers circled, almost as if he was idling the time. "The universe is unspeakably vast. There is no need to stay in a place that doesn't suit you. There is always a new place to go."

My chest tightened, and I suddenly felt the sting of tears in my eyes. I bowed my head, but before I could hold it back, a single fat tear fell on the screen. I tried to wipe it away, but he'd already seen it there, glowing atop some mysterious blue moon.

He gently lifted my chin. "What's wrong?"

"I don't belong out here," I said, scrubbing at my eyes.

His brow furrowed. "Why do you say that?"

"I'm nobody. I don't know anything," I said. "I'm a petty criminal on a dusty rock in a galaxy that—"

He put his hand over my mouth abruptly. Fury filled his eyes, and I recoiled. I hadn't seen him this furious since I tried to gouge his eye out. "How dare you?" I raised my eyebrows and tried to pull away, but he held me fast. "How dare you talk about yourself that way?" He shook his head and removed his hand, instead grabbing my hands and holding them tight. "You may have been born into the dust on Terra, but there is nowhere you cannot go now. Do you hear me?"

I nodded silently, my eyes still stinging.

"And don't ever let me hear you call yourself nobody again," he growled. "I won't have it…Lieutenant."

The title brought a warm flutter to life in my chest. "But I don't know anything about…well anything that isn't Earth," I said. "I'm not like you."

"No one knows anything until they learn," he said. The angry look on his face softened, and he stroked my cheek. "Ten years ago, I was hauling ore out of a mine on Kilaak. I had no idea what existed beyond the stars I could see through the smoke. We all come from somewhere." His brow lifted. "I can show you."

I heard a promise there. I wasn't sure if he was really making the offer, or if I wanted it so badly that I heard it. For now, I was someone different, and I wanted to believe in him. I dared to believe him. With a deep breath, I nodded. "Show me."

CHAPTER 14

Havoc

I DIDN'T KNOW WHAT VANI WAS DOING TO ME, NOR IF I SHOULD like it. It had been barely two days since she came crashing into my life and my ship, and I was utterly infatuated. If it was one of my brothers, I'd have told them to get their fill of fucking and send her on her way before she caused more trouble. It was one thing to enjoy her company here in the confines of my ship, but who knew what she would do when she had an opportunity. There was still a deep fear in her, and I couldn't trust her.

But gods, did I want to. Watching her face as she surveyed the stars, realizing that the universe was much bigger than the dusty prison where she'd spent her life...it made me want her even more. I wanted to be the one to hold her hand and show her the wonders of the world. I wanted to show her the sophisticated decadence of Niraj, the endless jungles of Agrinus, and the impossibly huge, gleaming shine of Firyanin. Unfettered by the dullness of Earth, that spark would grow into something incandescent.

"Captain, diagnostics are complete," Diana said. I looped my arm around Vani's waist and gently took the tablet from her as Diana gave her report. "Momentum drive is in optimal condition. I detect a minor shift in connection strength on Shielding Panel E17. Manual investigation recommended at your next refueling."

"Thank you, Diana," I said. "My flight plan?"

"We have ample fuel to arrive on Vakarios and launch into the atmosphere afterward. I have calculated several options, including refueling at Vakarios, as well as moving to Inan Prime or purchasing fuel at Gate AG B-2. Would you like further details?"

"No," I said. "Set a course for Vakarios. Adjust speed to give us three hours before my meeting. Will that require a change to the fuel plan?"

"A moment," she said. "No, Captain. Travel time to Vakarios will be approximately twenty-two hours. Now beginning encrypted message transmissions."

Finally, I returned my attention to Vani. She tilted her head. "What do we do for twenty-two hours?"

"I need sleep," I said. Adrenaline had long given way to exhaustion. At her flirtatious expression, I narrowed my eyes. "Actual sleep, not pretending to be asleep to see who's going to jump the other first. Can you handle that?"

A faint smile ghosted across her face. "Yes."

"Then we have to prepare for Vakarios," I said, a flutter of dread prickling over me. I nudged her off my lap, and she followed me into the narrow hall as I checked each of the small rooms of the ship. The armory remained locked. As much as I wanted to trust her, I wasn't ready to let her into my room packed with weapons.

"Is it that bad?" she asked.

"Who is the worst man in Dinesso's crew?" I asked.

She hesitated. "Rico." Her flinch was barely perceptible, but it infuriated me. I wondered what this Rico had done to make her flinch.

"I want you to assume that every man on Vakarios is at least as bad as Rico," I said.

"But you'll be there."

I paused and glanced back at her, baring my teeth. "Who says I'm not just as bad as he is?"

"Not to me, you're not," she said. "Surely not everyone there is so bad."

"Probably not, but assuming that they are will keep you alive," I said. "Even the Dominion doesn't touch Vakarios. The Bhazaran Cartel is the only law there, and they'll turn a blind eye to anything for the right cost." I checked the cargo bay and found all of my crates still strapped in tight. I had bought an extra case of guns and the grain alcohol from Henri, just in case something was damaged in transit. I was leaving nothing to chance.

"And I have to go there with you," she murmured.

"It would not have been my preference," I said. "There are places in the universe where women hold more power, but Vakarios is not one of them. Even the Diamondbacks send men to do their work on Vakarios."

"The Diamondbacks?"

"All female mercenary company," I said. Her eyes widened

with delight. "I'll put it this way. If their leader, Jalissa, ever met your Dinesso, he'd beg for mercy, and she'd blow him off the map with a smile on her face. And even Jalissa won't set foot on Vakarios."

Her smile faded.

"That's why I'm worried about you," I finished.

She just nodded solemnly and followed me through the ship to finish our post-jump checklist. Once I was satisfied that the Nomad was in peak condition, I finally returned to the small sleeping quarters. I stripped down, sat on the edge of the bed, and raised an eyebrow at Vani.

Despite the seriousness of our conversation, she gave me a wicked grin. She delicately plucked the thin straps from her shoulders, then gave a graceful little shimmy. Black silk slid over her breasts, then down over her soft hips. As she bent to pick it up, she turned to give me a view of her perfect bottom, and it was all I could do not to grab her and slam her down on my cock. "You don't like the nightgown I gave you?" I teased. "I'm offended."

"You like me naked," she said coyly. "But I'll put it back on if it hurts your feelings, Captain."

I grabbed her arm lightly. "Don't you dare."

"Captain, I have messages," Diana chirped.

Goddammit.

I grabbed Vani anyway and pulled her into my lap, busying myself with her breasts. She laughed and pulled my hand away. "Shouldn't you pay attention, Captain?"

"I can do two things at once," I said, returning my hand, finding her peaked nipple beneath my fingers again. She sighed, pushing into my grasp. "That's why I'm the captain, and you're the lieutenant. Go ahead, Diana." I certainly enjoyed the addition of Vani to my crew; I couldn't complain about having my hands full while I listened to messages.

Diana prattled on. I had a heavily coded message from Jalissa Cain about a smuggling job. The timing wouldn't work, so I sent her a quick and polite *not this time,* and moved on. There was a message from my brother, Mistral. He confirmed that he was on Phade, now, and would accompany me to the refugee settlement on Irasyne. There was also a message from Rhasat Glyck, the dealer I would meet at Vakarios. One of his underlings rattled off a confirmation of the location and time for our swap.

When Diana was done, I said, "Thank you, Diana. Please activate sleep mode."

"Good night, Captain. Sleep well," Diana said. The lights dimmed, and cool air blew through my quarters. I brought Vani back with me, curling my body around her.

"Are you going to stab me?" I whispered.

She chuckled. "No. But maybe you should hold me to be safe."

With several rounds of fucking, a chase through the ship, a launch, and an interstellar jump behind us, we were both exhausted. She fell asleep as soon as she hit the pillow, her body relaxing into me. I rested my head in the curve of her shoulder, breathing in her scent. There was no trace of Terra left on her, not the ever-present dust , nor the artificial perfume she'd worn to appeal to her targets.

She was something utterly different now. I breathed her in, held her inside me, and I drifted off in a cloud of nothing but Vani.

When I woke, I was confused and disoriented. My arms were empty, and I sat bolt upright in a dizzying motion. "Diana, daylight mode. What time is it?" I blurted. The lights flicked on, blinding me.

"Time is two twenty-one Ilmarinen Universal Time," Diana chirped. "We are approximately twelve hours from Vakarios."

I squinted and looked around. No Vani, and the cabin door was open. Goddammit. What the hell was she up to now?

"Any security alerts?"

"No, Captain," she said. I waited, trying to ignore Wraith's stern voice in my head and give her the benefit of the doubt. I'd count to ten and then grab a gun.

At seven, I caught a whiff of coffee in the air. Before I could investigate further, Vani tiptoed back into the cabin, wearing the black robe and nightgown I'd loaned her. Her shoulders slumped. "You're awake."

"Disappointed?"

"Yes. I was going to wake you up," she said, setting a cup of coffee next to me on the small table. Her wavy hair was tied back in a bouncy ponytail, filling my head with filthy thoughts. "I decided that would be one of my duties."

I was perfectly content to play along. "And how were you going to wake me up, Lieutenant?"

Her teeth tugged at her lip. "Want me to show you?"

"I think I do," I said.

"Then lay down and pretend to be asleep."

I laughed. "Only for you."

"Lights," she demanded.

"Diana, night mode," I said. This was ridiculous, but I could get into this kind of silliness.

"Yes, Captain. Good night," the computer said in her soothing voice.

The lights dimmed again, and I closed my eyes. My bed shifted as my companion crept back in, crawling under the blanket. Her lithe body slid between my legs, and without any fanfare, she licked me from root to tip. The warm rasp of her tongue on my cock brought me to life, awakening the steady pulse in my *dzirian*. "Oh, that's nice."

"Be asleep!" she protested, her voice vibrating against my thigh.

I held back a laugh. "I apologize," I said, lying back with my hand propped behind my head. If this was the height of her skullduggery, then thank the Wayfarers. I settled back, my muscles going loose and warm as she took me into the warm sweetness of her mouth. "Can I watch?"

She made a humming sound around me, sending a vibration down my shaft and into my balls. Despite her orders, I lifted the blanket to steal a peek. I groaned at the sight of her, flushed pink lips stretched around me, soft waves of hair tickling over my thighs. I rose off the bed when she opened wide and slid her tongue along the pulsing seam of the *dzirian*. It felt like there was a live wire in the tip of her tongue.

My breath shuddered out of me. "Gods of the void take you," I swore, grabbing a handful of the sheet. She just laughed a little, sending a shocking vibration through my shaft. I panted as she broke away and suckled and licked at my *dzirian*. "Don't tease."

She lifted her gaze and gave me a stern look from beneath the blanket. "You're supposed to be asleep."

"Vani, I would most certainly be awake by now," I said drily.

Her berry-kissed lips spread into a devious smile. She was in no hurry, licking and stroking and sucking in a decadent rhythm until I finally lost my cool.

"Vani," I groaned. "I'm gonna lose my mind."

"Ask me nicely," she said, caressing my *dzirian* with a perfect pressure. Her head tilted, and she laid a line of gentle kisses along my shaft.

"Please, angel," I said softly. That name was like hitting a switch in her brain, turning her into a fiend. She made wet, messy noises as she took me deep, until I hit the back of her throat. My hips rose as I came, letting out a long, happy sigh. I felt her tongue and throat working around me to take my seed.

She made a sound of satisfaction, a little *mmm* that nearly undid me, and slowly withdrew. Still holding me, she licked me clean, kissed the sensitive skin of my *dzirian*, then slowly lowered herself to lay on top of me. "Good morning, Captain."

"Good morning, angel," I said. Her smile was brighter than the stars, and I knew I was in serious trouble. "You can wake me up like that any time you like."

CHAPTER 15

Vani

After nearly two days of floating through space with nothing to do but talk and fuck, it was strange to have a ticking clock. Quite literally, as Havoc had Diana reminding him of the time every fifteen minutes. Though he'd clearly enjoyed my wakeup call, a grim tension settled over him as we rose and began our preparations for Vakarios. He dressed in dark pants and laid out a finely tailored black coat.

I let him pace, checking the cargo again before returning to me. He was gone for a while, and I finally ventured out of the cabin to find him in a room I hadn't seen yet. Behind the previously locked door, I found him examining two big cases full of weapons laid open on a small workbench. The scoundrel had an armory after all.

His violet eyes lifted to mine as he set out an arrangement of black straps. "Want to strap me in?" he said. "Closest you'll get to tying me up."

I grinned at him, and he raised his powerful arms to the side. He wore a snug black shirt that exposed those gorgeous biceps. I ran my hands up his arms. "I like this uniform, Captain."

"Glad to hear it," he replied.

I slid the nylon straps over each shoulder and tightened the buckles at his back. Hooking the buckle at his waist pulled the configuration tight, so he had a holster under each arm and one on his lower back. "Are you scared?"

"No," he said. "I am concerned for you."

"Got one of these for me?"

"No," he said. "Well, not exactly."

"Havoc..."

He ignored me and took a compact black weapon from the case, sliding it into one of the holsters under his arm. Then he lifted a rounded metal plate, placing it against his left forearm. He lifted his eyebrows and extended the arm to me. I took the cue and strapped it onto his muscular arm.

"What do you do when you don't have someone here to get you dressed?"

"I muddle through," he said. "It's much more fun with you here." Once the device was strapped down, he pried several loops from it and secured them around his fingers and thumb. Two of them connected at the base of his palm, and he connected a small silver device, no bigger than a coin.

"What's that?"

"Electric shock," he said. He thrust it toward me, and I darted back. He grinned. "I'm not going to use it on you. I'm creative, but there is absolutely no fun application of this thing." His brow furrowed, and then he rooted in a drawer. To my surprise, he took out a pair of black driving gloves with matte black studs on the knuckles and offered them to me.

"I thought I couldn't have a weapon," I said.

"I'm not letting you be defenseless," he said calmly. He held one out to me, then gently pried one of the studs loose. Beneath the flat cap were three wickedly sharp silver prongs. "You let me handle things, but if it gets out of control, this will get someone off you fast." He gently pressed his knuckle to my temple. "Boom. Flick the cap, hit them somewhere soft, and then get back. Just be quick. Once the cartridge activates, you have about three seconds to get clear or you get a dose of lightning up your ass, too."

"I don't think I'm into that," I said solemnly.

He chuckled and tilted my chin up. "I'm serious. Be careful. These are for an emergency only." He carefully replaced the cap and handed me the gloves. Each one had four large studs on it, and I realized this was a serious concession for him. Either he trusted me now, or he was far more scared of what could happen to me than what I could do to him. "Put them on after you get dressed."

"Captain, we are thirty minutes from entering the atmosphere at Vakarios," Diana said.

When he lifted his head again, his entire demeanor had changed. His shoulders shifted, and his chest rose. It was like watching him turn to stone.

This was the Havoc who had chased me down and punished me for drugging him, but it wasn't the one who'd held my hand as we hurtled through the stars. I liked them both, but I was glad this one was here if we were about to descend into danger. That hardness would keep us both alive.

"You'll be my companion on Vakarios," he said. He raised an eyebrow. "My pet."

"Your what?"

"It's not unusual for traders at Vakarios to bring companions. They think it makes them look more impressive," he said. He shut the cases, gestured for me to leave the room, and locked it behind him. I couldn't help noticing that it was one of the only rooms he kept locked, with its own security code. I kept that observation to myself and followed him into the central cabin.

My stomach twisted as he opened the drawer where we'd found the sex toys. He took out a black bag and laid it out. Inside was an assortment of cosmetics in black containers. "You are beautiful as you are, but-"

"I get it. I need to play the part," I said gently. He actually looked apologetic as I dumped out the bag's contents. I didn't recognize the languages on the containers, but it seemed that the basics were universal. While he talked, I used a black pencil to outline my eyes and brighten them.

"You will be absolutely submissive to me," he said. "If someone speaks to you, do not respond. If someone touches you, just touch my hand. It will only happen once."

My heart thumped. There was something beyond firm confidence in his voice. He was really worried, and that scared me. It made me want to protect him, but at the same time, I wanted to hide. I wanted no part of something that scared Havoc.

But I nodded my agreement, dipping my fingers in the light

pink powder to rouge my cheeks. Vakarios might have been an unknown, but accompanying a dangerous man to an illicit deal was right up my alley. I'd been Dinesso's arm candy plenty of times. "What should I do when you talk to your guy?"

"Follow my lead," he said. "Rhasat likes to have a drink or two and pretend that he gives a shit about anything but money. He likes to make people wait. It's his way of swinging his dick. You just stay quiet and close to me and ignore him."

I set aside the compact. "Hair?"

He glanced down at me and froze. His lashes fluttered. "I like it down, but...put it up. Like when you woke me up this morning."

I smirked at him and raked my hair into a high ponytail. "Good? Does it make you think filthy thoughts?"

I'd hoped for a little joke to ease his tension, but he didn't smile. "Keep it like that," he said.

"Can I ask what you're trading with this guy? Why is it so secret?"

"It's none of your business," he said coolly. Of course.

"Entering atmosphere in one minute," Diana said. I startled and looked around, but Havoc simply sat on the couch next to me and beckoned. Instinctively, I climbed into his lap, and his powerful arms closed around me.

"Hold on to me," he said, stroking my brow.

"I'm sure it'll—" I jolted as the ship gave a tremendous bump and rattled violently. There was a terrible roar of noise, but he just smiled at me. I closed my eyes and pressed my head into his shoulder, hoping my stomach didn't explode out of my mouth. Then the vibration ceased, and there was a light hum.

"Report, Diana," Havoc said, still gently stroking my back.

"All systems are optimal," Diana said. "Setting a course for Port Vakarios. Given wind conditions, arrival is expected in thirty-one minutes."

"Thank you, Diana. Please check my reservation at the hangar and alert Zovareti to have our hangar ready," he said. When I drew away from him, he smiled faintly. "You okay?"

I nodded. "I'm fine."

Then his face hardened again, and he lifted me to my feet. "Come here," he said. He took another black bag from the cabinet and dumped its contents on the couch. I didn't know whether to be excited or horrified at the array of leather and straps.

"You can't be serious," I said. There was no way that arrangement was going to cover enough of my body to go outside.

"It's not my fault that you came on my ship with nothing. I have one flimsy little nightgown and this," he said.

I picked up the web of thin leather and peered through one of the gaps at him. "You better buy me some real clothes when this is over."

His head tilted, a dangerous smile on his face. "And how do you intend to earn them?"

"I can cook and clean," I said. "Or make you some good cocktails if you have liquor on board. I can also deal cards and cheat without getting caught. Very useful."

He chuckled. "I thought you'd offer to fuck me."

"That's not much of a bargaining chip, considering I'll do that for free," I said frankly. "Very often and very vigorously. Several times a day, in multiple positions."

His hard expression finally broke and he laughed aloud.

Victory. "Tell you what, angel. If we survive this trade, I'll take you down to the markets at Ir-Nassa and buy you anything you want. Silks in every color you can imagine. And some very pretty lacy things that I can take off of you."

I liked the idea of a future with him. I wasn't stupid enough to think we'd be forever, but the thought that this fever dream didn't have to end anytime soon...it was a good one.

At his gesture, I reluctantly shed the black nightgown and replaced it with a sheer black bodysuit that left my legs bare and slid right up between my ass cheeks. He frowned at the array of leather straps, finally turning it and holding it for me to climb into.

Despite my protests, there was something exciting about it as he buckled and tightened each set of straps. The intricate array lifted my breasts, and there was a silver ring directly over my mound. More straps radiated from the ring to loop over my hips and thighs. The sheer material beneath barely covered me.

Then Havoc knelt at my feet, sliding a sheer black stocking up one leg. The ridge of his horn brushed my bottom as he hooked thin leather straps to the harness, then did the other leg. My whole body went weak at the feeling of his hands sliding up my legs. When he rose again, he grabbed a handful of the straps and pulled me into him.

"You look so fucking hot," he growled.

"Thank you," I breathed. His breath was hot against my neck, and he suddenly smacked my ass cheek, awakening the heat of that first fiery encounter. I moaned, surprising myself as I bent over for him. It was like he'd short-circuited my brain. "Shit. What was that for?"

"Because we both like it," he said. "Don't you?"

"N—" I stared back at him. *Honesty, Vani.* I liked that sweet burn. "I do."

"Stand up, Vani," he said roughly. He looped his arm around my waist and pulled me close. With a little grunt, he twisted my ponytail around his hand, just enough to send a message. My core ignited with desire. His warm lips brushed over my ear as he growled, "On Vakarios, you are mine. You do what I say."

I held my tongue. I wasn't just his on Vakarios. I was already his, here, there, as far as the stars spread across the universe. I nodded. "Yes, Captain."

A rich growl, almost a purr, rolled through him. "I like it when you call me that."

"Then I'll call you that," I said.

He kissed the back of my neck, but his teeth scraped my skin. "Vani, if anyone touches you, I'll fucking break them. Do you trust me?"

"Yes, Captain."

"Who's going to protect you?"

"You are."

"Good girl. Let's go."

CHAPTER 16

Havoc

If Terra was a dust heap, then Port Vakarios was a rotting garbage pile. With its rocky, dry surface, it had been inhospitable to life long before the drug runners and crime lords made it one of their hubs. A twisted pile of metal, comprised of half-constructed buildings and defunct spacecraft, formed the Port itself. Neon flickered within its depths, advertising the most decadent of pleasures.

My heart thumped as I watched it come into view. Despite making most of my living off illegal trade, I hated this place. There was decadence, and then there was depravity. If I wasn't one man with a non-combat ship, I'd have blown the whole place out of existence. I'd even tried to get Rhasat to make me a trade elsewhere, but he suspected it was a setup. So I was stuck here until I found another dealer or someone less suspicious killed him and took over his trade.

The Nomad jolted to a landing at the Traveler's Virtue, where I had a good relationship with Zovareti, the owner. Our good relationship meant I paid him extra, and he brought in a loading crew that wouldn't peek in the crates or sample the wares.

Landing on Vakarios was unpleasant at the best of times, but Vani added a whole layer of complication. She was a beacon of sheer lust. I hoped hanging her off my arm wasn't a drastic miscalculation.

As soon as I landed, Diana chirped an alarm. "Captain, I have an incoming communication from Rhasat Glyck."

I scowled as the screen lit up with the familiar face. Black tattoos crawled along his temples, a stark contrast to his berry-red skin. "Rhasat," I said drily. If he changed the plan, I was going to lose it.

"Havoc," he said warmly. "What do you say that we meet at Solo before we make the swap? They've got a hot pot you wouldn't believe."

I fucking knew it. "I'm not here for local cuisine. We meet at the warehouse as planned."

"Havoc, Havoc," he said. His voice scraped against my already raw nerves. "You want my gifts or not? I have a table already reserved. Don't insult a man's hospitality. See you shortly. I'll order an appetizer for you."

He cut off, and I swore in Zathari. "Motherfucker."

Vani touched my arm lightly. "He's setting you up."

I glanced at her and bit back my sharp retort. Two days off of Earth and she was suddenly an expert in intergalactic smuggling? "I know," I said calmly.

She pondered, then tugged at the lacy hem of her thigh-high

stockings. A coy smile tugged at her red-painted lips. "You could hide another weapon here."

I chuckled. "Clever girl. I'd need something bigger than you can fit there."

Her brow furrowed. "I'll watch your back."

With my apprehension dragging my nerves over a razor's edge, I nearly snapped at her. What the hell did this little woman from Terra think she could do? She was there to look pretty and hopefully not get us both killed. I was in this increasingly precarious situation because of her.

But that was my ego talking, and that same stupidity had gotten me into this. She wasn't just a pretty pair of tits and a wicked mouth. This little woman from Terra had tricked me several times over, and I'd learned repeatedly that she paid attention to everything around her. If I had any doubt of her quick wits, I only had to look at how she'd managed to get my ship out of the most secure hangar in the Prospects and convince my cutting-edge AI to let her have full control of the ship while I was unconscious. She'd also spent her whole life working for a man like Rhasat Glyck. Maybe she didn't know my world, but she sure as hell wasn't stupid. And I would be if I turned down an extra set of eyes. I nodded and waited until my temper had cooled to say, "Thank you, angel. Let's go."

She raised her eyebrows and bent over the couch slowly. "Give me another good one," she said.

"What?"

"You want them to know I'm yours? Leave a nice handprint," she said. "I like the sting."

"Fucking hell, you're something," I marveled. I palmed her ass. "Are you sure?"

"It's not like you to hesitate, Captain," she teased.

I tilted my head. "Believe it or not, I don't want to hurt you."

Her brow furrowed. Then her lips curved into a sly smile. "Then call it a deposit. Give me something to look forward to later." Her hips swished a little, tempting me.

"You better hold that ass still or we're not getting out of here on time," I growled. Then I braced my hand against her back and gave her a firm smack that jolted up my arm.

She yelped, then let out a charming laugh as her foot curled up. "Shit," she panted. "One more."

I waited, idly tracing a circle on her thigh. "Oh, I don't think you'll need it." There was already a pink imprint forming on her golden skin. She was tough, but her skin marked easily. I placed my hand in the outline and squeezed her cheek. "You've got a nice little mark now. I think it says 'This ass is property of Captain Havoc.'"

The smirk she threw me was like a match to rocket fuel. She tossed her ponytail, straightened, and brushed past me to the boarding ramp.

Despite my trepidation, I enjoyed watching Vani walk ahead of me down the ramp, with that perfect ass on display. There was a swishing rhythm to her hips, and she drew herself up taller. She was casting a spell, just like she'd done to me back in that shitty bar on Terra.

Gods, she was something.

The ramp descended into the cool, dry air of the hangar. The smoky smell of Vakarios greeted me immediately, as did a crew of men in red coveralls. As soon as we emerged, one of the men let out an appreciative howl and eyeballed Vani.

"How much for the pussy?" he asked.

"More than you'll ever touch in your life," I growled. "Where's Zovareti?"

As if I'd conjured him from thin air, Zovareti, a broad-shouldered Il-Teatha male, broke through his crew. His brilliant red skin nearly matched the coveralls, but his orange eyes alit with mirth. "Captain Havoc, welcome back," he said in his booming voice. He gave Vani an appreciative look, and his tendrils lit up pure red. "Pretty cargo."

"Thank you," I said, pulling her closer. "Picked it up on Terra."

"You selling?"

"Not yet," I said. "Just trading as planned."

He nodded. "I've got lot eight reserved for you. Nice and open, just the way you like."

I nodded to him, then glanced back at the ship. "Diana, lock down." The cargo bay closed, and I received a notification on my watch that the security protocols were activated.

Vani clutched my hand tight as I led her out of the hangar and onto the bustling corner outside the Traveler's Virtue. I put up one hand to hail a passing shuttle. When the gleaming silver vehicle pulled over, I held her hand so she could climb in. It stank of stale smoke and fried food.

"Where ya goin', boss?" the driver asked.

"Solo," I said. I swiped my burner chip over the reader to confirm payment. "I'll give you fifty extra to keep your mouth shut the whole time."

"You got it, boss," the driver said, whizzing into traffic.

I glanced over at Vani, who was wide-eyed as she looked out the window at the strange landscape. It wasn't all that different from parts of Terra, where the one-sided war with the Aengra had left their cities bent and broken.

But the streets of Vakarios bustled with visitors from all over the galaxies, from crimson-skinned Il-Teatha to the thin, reptilian Esheryash who looked like they'd crawled out of a swamp and put on expensive suits. We passed a brothel, where a Vaera woman danced slowly in a cage by the door. Dingy holographic signs advertised virtual brothels, where you could pay for a stint with a complex headset and immersive software that simulated a whole catalog of sex acts, from the innocent to the truly horrendous.

It didn't take long to reach Solo, which featured a neon projection of a cat eating from a bowl of noodles. Two of Rhasat's men waited outside. Their stiff posture and tailored suits were a strange contrast to the overly cute feline peeking over their shoulders.

One of the men was Vaera, like Rhasat, but the other was a huge, scarred Proxilar male who looked like he'd tried to go down on a jet engine. I gritted my teeth and held Vani's hand while she climbed out of the shuttle. Sure enough, the flat-nosed Proxilar snapped his head around. He'd smell a female from a mile away.

The Vaera bowed slightly. "Captain Havoc," he said. "And...unexpected guest."

"No guests," the Proxilar said. He reached out to touch Vani, and she shrank away, tucking her face into my shoulder. His face twisted in anger. "Come here, little pet. I'll take good care of you."

"Touch her and it'll be the last thing you do," I said. "Weigh it carefully."

"You didn't tell Boss Glyck you had company," the Proxilar said. "She can wait with me."

I wondered just how stupid he was. He answered my question within three seconds, when he ignored my warning. His thick, armored fingers closed around her arm. Her head flew up, a murderous glint in her eyes. "No," I said quietly. I had a feeling she was itching to shock something, and I'd prefer it happened after I closed my deal.

As he went to paw at her ponytail, I grabbed his wrist and twisted it around, snapping joints all the way up his arm in a delightful staccato. When he lunged, I drove my fist up into his nose. He staggered, and I closed the gap to seize his flabby throat.

"Out of respect for Mr. Glyck, I'll give you one chance," I said. "Apologize to me for touching my things."

"Fuck you—"

I squeezed hard enough to pierce his skin. My fingers dug under the armored plate and pressed into the thick cartilage of his windpipe. He made a choking sound and slapped at my arm. "Is that an apology for your kind? Where I come from, we start with 'I'm sorry.' Ending with 'sir' is a nice touch."

Give me a reason, motherfucker, I thought.

"Erkesh," the Vaera bodyguard said in a placating tone. "Captain Havoc asked you nicely."

"Sorry," Erkesh groaned.

I shoved him away and wiped my hand on the back of his ill-fitting jacket. "Fuck off."

The Vaera bowed again and gestured. "My apologies, sir. Mr. Glyck is inside waiting." Though he was smart enough not to touch, his eyes passed over Vani.

Her chest heaved, and she grabbed onto my arm again. Inside, the restaurant was surprisingly well-furnished and clean for a place on Vakarios. Another of Rhasat's men waited just inside, smiling brightly at me. "Mr. Glyck is ready for you, Captain."

We passed a secluded table where two men spoke over drinks. Her hand tightened on my arm, and I saw what she saw. A Vaera woman in a skintight bodysuit was on her knees under the table, servicing one of the men while he calmly carried out his business. In a place like this, they probably had girls and boys on the menu for the right price, right there between cock-tails and appetizers.

In a back room, Rhasat Glyck awaited. His gaudy gold-embroidered suit was a poor man's notion of a rich man's clothing. A series of gold ornaments lined his pointed red ears. As he looked up from his drink, he drew a deep breath to start delivering his usual load of bullshit. But the words dried up on his tongue as he caught sight of Vani. His amber eyes swept over her, and he made a beckoning gesture. "Captain, you come bearing gifts. How thoughtful."

"This is not for you," I said. I took the chair across from him, staring him down. There was no seat for Vani, so I patted my lap. She perched on my thigh. When she started toying idly with the hair at the back of my neck, I gritted my teeth to hide the shiver rippling down my spine. I gave her a stern look. "Stop."

Her green eyes flickered with hurt. I slid one hand under her and gave her the tiniest little pinch on her bottom. Her lips twitched, but she nodded and simply laid her head on my shoulder. Her touch was enough to make me stupid, and I couldn't afford to be anything less than sharp here. Just the smell of her was distracting, but I couldn't bring myself to send her to the floor.

"Please, eat with me," Rhasat said. There was a massive spread of food on the table, and I had to admit, it smelled good after a month of eating reconstituted meals that all tasted vaguely of eggs and over-cooked broccoli. "Does your pet eat?"

"She's a human," I said. "Of course she fucking eats."

"Apologies, apologies," Rhasat said. He raised an eyebrow. "You know, we've been business partners a long time, you and I."

"If you're going to ask for a taste, the answer is no," I said. "Go to Terra and get your own."

His eyes narrowed. "Then maybe I change our deal. Send it over here, or we go home unsatisfied."

CHAPTER 17

Vani

My heart raced as Rhasat Glyck demanded a taste of me. I couldn't be certain, but he had the deep crimson skin and delicately pointed ears of the Vaera. Most of the citizens of the Aengra Dominion were Vaera, and I'd met a rare few who dared to venture out to the Prospects. Unless Glyck had hidden superpowers, I had no doubt Havoc would win a fight. But it might not matter.

Everything had a price, after all. He'd made it very clear that closing this deal was his top priority. And if they decided that I would sweeten the deal, there wasn't a damn thing I could do about it.

Havoc tugged lightly on my ponytail, holding firmly without hurting me. My gaze slid to Rhasat, who was staring at me with lust painted all over his face. The glazed look was one I'd seen a thousand times in the Dahlia, on slack-jawed faces gazing up at the dancers.

Then Havoc kissed me, rough and deep. He nipped at my lip as he pulled back, and I let out a soft whimper. His pupils dilated. I had to admit that it was nice to have that power over him. "This one is mine," he snarled. "You want my leftovers?"

Rhasat snorted in derision. "A warm hole is a warm hole. What do you care what I do after you're finished with it?"

"I care because this is not the deal we made. I didn't come all this way so you could jeopardize our deal over a piece of human pussy," he said. "You are spitting in my face. You want my jacket, too? Maybe my shoes?"

"Come now, Captain," Rhasat said. "Don't be so goddamned dramatic. One might think you were attached. Deals change all the time."

I didn't want this, but this deal was important to him. And surely, there was nothing Rhasat wouldn't ask that I hadn't been forced into a hundred times at the Dahlia. I took a deep breath and said, "Captain, I'll—"

His eyes were full of genuine fury when he turned to me. "Silence, or I'll give you something better to do with your mouth."

Heat flared in my chest as I clamped my lips shut. That fury wasn't entirely an act.

"Obedient little pet," Rhasat said, clearly unbothered by Havoc's anger. "I'll throw in another fifteen percent if you give her to me. Plus ten in cash. What do you think?"

Havoc's eyes widened. "I'll think about it," he said. My heart raced as he dug into his meal. He ate deftly with slender chopsticks, and the two men conversed about commerce and politics on planets I'd never heard of, like they hadn't just discussed selling me. Now and again, Havoc held up a piece of meat or vegetables for me, and I ate it obediently. The food was good, but my stomach was in knots. Maybe Rhasat wouldn't want me if I threw up all over his fancy suit.

As they ate and drank, I noticed that Rhasat drained at least three glasses of dark brown liquor, while Havoc sipped at his, occasionally spilling a bit of it into an untouched bowl of soup on his side of the table. When a waiter came to offer him another drink, Havoc waved him off.

Eventually, they finished their conversation, and Rhasat placed his hands on the table, giving me a hungry look. "Well, what do you say to amending our deal?" My heart pounded, and I clasped my hands tight under the table to keep them off of Havoc.

"No," Havoc said flatly. "If for no other reason than to remind you that a deal is a deal. Renegotiating on the spot is a good way to ensure that we never work together again. Have your people meet mine at lot eight. As we agreed weeks ago."

Rhasat chuckled. "A hard man as always."

Havoc slid me off his lap, and I waited patiently for him. As he led me out of the restaurant, I felt hungry eyes following me. Most of the people here were men, with the occasional female companion like me. Some sat on laps, while other were under the tables. My cheeks heated as I imagined myself nestled between Havoc's powerful legs, one of his hands resting on my head while I swallowed his cock. Heat twisted through my core. While I was leering like a complete creep, I noticed one of the waiters touch his ear and then slide out the side door. My lust turned to sharp alertness.

I held Havoc's hand tightly as we emerged from the restaurant, where he hailed another shuttle. "Good evening, Captain Havoc," the bronze-skinned bodyguard said. The scaly one that had grabbed me was gone, probably tending to his shattered arm.

Havoc just grunted at him. The shuttle halted, and Havoc held my hand to help me in. I peered around his big frame, watching the front doors of the restaurant. The bodyguard turned and walked to the corner of the restaurant, where the waiter met him. The projected cat's tail flicked lazily over them as they spoke. Then the waiter disappeared around the side of the building, while the Vaera underling put a hand to his ear.

Sneaky son of a bitch.

Once Havoc was inside the shuttle, I whispered in his ear. "Someone's following us."

His brow furrowed. "Who?"

"Waiter from the restaurant," I said. As the shuttle lurched away from the sidewalk, I peered out the back window. Another shuttle was right behind us, but the waiter was on a hoverbike behind it. "He's behind us. Human sized. Copper skin, dark brown hair shaved on the sides."

A few minutes into our ride, the waiter turned sharply down a side street and disappeared. I updated Havoc, and he gave me a solemn nod. When we emerged from the shuttle, he gave me a sharp smack on the ass, and I giggled, tumbling into him. As I trailed after him, I fixed a vacuous smile on my face and surveyed the leering hangar crew for our tail. No sign of him yet.

The red-skinned man—Zovareti—greeted Havoc as we returned. "Captain," he greeted warmly. The long, thin tentacle-like strands framing his face had a soft orange glow, pulsing like a heartbeat. "Ready for your trade?"

"Have your crew meet me at the cargo bay," Havoc said.

My heart thrummed as we walked back into the big hangar where the Nomad waited. At the opposite end, a big set of metallic doors slid open and let in a wide beam of sunlight. Beyond the open door was a concrete yard with another hangar across from it. This was neutral territory for making a trade.

A crew of men in red coveralls crossed the open area, pushing a trio of handtrucks. When Havoc led me up to the Nomad, I froze. One of the men loading crates out of the Nomad was the waiter from the restaurant, now wearing red coveralls like the crew. Pure adrenaline shot through my system at the sight of him. I whirled and tucked my face into Havoc's chest.

"What is it now?" he said irritably, lowering his head. "I don't have time for your foolishness." His big hand cupped my jaw, turning my face up. His angry tone was all for show. As he stared down at me, his violet eyes were wide. His brows arched in a silent question.

Rising on my toes, I whispered. "Middle handtruck. Guy with the brown hair and the tattoo on his left hand. That's the one who followed us."

Pressed close to him, my hands were hidden. I carefully pried the cap from one of the studs on my right glove. He nodded and whispered, "Get your shoes off just in case. I promise you'll be fine."

I frowned at him and raised my voice. "But my feet hurt," I whined.

"Then take them off, for fuck's sake," he growled. "I've had enough of you bitching." I heard a snicker from one of the men hauling crates out of the Nomad.

I fixed a pout on my face and nudged off my high heels, curling my stocking-covered toes into the rough concrete. I clasped my hands behind my back to hide the glove.

Out in the open lot, another crew was approaching with a second set of handtrucks, all loaded down with silver crates. The waiter guided the crew to take Havoc's crates across to the other ship. The crew in red loaded the new crates into the Nomad's cargo bay while Havoc supervised.

Soon, the waiter returned to our hangar, holding out a tablet. "Need a confirmation, sir." His eyes raked over me.

"Get that for me, pet," Havoc said, watching the man intently. "And then we'll be on our way."

My heart pounded as I approached the impostor. The waiter's eyes widened just a little, his expression shifting subtly. I'd stared at way too many men who were thinking depraved thoughts about what they were going to do to me. I knew that look.

When I reached for the tablet, the man dropped it and grabbed one of the leather straps on my chest, yanking me closer. His other hand slid down, like he was going for a weapon in his pocket. I planted my knuckles into his temple, leaving the pronged cartridge buried in his copper skin. He released me to claw at his face, and I staggered back just as the cartridge activated. A blue flash ignited. He screamed and fell to the ground, blood streaming from his nose. An awful, warbling groan came from spit-flecked lips as he writhed. Then the blue light blinked out, and the man went flat.

In a blur of black and gray, Havoc lunged past me and

slammed his elbow down on the man's chest. He arched and let out a whining cry of pain. Havoc hauled him up by his collar and turned toward the frozen crew loading the Nomad.

"If any of you thought you were going to rob me, think again. I suggest you get back to work before I turn your nuts into earrings," he said, still glaring at the man.

There was a series of noisy thumps as the crew shoved the last crates into the Nomad. They sprinted out of the hangar.

"Sir, it's a misunderstanding, I don't know, I was just—" the waiter protested.

Havoc flexed his fingers and grabbed the man's crotch. A blue spark arced over the back of his hand from the weapon I'd put on him. The other man turned bright red and screamed. Havoc let him fall to the ground, twitching, a wet spot spreading on his coveralls. He knelt, putting his face so close that he could have kissed the waiter's blood-streaked face. "You tell Rhasat that this was his one and only fuck-up."

"Sir, I—"

Havoc glanced at me, then slid his hand up over the man's face, pressing his thumb to the man's eye. "You keep talking, you're going to deliver the message with one eye. I saw the way you looked at my pet."

The man let out a pitiful sob. "Yes, sir, I understand, I'm sorry," he blurted. "I'll tell him. I'm sorry. Please don't."

Havoc grabbed the man's hair and pulled him up to his knees. "Apologize for touching my pet. Now I'm going to have to clean her because you touched her."

"I'm sorry, sir, I'm so sorry," he babbled.

"You apologize to her."

The man's tear-filled eyes fell on me, and he clasped his hands together. "Please, miss, I'm sorry. I really am."

I nodded, and Havoc dropped him. Then he snapped his fingers at me and jerked his head toward the ship. I stared at him, not knowing whether to be horrified or completely in love. I scooped up my discarded shoes and hurried after Havoc as he stomped up the loading ramp and into the cargo bay. The waiter scrambled away from the ship as the ramp lifted behind us.

Heat radiated from Havoc as he stormed around the bay, investigating the crates. They were all askew in the middle of the floor, thanks to Havoc scaring the shit out of the loading crew. "Lazy fucks," he muttered, shoving the heavy crates out of the way to make a path. "Diana," he said sharply. "Give me a report on weight."

He opened one of the crates, revealing a neat array of brown cardboard boxes inside. After a quick glance at me, he opened the box to reveal small glass vials filled with clear liquid. Then he opened a white plastic case mounted to the wall and removed a handheld device with a glowing screen. He secured a sterile needle to the device, then typed rapidly on the surface. Carefully handling the vial, he popped the cap and slid the needle inside. His eyes narrowed intently as he watched the screen. Then it turned green, and he sighed heavily.

"Captain, the cargo weight is within acceptable margins of error," Diana said.

He popped the needle off and replaced it, then repeated the process with a vial from the next crate. One by one, he opened each crate and removed a sample vial. He was like a man possessed, still tense and angry. I didn't like him like this.

"Thank you, Diana," I said mildly. When he had checked a vial from each crate, he carefully loaded them back into neat stacks and strapped them in with cargo nets and ratchet straps. I considered offering my assistance, but I preferred to let him take out his foul mood on the hard-shelled cases and not me.

Finally, the cargo bay was as orderly and neat as the rest of the ship. Havoc glared up at the ceiling and snapped, "Diana, prepare for launch."

"Would you like to refuel on Vakarios or go to Inan Prime?" Diana asked.

"Get me off this rock," Havoc said.

"I'm sorry, Captain, I don't understand the response."

"Go to fucking Inan Prime," Havoc said. It was odd, but hearing him swear at Diana worried me more than watching him brutalize Rhasat's men.

"Please take us to Inan Prime, Diana," I added. He whirled on me, giving me a look of sheer fury. "What? Whatever you're mad at, it's not Diana." And I sure as hell hoped it wasn't me.

"Setting navigation plan for Inan Prime," Diana said. "Launch preparations will be complete in approximately seven minutes, Captain."

He stormed through the ship to the cockpit and sat in his chair, elbows propped on his knees. One leg bounced with nervous energy. I was afraid to touch him, for fear of triggering an explosion. "Diana, open a comms channel to Rhasat Glyck."

It only took a minute before the screen lit up, displaying the smarmy dealer's face. He grinned. "Captain Havoc, did you change your mind?"

"If you ever try to fuck me again, I will end you," Havoc said.

Rhasat's expression faltered. "It's just business, Captain."

"And when I slit your throat in that nice little penthouse in Votalar, it'll just be business," Havoc said. "Enjoy your stay on Vakarios."

All traces of the dealer's bluster failed. His eyes widened at the word *Votalar*. "Captain, you don't have to—"

Havoc slammed a hand against the control panel. The screen went black as he glared at me. "Sit down and prepare for launch."

CHAPTER 18

Vani

"Captain, we have achieved orbit," Diana reported. "Now setting a course to Inan Prime. To optimize fuel efficiency and maximize profit, the expected travel time is thirty-two hours."

He grumbled. "Thank you, Diana."

The tension in him was frightening. A million miles of space lay between us and the Dahlia, but I could have been walking down that familiar dark hall and staring at Dinesso's office door. There were times I was so careful, giving him exactly what I thought he wanted, and I still limped away with his anger stamped on my flesh. It was a terrifying way to live, always walking on a knife's edge, knowing you were fucked no matter what you did. Feeling this with Havoc, who had made me feel safe and stable for a few blissful days, was infinitely worse.

I glanced at him, but he was staring resolutely at the monitor, fingers drumming rapidly against the arm of his chair. His nostrils flared with each breath. With a deep breath, I unbuckled myself. My butt was sticking to the damn seat, and I was tired of having leather straps between my tits. I waved and said, "I'm getting out of this thing."

Before I made it out of the cockpit, a big hand twisted into the back of the leather harness and pulled me back. His warm lips grazed my neck. "I don't think so."

A chill prickled over me. "Oh, no?" He pushed me into the central cabin, still holding me firmly. My heart thrummed, but there was fear mixed into my anticipation. I contemplated my gloves and wondered if one of these little spark plugs would drop him like it did the waiter. I hoped it wouldn't come to that, but I'd learned to prepare for the worst.

"Diana, configure for High Top," he ordered. The devious silver device spun into place as we walked in, several curved plates forming a waist-high surface.

I dug in my heels, pushing back against his broad chest. "What did I do?" I complained. With the soft stockings on my legs, I had no traction, and I soon found myself bent over the small table. His broad thigh wedged between mine and shoved my legs apart. Silver bands secured my ankles. Another pair slid up, wrapping around my thighs. More bands grabbed my wrists and pulled them tight. Despite my fear, my whole body heated, and I felt a telltale wetness on my thighs. I needed to have a serious talk with my sex drive, because this was absurd.

Havoc circled me, stripping off his tailored coat. His violet eyes narrowed. "What did you do?" His voice dripped with quiet danger. I'd heard that edge in Dinesso's voice; it was a pool of gasoline just waiting for a match. My sweet dream was melting into grim reality.

"Stop it," I said sharply, surprised at the heat in my voice. I hadn't said *no* in years. His head tilted slightly. "I like fucking you. Don't make it a punishment. If you're mad, I'd rather you just hit me than this."

His hard expression melted into horror. "Fuck me, I didn't even think. Diana, release subject."

I was utterly confused as the device released me. He swiftly pulled me to his chest, where I listened to his heart pounding against my cheek. "I don't understand. You seem so angry."

He held me at arm's length and shook his head. "No," he said. "I'm just a fucking idiot. I'm not angry at you."

"Really?" I murmured.

With a little sigh, he sat on the couch and patted his thigh. I hesitantly sat in his lap, and his big arms wrapped around me. He brushed a soft kiss on my lips that did wonders to soothe my nerves. One finger traced a slow, wide circle on my thigh. "Absolutely not. I'm sorry I frightened you. I'm angry at that bastard Rhasat. I'm angry at myself for not noticing the guy who followed us. Gods of the void, Vani, you were so good, I can't even describe it."

I felt like my chest was going to explode with pride, even as I waited for the other shoe to drop. "I was?"

"You were fucking brilliant," he said, petting my hair. He tugged the elastic out of it and let the waves shake loose. The feeling of his fingers combing gently through my hair was heaven. "Clever. Observant. Absolutely perfect. When you dropped that little bastard, I could have kissed you right then."

"Then why the sex spider?"

His lips curved into a devious smile. "The sex spider?"

"Yes," I said. "Look at it."

He glanced over my shoulder at the array of silver limbs and tilted his head. "You're not wrong." He brushed a lock of hair from my face. "I wanted to celebrate finishing the job with you."

"By strapping me down while incredibly grumpy?"

One dark brow arched. "I think we both know you like it."

I huffed. "I like half of that. Next time, you should lead with 'I'm not mad.' The last time you grabbed me and threw me into that thing, I thought you were going to kill me."

He nodded. "It seems very obvious now that a much smarter woman has pointed it out, but my dick makes me stupid sometimes. I'm sorry," he said. A strange, haunted expression pulled his features into a grimace. "I wouldn't punish you like that. You're safe with me, Vani." He gestured broadly, then slid his hands over my hips. "When we're together, this is only for good."

I nodded solemnly. He looked far too serious, but it filled me with a strange sense of solid, reassuring warmth. I'd never had a man apologize for frightening me. This was all so strange and new.

I grasped his cheeks and kissed his smooth brow. Then I whispered in his ear. "Your dick makes me stupid sometimes, too." He laughed. Then I rose, strutted to the device, and bent over the small tabletop. His eyes widened. "Well, get over here, and show me what wicked things you have in mind."

"Are you sure?"

"If you don't, I'm going to see if Diana will do it for me," I teased. "I bet she can get creative with these extra limbs."

His lips curved in a delightful smile. "Diana, detain subject," he said. There was a buzz and a whir of activity around me as the silver bands secured me again. This time, I was aflutter with anticipation of what he had in mind. If Havoc intended to cele-brate, I had a feeling I was going to be wrung out and devoid of brain cells by the time he was done. His big hands slid up my legs, and he spanked me lightly.

"A celebration spanking?" I teased.

"You like it," he said, giving me another firm smack. I let out a low moan as the little spark of pain turned into a burning ember of pleasure. "Do you want me to have Diana run a report right now?"

I glanced at him. "She's busy flying the ship. Let her focus on more important things."

"You know, Lieutenant, you're right," he said solemnly. Then he slid his fingers under the leather straps and spread my slick folds open. My body pulsed around his warm fingers. "I can handle this one. My calculations say you like it."

"Fuck," I murmured, lowering my head. "Yes."

He kissed my neck, gently rubbing my skin before he gave me a sharp smack that rang out in the quiet. I gasped. After delivering another to the other side, his big hands rubbed out the burn as he leaned over to whisper in my ear. "Do you want me to stop? Remember what I told you. You can have what you want. Just be honest. I trust you."

"No," I growled, curling my toes. "Keep going."

"You were so good down there," he said. The low rumble of his voice was hypnotic. He spanked me again, and I involun-tarily jerked against the bindings. His hand slid between my legs, stroking my pussy. I strained to get closer to him, to squeeze his fingers between my thighs, but I couldn't go anywhere.

"I was good?" I'd never get tired of hearing that.

"So good. Fucking brilliant," he said, spanking the other side harder. He pressed his hips to me. "Did you see the woman sucking cock under the table?"

"Yes," I whispered, trying my best to rub against him. He was so close to where I wanted him, that magnificent cock straining against my cheeks.

"Did you want to do that for me?"

I was quiet, and he gave me another sharp tap. I blurted, "Yes. But not in front of everyone. I hated the way they looked at me."

"I would never share you like that," he said. When I turned to look at him, his violet eyes were practically glowing with lust. "You were going to let Rhasat touch you to save my deal, weren't you?"

I nodded. "I thought you would want that. This deal is obviously important."

"I would have cut off his dick before I let him put it near you," he said calmly. "Do you understand? You are mine. No one else gets to touch you. Never again."

My lips curved into a smile. "Yes, Captain."

"Say it," he said, grinding hard against me. "No one gets to touch you."

"No one gets to touch me," I said, holding that hard gaze.

His smile was almost vicious, as if he was staring down at the other predators he'd conquered to claim his prey. "What do you want from me, angel? Anything you want from me is yours."

"More, please," I said. I was ascending into that beautiful, hazy place where everything was just sensation. No need to think or worry about anything. I could just float on this feeling forever.

"Good girl," he said. "I like when you're honest."

Good girl.

I'd been called a lot of things in my life. Trash. Useless. Slut. Some of them had sunk so deep that I believed them. No one had ever called me a good girl, but hearing Havoc say it made me feel like I could be something good. Maybe here beyond the gravity of Earth, amongst the stars, I could be something different.

The slate is clean, Vani.

No past, just an infinite expanse of possibility in front of us.

He gave me another series of quick, light blows, leaving me tingling and almost dancing on my toes. As his rough hands skimmed over my burning cheeks, he murmured, "How do you feel?"

"So good," I said dreamily.

He chuckled. "Angel, I'm going to give you five more."

"And then?"

"And then I'm going to devour you," he said calmly. I nearly melted into a puddle. "Count for me."

He smacked me again, and I moaned, "One."

It made no sense, but that delightful burn turned into a buzzing euphoria that enveloped me from head to toe. Men had hurt me before, but it was from carelessness or cruelty. Havoc had discovered a spark in me that I didn't know was there, and he knew how to ignite it without hurting me. He treated me like I was something precious, not a piece of trash to toss out when he'd used me up.

I counted, letting out a peal of giddy laughter. "Three," I squealed, squirming away from the burning sensation. It was just on the verge of too much, like walking an electrified tightrope.

His fingers curled against me as he laid that broad chest to my back. "I can't wait to taste you."

I wiggled back against him. "Come on," I complained.

Then he laughed, pressing his hand to my back. "Patience, angel." He gave me another hard swat, then kissed my stinging cheek. "One more." I was breathless and panting by the time he gave me the last one and ordered Diana to release me.

Our hands were a fumbling tangle as he tried to unbuckle the leather harness. Between the two of us, we only managed to get our hands stuck under the straps, and I accidentally kneed him in the gut. We fell to the floor in a breathless heap of laughter.

Finally, he gave me a murderous look and pinned my hands over my head. "Hold still, you hellion. It's like you don't want me to get you naked."

I snickered as he finally got the buckles loose and peeled the web of leather off of me. His hunger was delightful as he stripped me bare and placed me on the plush couch like a throne. With him on his knees in front of me, I felt like a goddess. Instead of commanding me to keep my hands off, he brought my hands down and kissed them. Then without speaking, he brought my fingers up to his brow.

When I touched the velvety skin at the base of his horns, he shivered as if I'd grabbed his cock. "I can touch?" I whispered.

"I want you to touch," he growled. And I did. I traced the curve of them as his tongue plundered me, lashing and swirling until I was losing my mind. I let my finger dip into that one little imperfection, and then I held on tight, like I was steering a ship. He laughed against me and hiked my legs over his shoulders. His thick fingers slid inside me, curling up toward his tongue as he mastered me both inside and out.

And then that devious bastard teased me. He brought me to the edge, as I moaned *yes, yes, please* and broke away to say, "Not yet. Not yet, angel." I was nearly screaming with need when he finally pushed me into the abyss. Then I was flying into nothingness, untethered and free.

My hearing was half gone, but I could hear Diana saying, "Captain, is there a medical emergency? I detect sounds of distress."

His voice rumbled against my thigh. "Diana, please establish a voice profile for passenger Vani."

"Establishing," Diana said.

"Prior distress is an indicator of erotic climax," he said. "Get used to it."

"Yes, Captain," the ship agreed.

He lay flat on his back and brought me down to lay on his chest, panting. His heart thrummed against my cheek. "Like I said, I wasn't angry at you." He propped one arm under his head. "Believe me now?"

"I believe you," I said. "Captain."

CHAPTER 19

Havoc

WITH HOURS BETWEEN US AND VAKARIOS, I FINALLY RELAXED. IT didn't hurt that I still had the taste of Vani on my lips. As she sipped from a cup of reconstituted fruit juice, her face was wonderfully flushed.

"What now?" she asked. She'd showered and put on one of my shirts, which was practically a dress on her. I much preferred her naked, but I'd conceded after she tolerated the uncomfortable leather straps for the trip onto Vakarios. And there was something irresistible about seeing her in my clothing, the dark fabric skimming her thighs and barely covering that perfect bottom. Her cheeks were bright pink from my hand, but I'd given her what she wanted and not a bit more.

It had nearly broken me when she begged me not to fuck her as a punishment. That she thought I was capable of such a thing made me angry, but my anger faded to shame. That was my fault, not hers. And it was my responsibility to repair that and send that fear into the void.

"You want to fuck again already?" I asked. "I must not have worn you out enough."

"You are such a single-minded disaster," she teased. "There are other things we can do, you know."

"None as much fun," I lamented. "Come sit with me and I'll show you." She grinned and plopped into my lap. I kissed the side of her neck. "And don't blame me. You do this to me." Her smile widened, and she offered me a sip from her glass. I sipped at the sweet liquid and winced at the artificial taste. "Eventually, I'll take you somewhere with real fruit. You'll never want to drink this again."

"That sounds nice," she murmured. Though she smiled, I caught the hint of wistfulness in her eyes. Would she go with me? Or was this a lovely dream that was sure to end?

"I need to deliver my cargo to Irasyne," I said. "One more gate jump, and a few days' travel. Then I'm done."

"Is Irasyne terrible, like Vakarios?" Her nose wrinkled.

I shook my head. "Not at all. It's very beautiful, and the people are peaceful. Mostly. That's where the Zathari live now."

"Your people live there?"

My breath caught in my chest. "They do. I'm not welcome there."

Her brow furrowed. "Why?"

"Criminals and killers aren't welcome," I said.

"Then why are you going?"

"They need what's in the hold," I said.

Her head tilted, and she waited a few seconds before speaking, like she was weighing her words very carefully. "You're selling them drugs?" She had a good poker face, but I could tell she disapproved.

What surprised me was that I wanted her approval. There were only a handful of people in the universe whose opinions mattered to me, and somehow, she'd joined that fold. I wasn't sure when it happened, but her disapproval made me uneasy. "It's medicine. Antibiotics, specifically," I said. "The Zathari didn't originate on Irasyne, so they've come in contact with some new diseases that their bodies can't fight well. And they can't afford the prices to import it from Firyanin. *Alcamara* is a broad-spectrum drug. It kills most diseases without too many side effects."

"So you bring them medicine," she murmured. Her delicate fingers drifted up to touch my brow, feathering across the sensitive skin around the base of each horn. A shiver rolled down my spine. "How could anyone not welcome you?"

"I may be good at fucking and fighting, but I'm not a good man, Vani," I said. "When we escaped Kilaak, we killed people."

"Bad people?"

"Relatively, yes," I said. "And more when they chased us down. The people above them didn't like it. Me and my brothers have a price on our heads. We've all done bad things since then, so staying away from Irasyne keeps the others safer. It keeps the Dominion away from them." And they would spit on us, even as we protected them from afar. My brothers all had choice words for them, but under every *fuck them* was a throbbing, infected wound that would never heal. I'd never been allowed to enter those gates, and somehow, I was still homesick for a place I'd never been.

Her face was unspeakably sad. "How can you say you're not a good man?"

"I am not—"

Her eyes sharpened, and she covered my mouth. I recoiled, but she kept her small hand over my face, fingers digging firmly into my jaw. "How dare you talk that way about someone I care about?"

My head tilted, and hers followed in a comical mirror, as if she'd realized what she had blurted out. I gently plucked her hand away, then kissed her fingers. "You're a sweet girl, but you don't understand."

"Don't you dare patronize me," she said sharply as she yanked her hand away from me. She slid off my lap and paced furiously around the galley. "What happened to finding a new place and being something different? Was that bullshit? Or are big bad Zathari males beyond saving? If you get to tell me that I'm somebody, then I get to tell you that you're a good man."

She couldn't have surprised me more if she'd slapped me across the face. "Are you mouthing off to me?"

"I sure am," she said, leaning in. "You want to do something about it? Come on, Captain. Do something. I fucking dare you."

I grabbed her and silenced her with a ferocious kiss. As her tongue tangled with mine and her soft body melted into me, I realized that I could be worthy of this angel of the stars, or at least become better for the effort. For her, I could be the man she thought I was or die trying.

I pushed her away and stared up at her. Her eyes were glassy as she stared down at me, breathing hard. "Well? What do you have to say for yourself?" she demanded, her voice rough and breathy. "Are you done saying stupid things?"

"My name is Arumas Khel," I said, which was possibly the stupidest thing I'd ever said. Or maybe the smartest. Only time would tell.

Her jaw dropped, and I could see her fury turning to stunned wonder. "I thought you didn't tell people your name."

"I don't, but I want you to know it," I said. There was no way for her to understand how important this was, but her eyes welled with tears. She took my hand again and pressed it flat to her chest, so I could feel the soft pulse of her heart. I imagined that whispered name curling up inside her breast, safe and sound. The Wayfarers might not know my name, but now she did. Besides my brothers, she was the first to know it, and I hoped that I hadn't fucked up beyond saving.

"It's a pretty name. Arumas," she repeated softly. It was music on her lips. "What does it mean?"

I chuckled. "It means little brother. My brother Viper picked it out."

"How many brothers do you have?"

"My brothers are like your sisters," I said. "We weren't born together, but we found each other. There are..." I thought. "Thirteen. Ten Zathari, three others."

"That's a lot of brothers," she said. "Are they all scary like you?"

"Some are scarier," I said in a mock serious voice. "But they're not nearly as handsome."

"I believe it," she said. "Is Khel a family name?"

"We picked that, too," I said. "It means from the void. From nothingness."

Her brow furrowed. "Why did you pick it? It sounds so bleak."

"My people believe in spirits called the Wayfarers. They guide our souls out of the void and into existence. The void is a place of potential and creation. All light once came from darkness, just like plants grow from the dark soil and the sunrise comes from the night," I said. "It's not a bad thing."

And this gleaming little gem had come from the dirt and dust of Terra, as if the Wayfarers themselves had unearthed her just for me. Beautiful things often grew in the darkest of places.

Her eyes shone. She gently clasped my cheeks and kissed my brow gently. "Thank you for telling me your name. It makes me feel special."

I raised my eyebrows. "You are special. You're the only person who didn't have to escape from prison to learn it," I said wryly.

She rested her hands on my shoulders. "After we go to Irasyne—"

"We?"

"Are you going to get rid of me?"

"I don't think I could if I tried," I murmured.

She smiled. "After that, can we still go back to Earth?"

"For your sisters," I mused. She nodded. "I told you I'd take you. Tell me about them."

"Naela is very sweet," she said. "She's two years older than me, but she's still kind of innocent deep down." Her brow furrowed. "It lets them take advantage of her sometimes. But no matter what, she's still kind. Not like me."

"I like you just as you are," I said. "You have sharp edges. So do I."

She smiled shyly. "And Amira is younger. She's the one who was dancing on the stage when you came to the Dahlia and met me. So far, Dinesso and his men have left her alone. Partly because Naela and I keep them away from her. She's so beautiful and sweet, and it's just a matter of time before they break her, too." Her chest heaved. "Please promise me that we'll go back for them. I can't let them hurt her like they did me."

I tilted her chin up and met her determined gaze. "I gave you my promise already. The question is whether you want me to do it clean or dirty." Her brows arched. "I'll walk in and kill this Dinesso shitbag on the spot if that's what you want. Or I can make a trade for the girls."

"You'd kill him for me?"

I would do far worse. I would tear this universe to its foundations and leave a trail of destruction in my wake if she asked me to. It wasn't only that I wanted to make good on my promise to save her sisters. I wanted to give her a clean slate, to let her face the future knowing that no one was going to drag her down ever again. I'd fought and killed to protect my brothers, but this ferocious need to protect Vani was terrifying and barely under my control. "Yeah, I would. If that's what it takes to keep you safe."

Her eyes fell. "Make a trade," she said.

"Why would you spare him? All you've wanted is to get away."

She laughed bitterly. "I know it's stupid, but despite everything, I had a place to live. I always had a home and food on the table. And the lesser monsters were afraid of him. I've never known a life without him."

That might challenge my ability to keep my word. Knowing what this man had done to my Vani, I couldn't leave him alive.

But that was a worry for another time. I nodded solemnly. "After Irasyne, we'll go back to Earth."

"Couldn't we go now?" she asked. "He could have hurt them already."

My heart ached for her, but I shook my head. "I am a man of my word, Vani. They'll be expecting me on Irasyne. When I tell them I'll be there with a shipment, I do it."

Wraith, ever blunt and tactless, asked me once if I was trying to buy my way into Irasyne. It was a pointless pursuit, and we both knew it. But keeping my word mattered, and even if my hands were filthy, I was honoring the old ways and caring for my people the best I could.

Her posture stiffened. "It's not breaking your word, though. Are people going to die if they don't get medicine right away?"

"Vani—"

"Is your reputation for being on time more important than my sisters' lives?" she pressed.

I felt like she'd punched me in the gut. The surprise was followed closely by anger. "Don't mistake my affection for weakness, Vani. You don't get to dictate my schedule. And I'll remind you that you accepted my terms long before we left Earth."

"And you made your deal," she replied. "You met Glyck on time. Can't they wait a few more days?"

"No," I said sharply.

Her eyes narrowed, but she didn't respond. She rose. "I'll be back."

I watched her leave, contemplating. Perhaps being in space too long had made me soft and desperate. I needed to talk to Wraith or Mistral, who could cut through this lovesick fog in my brain. If I was watching Razor, endlessly optimistic and a little gullible, getting his dick wrapped around a Terran woman, what would I say?

Watch her carefully. Don't turn your back for long.

It really wouldn't be so bad to go back to Earth now. But the refuge on Irasyne had minimal technology. I scheduled my visits months in advance, and I had no way to communicate with them rapidly. By the time they got a message, I'd have already missed our meeting. Still...I kept them so well-stocked that it wouldn't endanger anyone to delay things by a week or so.

But I couldn't help being suspicious of Vani. Even though I'd promised her a clean slate, I was as fallible as the next man. And as much as I wanted to believe that she was infatuated with me, ready to follow wherever I want, I also believed that she was more than capable of running a long con.

"Captain?" Diana asked. "We are receiving a ping from the Ilmarinen system."

I frowned and said, "Continue in primary language and activate the Babel jammer."

Diana switched into Zathari, her tone clipped and precise. "It seems to be a locator. Should I respond?"

"Is it legitimate?"

"It appears to be," Diana said. It wasn't entirely unusual to receive an Ilmarinen ping. Part of using the gate system was accepting the risk of the massive intergalactic corporation knowing where you were. Every ship contacted the Ilmarinen system prior to a jump, meaning they couldn't use any signal blockers or stealth systems. Every jump was logged, so

Ilmarinen Interstellar could always determine which galaxy a registered ship was in.

If the system pinged you and got no response, they'd know you were off the radar. It wasn't illegal to go stealth, but going dark typically went hand-in-hand with illegal activity. Missing a ping increased your chances of getting stopped on a jump, which could be disastrous if you happened to be a Zathari smuggler with a bounty on his head for his involvement in a notorious prison escape a decade ago. Instead, a smart criminal did as much legally as possible.

This was probably a perfectly normal check. I got them on probably twenty percent of my jumps. Logically speaking, it was all but certain I'd receive one while I had Vani onboard. It was probably just standard.

But maybe it wasn't.

I didn't want to be suspicious of her. I wanted to trust that beautiful softness that bloomed from the brilliant blaze within. I wanted it all to be real, because I wanted to believe that I had found something so perfect.

But I would be an idiot to trust her completely. Her insistence on going back to Earth was logical, but it was troubling. And while that ping could have simply been a massive interstellar system keeping track of its customers, it could have been someone looking for my ship.

Or for her.

"Respond, Diana," I said. "Give them our location." I heard the sound of water from the cabin, and I quietly said, "Deactivate Babel jammer, Diana."

She returned and tilted her head. "Were you talking to

Diana?" Her face was scrubbed clean of the heavy makeup from Vakarios, leaving her rosy-cheeked and natural.

"I was sending a message to one of my brothers." Dishonesty turned my stomach, but I couldn't see any way around it. "Telling him I might have a guest when we meet on Phade." Every word felt like ash in my mouth.

She smiled brightly. "I can't wait."

My stomach twisted into a knot as I forced a smile. "I think you'll like him."

I hoped we made it that far.

CHAPTER 20

Havoc

FOR NEARLY TWO DAYS, WE WENT FROM THE CABIN TO MY quarters in a heady blur of long conversations interrupted by feverish bouts of sex. At some point, I thought I'd have to tap out from sheer exhaustion, but one look at Vani and my cock was reporting for duty yet again.

Over bland meals vastly improved by her presence, I told her about the mining pits of Kilaak, and how I had come by the chip on my left horn. She told me about the men that served Dinesso, and I learned that she'd named Rico the worst of the worst because he liked to put out his cigars on human skin. It was a game for him to try to make her cry.

The way she spoke of it was like she was telling me about learning to write her letters, as if it was a perfectly normal part of life. With each matter-of-fact tale, I knew, no matter what I had told her, I would kill them all for what they'd done to Vani and her sisters. There would be no mercy or deals. I couldn't walk away from men like Dinesso, knowing they were only going to find new victims. And I couldn't move forward, knowing that the men who'd scarred my angel were still breathing. My vow to protect her trumped my agreement to spare them. She'd have to understand.

We also spoke of far more pleasant things. I told her about the way my brothers had gravitated together on Kilaak, binding our ragged scraps together into something approximating a family. Every year, we all returned to Phade for the winter solstice, a sacred holiday to honor the Wayfarers. We'd celebrated it with shitty food and prison hooch back on Kilaak, and we'd continued to this day, though with much better food and wine.

In turn, she told me about how she and Naela had a tradition of finding books for each other. Her eyes gleamed when she talked about the glossy book filled with pictures of Earth before its decline, of vast green forests and turquoise seas and rainbow wildlife. Her sister cried over it and hid it under her mattress to protect it.

Vani also had a wicked streak, and she was uncannily good at imitating voices. She made me laugh with her delicate impression of Diana, down to her precise diction and faint accent, and once had me nearly convinced that Diana was requesting me to fuck her silly in the galley. Her quick wits delighted me to no end.

But I was wary, too, as she asked endless questions of how traveling between gates worked, how the ship stored messages to be relayed when entering a new galaxy, and critically, how long it would take us to return to Earth after Irasyne.

Maybe she was curious, and maybe she was preparing for something. I hated that I couldn't be sure. My growing distrust hung over me like a stormcloud. I hated pretending that I was unbothered, and each smile and kind word felt like a lie. The deception, subtle as it was, made my stomach churn.

Our second day of travel from Vakarios brought Inan Prime into sight. Grim, gray wastes greeted us as we descended through the atmosphere, headed for the fueling station.

Well before I was born, the Aengra Dominion had scraped Inan Prime clean of its rich deposits to be refined for fuel for Ilmarinen Interstellar and its jump gates. Though it was no longer inhabited, Inan Prime remained a popular stop for travelers passing through the system. From here, it was only a short flight to Xhaaro, a planet that had been mysteriously abandoned centuries ago. Collectors and museums throughout the Dominion became obsessed with its lost history, creating a lucrative market for intact artifacts, as well as a cottage industry for elaborate fakes. My brothers Wraith and Razor had gone on several treasure-hunting expeditions to Xhaaro on behalf of wealthy collectors. Between the radiation and the mutated creatures living on its surface, it sounded like a miserable hellhole, but the two of them were insane enough to enjoy it.

With the rise of travel to Xhaaro, Inan Prime had become a prized stop for ships passing through the system and a rest stop for those on their way to and from Xhaaro. Ard-Alkur Station was the primary point of interest nowadays, owned by a private fueling operation in the northern hemisphere. A small spaceport surrounded the fueling station, with a bar and a trader who stocked basics and offered simple ship repairs.

"Can we get out?" Vani asked as Diana guided the ship in for a landing at the station.

"There's nothing to see," I said. "Inan Prime is a hunk of rock and nothing more."

"But it's a hunk of rock I've never seen," she said. There was an earnest curiosity in her eyes that I couldn't resist. And considering her only trip off my ship since leaving Earth was into the filth of Vakarios, she deserved a change of scenery.

"All right," I agreed reluctantly. Fueling took time, regardless of whether we waited onboard or left the ship. I opened the shields on the cockpit windows so she could see. We sailed over an expanse of petrified trees, a dry riverbed, and finally, another small station with runways and landing pads radiating out from the central hub like the spokes of a wheel. "Open hailing frequencies, Diana."

"Yes, Captain," she said.

A brusque male voice issued over the speakers. "Craft IMS-X21, you are requested to land at pad seventeen. Please signal your understanding and acceptance of protocols on Inan Prime."

"Accepted," I said. "Thank you."

"Please authorize automated guidance," the voice said.

"Authorized," I said. "Diana, confirm authorization."

There was a little jolt, and Diana replied, "Now connected to landing system. Expected landing in three minutes."

Vani was on the edge of her seat as she watched the ground rising beneath us. Her eyes closed for only a split second when we landed, and then she lurched out of her seat. She'd fashioned an outfit from one of my black shirts, soft black tights, and the sash from the borrowed nightgown.

When Diana cleared us to move around, Vani headed toward the back of the ship. I frowned when she stopped at the door to the armory and looked at me expectantly. "What do you need?" I asked warily.

"Can I use those gloves again?" she asked.

I shook my head. "You don't need them here."

Her brow furrowed. "But I'm defenseless."

"You came on my ship without a weapon," I reminded her. My eyes drifted down. "Well, except the one under that shirt."

Her lips curved slightly, but there was a look of frustration in her eyes. "You still don't trust me."

"This is a trade station in the middle of nowhere," I said. "You don't have anything to be concerned about."

Her hand snaked into my jacket and rested on the holster at my hip. I instinctively covered her hand, my heart pounding. "That's why you're carrying, huh?" she asked. "I just want to be able to protect myself if something happens."

Or did she want to put me down and finally take the Nomad? I plucked her hand off my gun, then kissed her fingers. "You've got me to protect you."

"I thought we had a clean slate," she said quietly. "But you still don't trust me after everything."

Even without a weapon, she'd just carved my heart right out of my chest. Worse, I couldn't argue—I didn't trust her.

Her shoulders rose as she took a deep breath. "Let's go."

"Wait," I ordered. I fetched one of my tailored coats and snugged it around her. It was practically a dress on her, but I liked the look of her in my things. I also hoped it would somehow erase the pain of my distrust. "Inan Prime is very cold."

Tension still hung thick and heavy between us, but she clutched my hand tight as we waited at the boarding ramp.

"Captain, please wait for gangplank connection to be confirmed," Diana said. There was a jolt from outside the ship, then a rush of air. The ship sank slightly on its landing gears, and Diana let out a quiet chime. "Connection confirmed. Please be careful."

Vani was practically bouncing on her toes as the boarding ramp descended and let out a quiet hiss. A rush of cold air billowed over us, and she wedged in close to me. A translucent corridor was sealed to the door, stretching all the way to the central hub of the station.

"What the..." Vani said, staring up at the low, plastic ceiling.

"The air here is toxic in large quantities," I explained. Metal doors sealed behind us and let out a noisy hiss as they vented into the outer atmosphere. Huge, plate glass windows gave us a view of the barren planet beyond. With one hand on the fogged glass, she stared in wonder. It was easy to forget what it was like when everything was new, but I'd been just like her when we left Kilaak.

"You trust them with the Nomad?" she asked. A crew of workers in dark coveralls and sealed face masks were surrounding the ship for refueling.

"I don't trust anyone with her," I said frankly. "But we have to get fuel somewhere. And I'd rather it was here than paying triple the cost at the Ilmarinen station."

Inside Ard-Alkur Station was a small but thriving market-place. The smells of frying food and cooking spices filled the air. I could smell the sweet but pungent smell of Sahemnar cuisine. For a culture that was historically uninterested in colonization, somehow their cuisine had made it to nearly every galaxy I'd visited.

I let Vani go as she wandered into one of the shops to admire a display of dresses. There was a marketplace in Ir-Nassa a hundred times this size, to say nothing of the endless shops and boutiques in Aliaros. But she was utterly spellbound. It was every bit as beautiful as I'd imagined it would be, like watching a flower bloom. There was wonder in her eyes and a soft smile on her face as she held up a dress to her frame, looking down at it as if she was trying to imagine herself in it. She looked up and caught me staring. Her smile widened into a brilliant grin, teeth tugging at her lip.

The feeling that gripped me was so unfamiliar I couldn't even wrap my head around what it was. It was warm affection, pride that I'd brought her here, and a nearly uncontrollable desire to run to her side. It made me feel soft and strange, but I liked it. I'd killed enemies, pulled off lucrative smuggling runs, and outrun the bounty hunters of Deeprun for a decade, but watching her with that dress in her hands made me feel like a conqueror.

Vani held up a bold red dress with high slits on either side. Her eyebrows raised in a silent question. I nodded, and I was rewarded with another of those supernova smiles. I held up two fingers, and she picked out a green one. I tilted my head, and she held up a dark blue one with long sleeves and a plunging neckline. The rich, twilight color was my favorite. I gave her an approving look and nodded.

My watch buzzed with an alert from Diana, and I inserted a small earpiece into my ear that synced to the system. "Diana?"

"Captain, I have received another ping to our location systems," the AI said.

"From Ilmarinen?"

"Yes, Captain," she said. "Shall I accept?"

I hesitated, looking out at my ship. With another jump ahead, I didn't want to run the risk of being flagged. Being late would wound my pride, but getting investigated by Ilmarinen could be a much bigger problem. It would be exponentially harder to deliver my cargo if I was on my way back to prison. "Accept it."

"Yes, Captain," she said.

Hurrying back into the shop, I found Vani holding two pairs of earrings, frowning like she was trying to decide. "Get them both," I said, kissing the top of her head. "Let's eat and get back to the ship."

She nodded, hanging back as I took a thin fiber bag from a dispenser, put her items into it, and walked out. She tugged on my arm. "Are you stealing?" she whispered.

I snorted a laugh. "Everything's chipped. It'll charge directly to my account when we leave."

"Oh, right," she murmured, taking the bag from me and clutching it to her chest. "Thank you."

One of the small restaurants was a noodle stand with a conveyor belt carrying colorful dishes around a steaming grill. I grabbed a few bowls, handed them to Vani, and grabbed two more before leading her to a cozy table that overlooked the vast wasteland beyond the station. While I ate, she watched a massive Chariot class ship coming in for a landing. Red and blue lights twinkled on its belly, casting a strobing glow over our table.

I nudged her. "Don't let it get cold," I said.

She shook herself and picked up a set of chopsticks, deftly maneuvering a wad of seasoned noodles into her mouth. One of them snapped up to her cheek, and her eyes widened in embarrassment. Without missing a beat, I leaned forward and kissed her cheek, licking it clean. Her eyebrow arched. "If you're going to do that, I'm going to dump this whole bowl on myself."

"Do it," I said. "If you think I won't take the bait, you're sadly mistaken. I will lay you out on this table in front of the whole damned station."

Her lips pursed in a mischievous smile. "No, you won't."

"Try me," I replied. I might get arrested, but it would be worth it to lick her clean and hear her squeals echoing off the walls.

She grinned at me and peered into my bowl. I'd found a decent-looking *viniiret*, a Sahemnar street dish of dried fruit, mashed grain, and savory strips of dried meat with a spicy-sweet sauce. "Can I taste?"

"Of course." I pushed the bowl toward her and watched her fish out a piece of meat. Her eyes closed in quiet bliss as she chewed.

"Oh, God, that's good," she murmured. Her tongue darted out to catch a drop of the thick brown sauce from the end of her utensil. "Where is this from?"

"It's Sahemnar cuisine," I said. "Well, according to the natives, this is a bastardized version, but it's still good. They're from Firyanin. Same galaxy as my home on Phade." I pushed my other dish closer, letting her share. "When I visit home, there's a couple of authentic Sahemnar restaurants just down the street. I keep them stocked in expensive spices, so they'll cook anything we like."

"Can we go there sometime?" she asked.

"We can," I said quietly. *We.* I liked that word more than I expected.

It was strange how much I enjoyed watching her eat. It wasn't just the bliss on her face; I could almost feel her joy and surprise at each new flavor, the tiny panic at the deceptively spicy dumplings, and the airy sweetness of a whipped fruit mousse. I took a bite of the fluffy pink dessert, then spooned a bit more of it and offered it to her. Never breaking my gaze, she rose to eat it, smiling.

"What would you prefer I call you in public?" she asked suddenly.

"Havoc is fine," I said. "My name is only for *shan-harah*." Our names were entrusted to our closest friends, lovers, and family. It was an expression of trust that was nearly sacred.

"And that includes me now," she said, her voicing lilting in a question.

My head tilted. "I think it does." But I couldn't help wondering if I'd made a mistake. Before I could consider it further, my watch buzzed again. Instead of a generic message from Diana alerting me to the fuel's percentage, there was a flashing red indicator. Adrenaline spiked through my system. "Diana, report," I said.

"Security update, Captain," Diana said. "Unauthorized personnel in proximity."

"Use deterrent measures," I said. My warm comfort evaporated into cold dread. I craned my neck, but we were on the wrong side of the station to see the Nomad.

"Negative, Captain. Ilmarinen personnel present," she said. "Per acceptance of your flight license, I cannot use hostile countermeasures on Ilmarinen personnel."

"Dammit," I swore. Vani's eyes were wide and filled with fear. "Are they serving a warrant?"

"I do not know, Captain. I have sealed the cargo bay, but your presence is advised," she said.

"I'm on my way."

I stole a look at Vani. I couldn't leave her here but taking her with me was no better. And fuck everything, but I couldn't help wondering if this had something to do with her.

It couldn't.

"Take me with you," she said, as if she heard the conflict in my head. "What's happening?"

"I don't know. Just follow my lead." I swiped my wrist over a scanner on the table, then grabbed her hand to hurry back to the hangar.

My heart pounded as I took stock of what I was carrying. Technically *alcamara* was a controlled substance in parts of the Dominion, but they had far better things to deal with than a cargo hold full of antibiotics. At worst, that was a hefty fine and a slap on the wrist. No way Rhasat would have ratted me out; not if he wanted to ever make another deal on Vakarios again. The Nomad's registration and my flight license were both under a fake name with impeccable papers, so this shouldn't have anything to do with Kilaak. The bastards that ran that hellhole would have to work a lot harder to find me than a simple ping through the Ilmarinen network.

I tried to tell myself it was nothing. Just a routine inspection. Hell, maybe some Ilmarinen officer just happened to be at the station and wanted to admire the Nomad and her sexy curves.

Yeah, right.

We reached the airlock as the doors hissed open. Two men in dark blue coveralls emerged. My eyes skimmed over them. Ilmarinen uniforms. Behind them was a broad-shouldered human in a dark suit like the ones I'd just seen on Terra. Vani stopped dead in her tracks, her hand falling out of mine.

"Rico," she breathed, her entire frame shrinking as she gaped at him.

The Terran man smiled and stepped forward. "Vani, my girl. Good work."

CHAPTER 21

Vani

THE SWEETNESS OF THE EXOTIC DESSERT TURNED TO ASH ON MY tongue at the sight of Rico. One of Dinesso's enforcers, he was worlds away from where he belonged. I took a step behind Havoc, but instead of shielding me, he turned to give me a look of absolute fury. "What did you do?" he asked.

"I didn't do anything," I protested. Of all the responses he could have given, that was not the one I expected.

"Grab the Zathari," Rico said. "The boss is paying good money for big ones to fight at the stadium." His dark, shark-like eyes fell on me, and I took a big step back. "And he wants to reward you for a job well done, Vani."

The men in the blue uniforms converged on Havoc, which was a mistake. The first one barely touched him before he was hurled into a bone-crunching heap against the wall. Havoc's violet eyes were full of fury as he turned on the other one. The uniformed man drew a silver, rod-like weapon with electricity crackling across its sharp tip.

In a blur, Havoc spun around the second man, grabbed his weapon, and jammed it into the small of his back, giving him a ferocious shock. The man fell flat on his face, trembling.

I dashed for Havoc, but Rico grabbed my coat and yanked me back. "Havoc!" I shouted, my arms pinwheeling as I tried to run to him.

Havoc's head whipped toward me, but his expression was a slap in the face. It wasn't protective rage, but utter betrayal. In that moment of distraction, the doors slid open again. A group of four men in dark blue coveralls emerged, all armed to the teeth. One raised a long gun. Thunder cracked. and Havoc hurtled back against the opposite wall and slumped.

"No!" I whispered. He stared in slack-jawed disbelief at the glowing slug on his chest. Gritting his teeth, he plucked the flattened metal off and threw it aside. He drew his own weapon and aimed it at the one who'd just shot at him. As he did, a wiry man slid from the pack and darted to his side.

"Aim for the fucking horns," someone yelled.

Havoc swept his leg under the one who came from his side, but as he did, someone fired another shot at his head. The electrified slug molded to his forehead and wrapped around one of his horns. His eyes rolled back, and he hit the ground, twitching violently.

I was frozen in horror. Cold, Calculating Vani was already way ahead. Havoc was down, but if I played along, I could get my hands on some of his toys on the ship. He kept the armory locked, but he had guns stashed all over the ship. He thought I hadn't noticed, but I kept my hands off out of respect for the tiny seedling of trust I'd thought was growing between us.

Forcing a smile, I looked up at Rico and gently adjusted his collar. "It took you long enough to find me," I said. My stomach threatened to eject itself as I fell into the simpering act.

His brow arched. "We figured the horned fuck left you to rot in the desert. Should have known you'd figure out how to keep yourself alive. Like a fuckin' cockroach."

I smiled as if it was the sweetest compliment I'd ever heard. "I told Nesso I'd get the ship, didn't I?"

"Did you have to fuck him?"

"I've done worse things," I said with a shrug. His nostrils flared.

Across the hall, a pair of mercenaries were already dragging Havoc through the doors and down the gangplank. Cold air billowed from the open doorway. I could feel a pulsing ache in my head, as if someone had hit me just like they had Havoc. His breathing was ragged. Whatever they'd hit him with was still glowing, sending an electric shock into him. His violet eyes were open and unfocused.

I'm so sorry.

I prayed that he was too out of it to see me cozying up to Rico. It was for us, and I would beg for his forgiveness if we managed to survive.

Rico grabbed me around the waist, forcing me to walk at an awkward angle down the frigid gangplank. His fingers dug into my side hard enough to tell me he wasn't completely buying my act. I tried to remain calm, envisioning the path I would take on the Nomad.

"Get him wired up," one of the mercenaries yelled from inside the ship.

As I climbed the boarding ramp, I saw the mercenaries manhandling Havoc in the lounge, binding his wrists tight behind his back. One of them knelt and slid a needle into the base of his left horn. A thin wire connected it to a small device, which the man secured to Havoc's horn with a strap. Havoc groaned, then jolted as a current arced into the needle. The mercenary pried the glowing slug off his horn, and Havoc went limp, breathing hard. His eyes found mine, and I felt like he'd punched me in the gut. It wasn't anger, but raw pain. And I knew somehow that it wasn't the pain of them electrocuting him, but the pain of betrayal.

It wasn't me. I wanted to scream. I had been his angel, had done everything I could to be worthy of his trust and regard.

The mercenary handed Rico a black remote. "If he gets too excited, hit the button," he said. "You want to keep a Zathari under control, it's drugs or electricity. Don't waste your time hitting him."

Rico tilted his head and pressed the button. Havoc's body went rigid, his eyes rolling back until all I saw was pure white.

My own body tightened in sympathy as an awful groan erupted from his chest. "Leave him alone," I blurted. "He's already down."

Rico gave me an odd look. "You like the ugly fucker?"

"If you keep that up, he's going to piss himself and then the ship will smell," I said, hoping my fury didn't seep through.

As if to give me an extra *fuck you*, Rico hit the button again. "Can't let him get away with stealing our Vani."

"Stop it," I hissed.

The man who'd wired Havoc looked me over. "Her next," he said, taking another set of plastic cuffs from his belt.

"Wait," I protested. "You can trust me. I promised Nesso I'd get the ship, didn't I?"

Rico shrugged. "If it was up to me, you'd spend the flight with my dick in your mouth, but the boss gave very clear orders."

This was going south in a hurry. Playing along was no longer an option. The mercenary took a step toward me, and I shoved Rico toward the approaching mercenary and bolted down the narrow hall into the cockpit. "Diana, the captain has a medical emergency," I said. "Give me temporary command."

"Yes, Passenger Vani," Diana said.

"Close cockpit door," I said. The door slid shut behind me, rattling angrily as Rico pounded on it.

"Open this fuckin' door, Vani!" he bellowed.

I felt under the pilot's seat until I found the gun. My heart pounded. I checked the indicator and found that it was set to *stun*.

"Diana, can you turn off the oxygen flow to the rest of the ship?" I asked.

"I'm sorry, Passenger Vani, but that would violate my protective programming," she said.

"Fuck me running," I swore. I kicked off my shoes and planted my feet, ready to go through the door. "Turn off the lights. Take the whole ship to sleep mode."

"I cannot enter sleep mode while the Captain has a medical emergency," Diana said. No wonder he liked Diana so much. She was literally programmed to protect him at all costs, even if it meant letting her ship and its captain fall into the hands of the worst men Earth had to offer.

"I guess I have to do this myself," I muttered. "Open the cockpit door."

"Yes, Passenger Vani," she said helpfully.

No hesitation.

As soon as the door opened, I squeezed the trigger. A little shockwave burst from the weapon and one blue-clad mercenary went down in a heap. Another pull, and the one behind him went down. There was a blur of blue as someone else darted out of sight.

I leaped over the fallen men and bolted for Havoc. He was barely conscious, his eyes heavy and hazy. I pried uselessly at the plastic bindings on his wrists, then realized he'd be more useful if he was conscious. Grabbing the rubber-coated wire buried in his hair, I yanked the needle out of his skin. He let out a groan that rose into a growl.

There he was.

"Havoc, we have to—"

A hand twisted into my hair and pulled me away. Rico's breath was hot on my ear as he growled, "You're going to fucking regret that," he said.

Searing pain rippled up my spine as I twisted in his grasp and jammed the gun under his chin. I pulled the trigger, and he went rigid. "Fuck you," I bellowed at him. God, it was satisfying to see him go down.

I was still gloating when a hand closed around my throat and another grabbed my wrist. Bones crunched as one of the mercenaries twisted my wrist and forced me to drop the gun. He threw me down on the couch where Havoc had made love to me half a dozen times. "Diana!" I bellowed as the man yanked my wrists together and bound them. "Call for assistance. Captain Havoc is under attack!"

"Goddamn, you're a handful," the man complained. "Nayvan, get me something to shut her up."

"Passenger Vani, I can call for local law enforcement to assist the Captain," Diana said.

"Yes, please—" A piece of cloth filled my mouth, tied roughly behind my head. I screamed in frustration against the dirty fabric.

The mercenary finished tying my ankles, then bound them to my hands behind me so my body was practically tied in a knot. He let out a heavy sigh. "We ought to get paid extra for this shit. Get this thing off the ground."

"Commands not recognized," Diana said from the cockpit.

Then a strange voice said, "Override code IIP-A-89. Ilmarinen inspection protocols."

"Ilmarinen inspection protocols recognized," Diana said helpfully. "Welcome aboard the Nomad."

CHAPTER 22

Havoc

AFTER GETTING A HUNDRED THOUSAND VOLTS STRAIGHT INTO MY jaw and pissing myself the first time, I quickly realized that I was in big fucking trouble. I felt like I'd gone through a gate with no shielding, with the universe tearing me apart and reforming me in the wrong configuration.

Now that he was conscious again, the dark-haired one with the Terran clothes and Vani's name in his mouth was having fun with that box. I'd quit protesting long ago, but he still did it every few minutes and laughed uproariously every time I went rigid, muscles trembling as they threatened to snap my joints.

And worse, Vani was right there, bound and helpless. Her eyes pleaded with me. I'd held her in this very cabin, listening to her heart beat steadily as I swore to her that I would protect her. And the worst part was that I still didn't know if she'd betrayed me. She'd cozied right up to Rico, the one she'd said was the worst of the worst.

I told you I'd get the ship, didn't I? she'd purred, as smooth and sweet as could be. I could hear that voice echoing in my skull, scraping every nerve. *You can trust me.*

"Preparing for jump," Diana said.

"Hey!" I bellowed.

Vani's eyes squeezed shut. Even though I was furious at her and myself, I still needed to hold her and protect her. The gravity generator switched off as the ship was drawn into the jump gate's field. "Get in here!"

But they ignored me, and the ship vibrated violently. Her body drifted a few inches above the couch.

"Deep breath, Vani," I roared at her over the noise of the ship. She sucked in a deep breath around the gag, but she was panicking, looking for something to hold onto. My hand should have been there to anchor her, but six feet might as well have been six miles. There was a single chime just before the sling-shot threw us forward into the nothingness between gates. "Just hold on, angel."

It felt like the world folded in, crushing us to a single atom. I forced myself to breathe out, but she was choking. I managed to flip onto my back and catch that stupid wire between my head and my shoulder. It tore out of my skin. "Hey! Get the fuck in here!"

Buckles clattered from the cockpit, and the dark haired one who'd put his hands on Vani stormed in. "You don't give the orders."

"You want her alive for your boss, you better get that out of her mouth," I seethed. "Just breathe, angel."

He gave me an odd look, then yanked the gag out of her mouth. Tears streamed down her cheeks as she sobbed in terrible, hiccupping cries. She was hyperventilating as pure terror took hold. "Fuck, Vani, you're gone for a week, and you turn into a crying little bitch?"

"Why don't you see how you handle a jump when you can't breathe, you cowardly fuck," I growled.

His dark eyes narrowed, and he grabbed the black box. Shit. I'd hoped he wouldn't notice, but he grabbed the box and knelt on my back. He was less deft than the mercenary, and he shoved the needle back into the base of my horn, scraping against the bone. I roared in pain as he gave me another wicked shock.

Then he settled back, resting his elbow on Vani's back like she was nothing more than furniture. Her bloodshot eyes pleaded with me, her beautiful face contorted in anguish. Her head shook, and I could almost hear her pleading.

Why aren't you doing something?

I wanted to comfort her, but I didn't dare give this waste of skin any more reason to hurt her. Right now was time to play it safe until there was a better set of circumstances.

"Nobody's ever called this little slut an angel," he said. He smacked her ass.

She just closed her eyes.

"Ain't that right?" He tilted his head. "She led us right to you, just like she was supposed to."

Her eyes flew open, and she shook her head. "I didn't," she protested. Then her eyes flicked to the Malzek device in the middle of the room. Her eyes searched mine, and I shook my head. No telling what this fuck would do with it. Given what she'd told me about Dinesso and his men, it could end badly for her, and I would never forgive myself.

"I told Dinesso the goat man probably killed you," Rico said. "Fucked you good and left you in the desert to rot. But the crew he hired picked up your signals at the jump gate loud and clear. Watched you jump right on out of the galaxy."

"I didn't—"

His big hand covered her face, pinching her nose as he covered her mouth. "Man, you put up with her talking all this time? Fuckin' women, man." Her eyes rolled back as she struggled in vain. My chest ached, my heart pounding painfully as I watched. "Good for one thing, right?" He ignored her desperate, muffled cries, and she eventually went limp.

At least when they'd hurt my sister, I could intervene. Nothing in my life had hurt quite like watching Vani struggle, knowing that she wanted me to protect her. I'd promised her that none of these men would ever hurt her again. To watch my own promise shattered was a nightmare.

I decided that he was going to be the first one I killed. And it was going to hurt. I wouldn't do him the mercy of making it quick. Even if Vani had betrayed me, he didn't get to touch her that way. He didn't get to drag her back into the dust.

There were a dozen possibilities for how they'd tracked me down, but Wraith would have told me, in no uncertain terms, *the simplest way is the truth, little brother.* I didn't know how she'd done it, but she had to have reported back to them.

As my ship hurtled back to the dusty rock of Terra, my mind spun through the last week, a heady blur of pleasure. There was Vani with my tablet, reading data files on planet after planet. She'd tricked me once; maybe all her innocent questions were for show. While she was shopping, I'd turned my back on her for at least five minutes. She could have made contact then. Hell, maybe she'd just put a damn tracker on my ship the second she boarded, and every second of this had been one long con.

I didn't want it to be true, but there were a lot of things in this life I didn't want. That hadn't stopped a goddamn one of them from happening.

She was unconscious for much of the descent to Earth, but the violent shaking as the Nomad re-entered Earth's atmosphere shook her awake. As soon as her eyes opened, she yelled for Diana. I had to give it to her. She was persistent. And Rico rewarded her for it by shoving her face into the cushion.

Maybe it was her body language, screaming aloud what her voice couldn't, but I could almost hear her begging in my head. It was deafening.

Havoc Havoc Havoc get him off me, I can't breathe, please protect me

"Hey, fuckface, leave her alone," I said. "You want to fuck with someone, I'm a lot bigger target."

"Ah, the goat man's protective. That's sweet. Did she get you hooked on Earth pussy?" He leaned in and wrinkled his nose. "It's not that good."

"It's all good pussy if you know what to do with it," I replied. "Did she call you to come get my ship?"

"Call came through loud and clear," he replied. He raised his eyes, bracing himself as the ship landed roughly. I cringed. "Pretty little ship."

"What are you going to do with her?"

"The ship or the slut?"

"Either," I said.

He leaned over on his elbows. "Whatever the boss wants."

The human mercenary who'd piloted my ship returned from the cockpit. "Call your boss for a transport." The dark-haired man nodded and stepped out of the cabin, leaving me alone with Vani.

"Vani," I said quietly. "Be honest. Did you sell me out?"

Her head lifted, and I hated myself for even asking her. I felt the pain of it, like someone had stabbed me in the chest. "I didn't. I swear," she protested, her voice scraped raw. "I've been honest with you, just like you asked."

The mercenary returned and sliced the plastic cable binding her hands and feet. She let out a groan as it released the sharp angle on her legs, and he picked her up roughly. "Your boss is ready to see you," he said, patting her on the ass.

"Havoc, please," she murmured. "You have to believe me."

But I was silent as I watched her go. "Diana, lock down the cargo bay."

"My apologies, Captain, but I cannot override Ilmarinen protocols," she said.

"That asshole isn't Ilmarinen, Diana," I said. "Someone sold him a code." Counterfeit codes were rare. If he got busted, he'd probably be sent to Kilaak, if one of the Ilmarinen investigators didn't simply make him disappear.

"I'm sorry, Captain, but I cannot override—"

"Diana, come on," I pleaded.

While I was still pleading with her disembodied voice, a couple of Terran males shuffled onto my ship and dragged me out, dumping me unceremoniously onto a dust-covered landing pad. I tried in vain to get up, but one of them planted a heavy foot in the middle of my back, leaning his full weight onto me as he waited. Hot sand scraped against my skin, and my lungs filled with the dry, hot air of the Prospects.

Soon, I heard the rumbling roar of an engine, and a couple of the men lifted me into the back of a truck. One hot, sand-filled ride later, there were rough hands dragging me out of the truck again. A silver dome rose against the skyline, with the broken outline of what might have been a helmet on it. They threw me on a rolling cart like cargo, then took me through an open gate.

Down a long, curving concrete hallway, there was a large open area filled with cells. It smelled like piss and unwashed bodies, which reminded me of nearly fifteen years on Kilaak. Several of the cages were occupied. Mostly human, but I saw the unmistakable frame of a Proxilar.

The humans tossed me into an empty cell and slammed the door. "Cut me loose," I demanded.

"When it's time to fight," one of them said.

Great. I had no doubt I could win a fight. Humans, especially the ones on Terra, were stupid. If they unleashed me to fight, I'd just break the hell out. I wasn't usually one to get worked up. Life was going to kick your teeth in sometimes, and there was jackshit you could do about it. But I was worried about what they'd do with the Nomad in the meantime, and increasingly, what they would do to Vani.

But a constant fear gnawed at my belly. It felt foreign, as if a parasite had taken root. Every time I thought of Vani, the sick, crawling sensation intensified. I could almost hear her voice in my head, protesting. *It wasn't me. I wouldn't do that to you.*

It was just what I wanted to believe. I wanted to believe that she was my angel, that my name was safe with her. That I hadn't been unspeakably stupid to put my trust in her.

I could have prevented all of this. She'd asked for a weapon before we went to the station. We'd be happily on our way to Irasyne right now if I'd just trusted her. Then again, maybe she'd have left me in a heap for her mercenary buddies to scoop up.

I'd been sitting on the hard concrete floor for no more than an hour when a human male with salt-and-pepper hair came to visit. Two men, including the dark-haired prick who'd roughed up Vani, flanked him. My eyes slid over the man in the suit. "You must be Dinesso."

He smiled, his teeth straight and white. Creases surrounded his soulless, dark eyes. I knew an expensive, tailored suit when I saw one; he was a wealthy man who knew how to look the part, not a poor man trying to look rich. "And you must be the Zathari with the beautiful ship."

"I am," I said. "Take good care of her. I'll need her back soon. Got a schedule to keep."

Dinesso chuckled. "I don't think so. She's mine now. Law of the universe, yes?"

"No, she isn't," I said calmly. "And when I get out of here, I'm going to show you how badly you've fucked up."

The well-dressed man gave a mock shudder. "Oh, frightening," he said. "Does that usually work for you?"

I tilted my head. "Where's Vani?" Those hands had hurt my Vani, long before I even knew she was a twinkle in the universe, and he was going to suffer for it.

"She's getting her reward for a job well done," Dinesso said. "What's in the cargo hold?"

"Antibiotics," I said. "Nothing useful to you."

He raised an eyebrow. "What's really in the hold? Narcotics? Guns?"

"Antibiotics. You can shoot it, if you want, but the best you'll get is a case of the shits," I said again. I regarded the men behind Dinesso. Rico, I knew. "Are you Luka?" The heavy-set blond flinched. He looked like three hundred pounds of muscle with the brain cells of a particularly ungifted squirrel.

That one would be the next to go after Rico. He was the one who'd carved his initial onto her skin. Maybe I'd carve my name into him before I finished him off. My full name, since he had plenty of real estate, and I had plenty of rage.

Dinesso spread his hands. "Welcome to Earth, Mr. Havoc. I think you're going to do nicely here."

"I won't be here long," I said. "If you want to save yourself some trouble, bring me Vani and my ship."

He laughed. "I don't think so. I look forward to seeing what you can do in a fight. Get some rest. Wouldn't want you too tired for your first match."

CHAPTER 23

Vani

THE WHIPCRACK OF A HARD SLAP RANG OUT IN THE SMALL, DINGY room. Tears pricked at my eyes, and I found myself wishing I'd go unconscious again. I should have known better than to think I could rise from the dust. To soar through the stars, seeing the whole universe unfolding before me, with Havoc at my side...it was just a cruel, sweet dream that had crashed back to Earth.

From the dust I had come, and to the dust I had returned. I was never meant to have anything else.

I pulled in vain at my bound wrists, but Rico had been thorough, tying them to the heavy arms of the chair. He'd delivered me to one of the back rooms of the Dahlia, just down the hall from Dinesso's office.

The boss himself had stopped in long enough to tell me that he'd be back, which was most certainly a threat, and left me in the hands of Dmitri and Jakob. They hadn't suffered one bit for my absence, but they hardly needed an excuse to beat the shit of someone, especially a woman tied to a chair.

There was nothing for me to give them. They had Havoc. They had the Nomad. They just wanted to put me back in my place, so I would remember where I belonged.

Dmitri circled me, shaking out his hand. Then he grabbed my hair, twisting it hard around his fist. "You could convince me to go easy on you," he said. "Like old times. Use that mouth to ask nicely, and maybe I'll listen."

"If you put your sad excuse for a dick anywhere near me, I'll bite it off," I retorted. His glassy eyes went wild with anger, and he slapped me again. Something popped in my ear, sending a stab of agony through my skull. I cried out, then let out a manic laugh. I liked the rage in his eyes. I liked knowing that he was shocked at what he'd found.

The girl who left Earth was never coming back.

My angel. My good girl.

I wanted to believe that somehow, Havoc was going to come for me. That he was going to cut through these bastards the way he'd cut through the men who imprisoned him on Kilaak.

But after everything, he thought I'd betrayed him. Because of stupid Rico. No. Not entirely because of stupid Rico. Because I'd manipulated him, lied to him, and attacked him not once, not twice, but three times.

No wonder he didn't trust me. I hadn't earned it, and whatever good will I'd gained with him was gone. That hurt far more than Dmitri's fist. Bruises would heal. Havoc's distrust had carved something out of me, and I felt like I was hemorrhaging out. Every good thing I'd felt for the last few days was seeping into the dust.

It wasn't me, I thought desperately. If I could just see him and tell him, let him look in my eyes and listen to my heartbeat while I told him the truth.

As the thought ran through my head—*it wasn't me, I swear it wasn't me*—I could have sworn that I felt something respond. I could feel him touching me, that big hand on my back.

Stay alive, Vani. I'll come for you.

His deep voice rumbled through my head, almost as if he was talking to me, the way he did when we lay in each other's arms and talked for hours. Maybe Dmitri had split something open in my brain that made me hear voices.

Dmitri rolled up his sleeves. "You used to be so well-behaved, Vani. Someone needs to teach that mouth manners again."

"It won't be you," I told him. As he wound up for another blow, I kicked him in the knee, eliciting a noisy crunch of bone. His face went red as he staggered back and cursed. A foul stream of curses poured over his chapped lips.

"I'm gonna kill the bitch," he seethed. "Get a knife. See how smart that mouth is when I peel her fuckin' lips off."

Jakob smacked Dmitri's broad chest. "You know the rules. Dinesso didn't decide what he's going to do with her yet. You fuck up her face, and he can't use her." He balled one fist, placing it right beneath my ribs. Then he pulled back and punched me so hard I retched. As I gasped for air, he laughed. "Don't worry. I can keep you pretty."

The world around me was hazy and fractured. I woke with a start, looking instinctively for Havoc. No warm body curled up against mine. As I started to call for Diana, my teeth brushed the bloody gash on my lower lip.

Pain lanced through me, radiating from my ribs and my sides. I let out a hitching cry as I struggled in vain against the bindings on my wrists. I wasn't in that perfect little refuge. I was back in the dust. The stars were gone.

He was gone.

And the man who'd held me down for my whole life was walking into the room. Dust streaked his tailored pants. Dinesso set a folding chair in front of me and sat in it, folding his legs neatly. "Vani, Vani, Vani," he murmured, clicking his tongue. "What happened, my pretty little bird?" He took a handkerchief from his pocket, then lightly dabbed at my split, swollen lip. "I told those morons not to hurt your face."

"Thanks for the concern," I mumbled. As if he was showing kindness, rather than making sure he could still use me. He liked the pain and how it humbled us, but he didn't like looking at the evidence of it. I'd never figured out if it made him feel guilty, or if the sight of imperfections angered him.

"When you didn't return, I thought the Zathari must have killed you. I was very sad," he said. His voice dripped with absolute indifference. "Imagine my surprise when you went through the Ilmarinen gate."

Confusion sprang to life amidst the pain. "How did you know about the gate?"

He reached over and pressed one finger into my bicep. "All my girls are tagged. It's a careless man who loses track of his treasures. I had Luka put a tracker on each of those syringes, too, just in case he dumped your body."

Horror washed over me. "So you followed me."

He shrugged. "My hired mercenaries did. It's easy enough to report a missing person," he said. "When you didn't come back, I assumed that he'd taken you prisoner. Once he made the jump into the Abeona Galaxy, they knew where he'd likely refuel."

"Where is he?" I asked quietly.

"He's going to earn his keep at the stadium," he said. "But I'm more concerned about you. Rico swore you tried to help him. I told him that simply couldn't be true. Surely, you were just trying to protect yourself from the big gray brute, weren't you?"

I should just go along with him. Beg his forgiveness, even if it meant getting on my knees. Havoc would understand self-preservation. But I couldn't do it.

Honesty, Vani. Honesty is everything.

Instead, I set my jaw and stared straight ahead. Dinesso sighed dramatically and rose, circling me slowly. I tried to control my breath as he placed his hands on my aching shoulders, then slowly hooked one arm around my neck. In one of his favorite moves, he covered my mouth, pinching my nose and sealing off my airways. He was a master of inflicting suffering without leaving a mark.

"Then I'm going to have to remind you where you belong," he said calmly. I twisted in his grasp, but he was so strong. "It may take some time, Vani, but I'm a patient man, aren't I?" My head pounded, but he leaned in, applying pressure to my throat.

As I was struggling to keep calm, I felt Havoc's hand on my back again, as if a single finger traced my spine. His voice was an unintelligible shout at first, but then I heard, clear as if he had shouted in my ear.

Where are you? Answer me, Vani.

There was a strange intensity to it. It wasn't a memory or a fantasy. It was real and tangible, like the crush of gravity when we burst through Earth's hold and into the vast expanse. He was here somehow.

I whimpered against Dinesso's hand, and he finally released me. As I coughed and gasped for air, he stroked my hair gently. "Breathe, sweet girl," he said. "You know this hurts me more than it hurts you. You know that you've always been my favorite. And I know you'll work so hard to make this up to your Nesso, won't you?"

"Thank you," I said roughly. "I was just—"

His fist hammered into my lower back, and my entire belly turned to lava. I couldn't even cry, just shook with silent sobs as white-hot pain gripped me. "You belong to me, Vani Adros," he said in my ear. "I fed you. I protected you. When your cunt of a mother abandoned you, I could have thrown you onto the street, but I sheltered you. I have been nothing but good to you. Do you even care about the pain you caused me?"

"I'm sorry," I gasped.

"You have not even begun to be sorry," he said. His hand covered my face again, and I closed my eyes, trying not to panic. I tried to listen for Havoc's voice.

I promise it will end. It will be over faster than you realize.

It was insane, but I tried to picture him, those beautiful violet eyes and dark gray skin. The look on his face when I touched his horns, and that shy, almost vulnerable expression when he finally gave me his real name. When he trusted me. When I was good.

I could feel him touching my fingertips, even as my heart pounded and my lungs screamed for air.

I'm in the Dahlia. Back room.

But there was nothing in return. I was a fool to expect a response. It was just my mind, desperate as a caged animal, looking for the one thing that would give me comfort. But I was no longer his angel. I had fallen back to Earth, and as the dark closed in, I knew that this was where I would stay. I would die here, and it was stupid to have dreamed it could ever be another way.

Something cold touched my face, and I jerked awake, barely suppressing a whimper. I wasn't going to let them have one more ounce of my pain. That was mine.

But when I opened my eyes, it was sweet Naela bending over me, her straight red hair loose around her face. Her brow furrowed in concern. "Hey, cupcake," she whispered. She used a wet cloth to dab at my split lip. "I thought you'd gotten out of here for good."

"Me too," I whispered. "We were going to come back for you."

"We?" she asked.

"The Zathari. He's a good man." I bowed my head. "But they followed me. Nesso put a tracker in me. In us, I guess."

Naela's eyes widened. Then she shook her head. "He was so mad when you didn't come back."

"Did he hurt you?" I asked. "I'm so sorry." I'd been floating through space, having the time of my life, while she was here suffering.

"It's not your fault." Her eyes narrowed. "You think the big guy will take all of us?"

"That was the plan," I said.

"So, what do we do?"

I thought for a while, closing my eyes as Naela gently combed my hair back. Her fingers were soothing as she combed out my disheveled locks and tamed them into a neat braid. "Have you seen him?"

"Not yet. They took him right to the stadium. The boys are selling tickets and taking bets on the horned freak." I started to protest, but she interrupted. "Their words, not mine. He's favored to win, so I'm sure they're going to mess with him so they can collect."

"When Rico grabbed us, all the mercenaries with him had some kind of electric weapon. His skin is really tough." I closed my eyes, trying to recall what the merc had said. "Rico had a remote, with a needle under his skin to keep him under control."

"No remote, no control," she mused.

I nodded. "It's a start. But please, don't get yourself hurt for me."

"If I can't get hurt for you, there's no one else. You're all I've got." She kissed my forehead. "I hope your boyfriend is as good as you say."

CHAPTER 24

Havoc

THE GOOD PEOPLE OF EARTH TURNED OUT IN DROVES TO WATCH two aliens beat each other to death. Their bloodthirsty screams were a nonstop roar. Across a long sandy pit from me was the Proxilar male, easily twice as broad and a foot taller than me. With a flat, scarred nose and bulbous forehead, he was ugly even by Proxilar standards.

As an image of my face appeared on a massive screen, a voice boomed over the crowd. "And here to fight the reigning champion, we have a horned beast from the far reaches of the Vela Cluster, as vicious as he is hideous."

First, that was fucking rude. I might be vicious under the right circumstances, but I was far from hideous. There were plenty of satisfied women from here to Thegara that liked me enough to come back for seconds and thirds. Second, why were humans so damned simple and predictable? They caught an alien with a shred of upper body strength, and their first instinct was to put him in a pit and watch him beat the shit out of another alien.

I was brilliant at math. Did it occur to these assholes to ask me to take a look at their books? I'd have bet a thousand credits that Dinesso had at least one asshole skimming money from his operation, and I'd have spotted it easily. Shit, I could have spent an hour adjusting the pricing at the Anchor Drop and raised their profits by ten percent. But did they ask?

No. Of course they fucking didn't.

Instead, they sent a scantily clad girl in a black uniform to slather burning silver paint on my chest. I'd considered grabbing her and using her as a hostage. But judging by what Vani had told me, Dinesso wouldn't give two shits if I pulled her arms off and wore her ribcage as a hat. Once she left, they drugged me, drilled a needle into the base of my horn, sent for a medic after I broke the first guy's arm, and got me wired up.

And then they did the most predictable fucking thing they could have done and sold tickets to watch me fling my fists like a trained animal.

Then again, I couldn't judge too harshly. People all over the universe loved blood sports. And on a planet like Terra, I had to admit that it made a little sense. If it was fun to watch two humans fight to the death, it must be exponentially more so to watch two aliens do it.

A deafening bell rang, and the crowd erupted in screams. The Proxilar lurched toward me, thundering with that heavy, earth-shaking gait. While I waited and watched, a current arced through my head. As soon as I reached up to touch it, another jolt ran through me, and I nearly fell to my knees.

Digging my bare feet into the sand, I waited out the lumbering beast. When he was within ten yards, I sprinted for him and slid in the sand, driving my foot into his shin. His armored hide protected his bone, but momentum was a bitch. With a surprised *hurk*, he went down in a spray of sand.

I pounced on him and twisted one of his massive arms behind his back. He wriggled and roared. "Hey, asshole," I growled. "Work with me and I'll get you out of here."

"Fuck you," he snarled. Using his other arm, he shoved himself upright, reached back, and grabbed one of my horns. I bellowed in pain as he swung me over his shoulder and slammed me to the ground. Air rushed from my lungs. The crowd roared their approval. I was stunned for a split second and reached up to make sure the damned thing was still attached.

Two horns. Thank the Wayfarers.

As I rolled to my feet, another powerful electric shock rolled through me and I flattened, my whole body locking down. My muscles didn't respond as the Proxilar pounced on me, raining heavy blows onto my face. The first hit to my nose woke me up, and I threw up my arms to shield my face.

"Kill him!" someone screamed from just above us.

I slammed my head into the Proxilar's face. We were both genetically built to survive, but my skull triumphed over his nose, which erupted with a hot spray of blood. As he reeled, I thrust my hand up to grab his throat. My fingers pried under the heavy armor plate on his neck, and his yellow eyes flew open.

"I'll spare you," I said, trying not to think about the hot

oozing substance under his neckplate. "You and me can get out of here."

"No you and me," he wheezed.

"Are you stupid?" I spat.

"You're stupid," he retorted.

Great talk. Despite his lack of contribution to his species' continued evolution, I didn't want to kill him. I wanted to spit in the faces of the fucks who'd put me here.

I drove my fist into his face, then dropped him in a groaning heap.

Apparently, Dinesso didn't like that. A shock rolled down my spine, and I fell over like a stone statue. The Proxilar pounced on me, pounding his meaty fists down into my bare back. My skin was tough, but that much force still fucking hurt. I played dead, letting myself go flat. The crowd screamed for blood.

Kill him! Kill him!

When his weight shifted for him to proclaim an unearned victory, I threw him off and pounced. I locked my arms around his thick neck and twisted violently. The tearing crack of his spine resonated through my chest, and I fell back, breathless. The crowd surged to their feet, screaming and cheering.

These people needed to get laid or something. I loved to fight as much as any Zathari, but watching two unwilling competitors fight to the death made no sense to me.

I extricated myself and rose, staring up at the glass-walled box at the top of the packed stadium. A vidscreen mounted at one end of the stadium showed a high-res image of my face, unbloodied by the Proxilar's blows. If they wanted blood, they'd picked the wrong two aliens for it.

Armed with electrified prods, a squad of men in tactical gear surrounded me and herded me back to the gate where I'd entered the stadium. No sooner had I stepped through the rusted gates than another shock rolled over me. The concrete rushed up to meet me.

A familiar voice chuckled. "Good fight, goat man," Rico said. Something wrapped around my horns, and there was a noisy clank of chain. It yanked, and a ferocious pain radiated from it. It was like getting kicked in the balls and getting a stiletto through my eardrum at the same time. The motherfucker had leashed me.

I reached up to grab the chain, but another vicious shock sent me back to my knees. Spittle flecked from my lips as I convulsed.

"Just go back to your cage like a good little goat," Rico said. Sadistic little shit.

Arms hooked under me and dragged me back to the cell. They tossed me back in, and I slammed into the bars to grab at them. Rico and his men laughed as they backed away, easily dodging my grasping fingers.

With every insult, I was calculating how much worse I was going to make it for Rico before he died. If I could make it happen, I was going to stick this needle into his dick and shock him until it exploded. I didn't care if Vani had betrayed me or not; he had that coming.

Since arriving on Earth, I hadn't seen Vani. But lying in that cell overnight, I'd entertained a dangerous thought. I'd heard her in my head. And maybe it was just my imagination. Thinking about her buried me in shame and guilt, so of course I imagined her scared and begging for me to help her.

And maybe it was something entirely different.

I'd given her my real name because she had awakened something in me. It felt right, like nothing ever had before. Wraith said starbonding was nothing more than romantic nonsense for Zathari who'd never gotten their dicks wet or their hands dirty. But the stories claimed that starbound mates were so intricately woven together that they could sense each other from far away. It let warriors fight while knowing their mates were safe, and it let them connect so intimately that they felt each other's pleasure and pain.

I'd never met anyone who'd experienced it. I'd also never met a human who made me want to share my name. No one had ever made me feel so soft and so powerful at the same time.

Anything could happen.

Outside, there were more roars as another match began. Despite the noise, I drifted off into a fitful sleep. When I woke, it was quiet. The cell across from me was empty, and I couldn't see past a short expanse of concrete on either side.

Soft steps padded down the hall, and I soon saw the source. A redhead in a skimpy outfit set a paper bag in front of the cell, and used a broom to push it close to me.

"I'm not hungry," I growled at her. "Unless you want to bring me your boss's balls as a snack."

She frowned at me. "Read the bag."

I bared my teeth. "I don't take orders from you." Her brown eyes narrowed, clearly unfazed. It was hard to be intimidating when I was on the wrong side of the bars with an electric current that sucked the strength out of me.

There was something about the pretty redhead that felt oddly familiar. Her black outfit and red-painted lips were identical to Vani's when I first met her, but that wasn't it. There was a proud posture and hard edge that felt like an echo of my Vani. I sensed grim resolve that had come through a difficult life.

I snatched the bag. Inside was a wrapped sandwich. I slowly turned the bag over and found a note in neat, feminine handwriting.

I'll get you out of here. Keep quiet, and keep your hands to yourself. Do we have a deal?

My eyes widened as I looked up at her. "How do I know you're not tricking me?"

"I guess you don't," she replied. Then she slid her hand under her short skirt. She was gorgeous, but she wasn't my girl. But she didn't make an offer, instead withdrawing a small black box from beneath her clothing. "You want this?"

"Is that..." I pointed up to my horn.

"Yep. If I get close to you, are you going to hurt me?" Her head tilted. "Vani told me you were a good man."

My heart tore open at the sound of her name. I wasn't a good man. I'd failed her. "I'm not going to hurt you."

Then she sank to her knees, inching close to the bars. Her dark eyes were wide and fearful, but she held my gaze. "If I help you, then you get Vani and the rest of us out."

"How many?"

"Four, counting Vani," she said.

"She told me about two. Are you Naela or Amira?"

"Naela," she said, her gaze softening. "She talked to you about me?"

I nodded. "She cares a lot about you two, but she never mentioned a third."

"When Vani left, Dinesso brought Karysse from one of the

other clubs to serve drinks. So far, they haven't hurt her, but Luka and Jakob have their eyes on her. And it's only a matter of time before they hurt Amira," Naela said quietly. "They're talking about auctioning her off and selling tickets to watch the winner..." She shook her head. "You know."

"Not if I have anything to do with it."

Her lips pursed in a smile. Then she tapped her forehead. "I can disconnect the wire so Rico can't hurt you."

"He'll notice the box is gone," I said.

Her gaze drifted down. "I'll get it back before he does. He won't be thinking clearly."

My throat tightened, and I grabbed her wrist. In a surprisingly fast motion, she yanked free and backed away from the cage. I put up my hands in a show of surrender. "I'm sorry. Don't let that asshole hurt you for me."

"This isn't for you. It's for Vani and the others. You're just the weapon," she said, inching closer again. "No offense."

It made me like her instantly. "None taken," I said. "I've been called far worse things. I'll be a weapon for you if that's what it takes."

She beckoned to me, and I leaned closer to the bars. I hated having anyone touch the sensitive skin surrounding my horns. That was only for Vani as far as I was concerned. But Naela was gentle. She twisted the dial on the remote, then feathered her finger over the needle buried under my skin. Her body tensed, like she was waiting for a shock. Then she grinned and got to work. From under her skirt, she brought a pair of pliers and wire snips.

"What else do you have under there?"

"You couldn't even imagine," she said. "I'm sorry if I hurt you."

"Don't apologize," I said. "How's Vani?"

She paused and pulled away, looking at me closely. "You really do care about her."

"Yeah, I do," I said. "I like her a lot."

Her lips quirked into a smile. "Good." She manhandled my horns to pull my head down to the bars. It took all my willpower not to slap her hands away, but I bit my tongue. Her fingers raked through my hair to expose the needle. Her sharp-nosed snips grazed the soft skin and sent a sharp pain skittering down my back. I gripped the bars as she worked. "Vani's...not good. Dinesso is teaching her a lesson."

A growl rumbled up from my throat. "What does that mean?"

"It means he's punishing her," Naela said.

"Did he put his hands on her?"

"What do you think punishing her means?" Naela said sharply. "She's hurting, but she's a fighter. And honestly, she's been through worse." She still held my horns, pulling my head up. "Are you going to do something about it?"

"You're fuckin' right I am," I said.

Her sharp smile was an echo of Vani's. "Good." Her eyes filled with fear as she took a deep breath. "I'm going to cut the wires. If I—"

"Do it," I said sharply. "Don't explain."

I braced myself, but there was only a tiny scrape against my skin and the distinctive sound of a wire being cut. She let out a heavy sigh and sat back on her heels. "Thank God," she sighed. She worked for another minute, then took a tiny tube from her bra. Her eyes followed mine. "What?" She opened the tube to reveal a tiny brush. Then she applied a thin coat to the wire. "I'm gluing it down so no one will notice it's been cut. I trimmed the wires back under the rubber so they shouldn't touch your skin. The needle is in your skin still, but it's not connected to anything. No more shock."

"Clever girl," I said. "You know a lot about electronics?"

"I know a little about a lot of things," she said. Then she gathered her tools and gave me a look. "Close your eyes, please."

The shyness definitely wasn't Vani. I smirked and complied. There was a pop that had to be a stocking snapping against her thigh. "Thank you, Naela."

"You can open your eyes." I opened my eyes and reached for the bag, but she lightly tapped my hand. "Don't eat it. It's drugged. They're slowing you down."

"You carrying some snacks under your skirt, too?"

Her cheeks reddened. "I, uh—"

"Gods of the outer reach," I muttered. "For once, I didn't mean that the way it sounded."

She chuckled and folded her hands neatly in her lap. "They're going to bring you out to fight again tomorrow. Not at the stadium, but at one of Dinesso's clubs. The Marksman. They do cage matches so people can see the blood up close." Her nose wrinkled. "He'll be there with a bunch of his boys to make sure all the gamblers pay up."

"Then it'll be easy for me to kill them," I said.

She nodded. "That's the idea."

"Will Vani be there?"

"I haven't heard either way," Naela said. "Dinesso is keeping her at the Dahlia right now, but they're not far apart."

Her brow furrowed. "Amira and Karysse will be at the Dahlia."

"What about you?"

"Probably tending the bar," she said. "But if you promise to take care of Vani, I'll get myself and the others to the hangar."

"You're a brave little thing," I said.

Her eyes were sad. "Not always. Vani protected me from a lot of bad things here. She got in their way sometimes, so they'd forget about me and hurt her instead," she said. "I wish I hadn't let her do it, but I did. This is all I can think of to do for her."

I hesitated, then put my hand through the bars. Her small hand hovered over it, shaking a little. Finally, she let her palm rest against mine. "Can you answer something for me? Rico said she led them right to me."

Her brow furrowed. "I don't know. Dinesso was mad when she didn't come back, so she clearly didn't do what he expected," Naela said. "Dinesso put a tracker in her somehow. She says she didn't know about it."

"Maybe she lied to you."

She scowled. "Maybe she did. And maybe she did a bad thing because she was afraid of a much worse thing. We've all done bad things to keep each other and ourselves alive. Do you care about her or not?"

I was quiet for a while. Care about her? That wasn't even close to the right word. I adored her. I wanted her. I needed her like nothing I'd ever needed. And I wasn't brave enough to say it anywhere but in the silence of my mind, but I was pretty sure I loved her. "Yeah, I do."

"Then I guess you have to decide if what she did is so bad that you can't forgive her for it," she said. "But I'll tell you this.

Whatever you think she did to you, the scales are still in her favor. She deserves much better than this place. She's an angel, and if you don't see it, then you're an idiot who doesn't deserve her." Her eyes widened, as if she'd startled herself with her vehement rebuke.

When she said *angel*, I felt like the little Terran woman had reached into my chest and yanked my heart out. "Thanks, Naela." I gently raised her hand and kissed the back of it. Her lips curved in a smile. "Any of the men here you want saved?"

Vani had told me how sweet Naela was. I wasn't sure *sweet* was quite the word for it, but I saw that tenderness that Vani clearly cherished about her sister. I could see the woman who'd baked birthday cakes in secret and tended to Vani when she was battered and bruised. But there also was something wonderfully sharp and deadly in Naela. "Let them all rot," Naela said calmly. "Good night, Havoc. I'll be ready tomorrow."

I watched her go, and I wondered how it was that two Terran women had managed to turn me inside out so easily. Vani had told me about how Dinesso and his men treated her, but she'd been vague about the details, almost like she was protecting me from knowing what she'd been through. Whatever she'd decided to do, she didn't make her choice in a vacuum. Decades of pain weighed her down.

Could I forgive a betrayal? Could I forgive her for selling my ship out from under me and lying to my face for days?

And maybe that wasn't the question I needed to be asking.

Was I so stupid that I could value a hunk of wires and steel more than a mate who had somehow found me even without the Wayfarers to guide her?

Fuck the Nomad.

There were a million ships in the universe, and there was exactly one Vani. She was mine now, and let the wrath of all the gods fall on the fool who tried to take her from me.

I closed my eyes, picturing the way her face lit up when she laughed at me, the solemn wonder when she rode me and touched my face like it was the most beautiful thing she'd ever seen. I saw her standing in that mundane little boutique on a cold planet, glowing with delight as she picked out something beautiful for herself.

Something pulled deep within my chest. It hurt, a pulsing, throbbing ache that matched my heartbeat.

Vani! It's me. Can you hear me?

I felt a sense of surprise, then a phantom feathering of fingers on my brow. The pain in my chest intensified, and I realized that I was feeling her pain. Dull pains poked at my ribs, at my back, in my shoulders. They had hurt my angel.

Is this a dream?

I smiled. Even inside my head, the sound of her voice was soothing. *Not a dream. I'm coming for you. We're going to take your sisters and get the fuck off of Terra.*

I'm ready when you are.

There was a long quiet, but I still felt her touch, as surely as if she was there in the cell. I could just barely smell something sweet, the feminine scent of her.

How the hell can I hear you in my head?

You're my mate.

Another pause, the touch intensified, and I felt a pulse of heat in my cock, as if she was reaching for me.

Of course I am.

I smiled up at the ceiling. When I got us out of here, I was going to make sure she never forgot it. I considered asking her for the truth. I decided it didn't matter. *Are you safe?*

She was quiet for a long time.

Vani! I wasn't sure if I managed to shout, but my head ached with the effort of it.

Another long stretch of quiet, and then her voice was barely a whisper. *I hear you. I'm so tired. I'm okay. Are you?*

I'm fine. You do whatever you have to do to stay alive, angel. Don't protect me.

Another long stretch, and then I felt a sense of relief. There were no words, but a warm sensation, and a phantom weight, as if she was lying in my lap. *I'll see you soon.*

Bet on it.

CHAPTER 25

Havoc

BY THE NEXT DAY, I WAS FEELING BACK TO MYSELF. MY STOMACH was gnawing at my spine from hunger, but I hadn't realized how much the drugs were holding me back. Just as Naela had warned me, Rico and his men came to retrieve me later in the evening. I played along, letting out a pained groan when he brought up that stupid box to zap me just for the hell of it.

With my wrists chained tight, I rode in the back of a truck through the Prospects. The open bed gave me a view of the city. In the distance, I saw the signal tower at the Anchor Drop, which let me orient myself. We weren't far from the Dahlia.

When we reached the Marksman, two men released my wrists and led me down into a cramped back room with a steel sliding door. From beyond it, I could hear a roaring crowd, eager for blood. They were going to get it tonight. I was going to tear a bloody path through whatever stood between me and my mate.

Mate. I rolled the strange, huge word around in my mouth. It fit. And even if it wasn't real, the Wayfarers themselves weren't going to deny me. They could rewrite fate to fit around us.

Outside, there was booming music while an announcer hyped the audience with a dramatic spiel about the savagery of the Zathari. Fuck them. My people were warriors, but they were also poets and sculptors and healers. And they sure as hell didn't put each other in pits to watch them fight to the death.

But Arumas Khel...he could be a savage if that was what it took. I would wreak absolute havoc on every one of them.

The door scraped open, and I emerged into a narrow hallway. Beyond it, the roaring crowd was no longer muffled. I sniffed the air. Cheap beer, whiskey, and something so sweet and familiar.

My vision sheared, and I was suddenly in the crowd, looking down at a caged-in pit. My body hurt, and I was terrified.

The world swirled around me again, and I was leaning against a cold metal wall. What the fuck was that?

I burst out of the hall and into a pool of blinding light. Just as I did, a gong sounded, and a wiry human male tackled me.

It hardly seemed fair to pit me against a human.

When the first shockwave slammed into me, it all made a bit more sense. The shimmering wave threw me clear off my feet and smashed me into the metal wall of the cage. Stars flashed in my vision.

The human stalked toward me, blue eyes brightening to white. "Sorry, mate," he said. "Not personal, but it's you or me."

"Could be neither," I groaned. I didn't know what the hell he was, but he wasn't human. If I didn't know better, I'd think he was a machine. He rushed me, and I tackled his legs, slamming him to the ground. His arms swung wildly, but I deftly locked both shoulder joints and lifted him up. I swung him around like I was displaying him to the crowd. People jeered and screamed. "I'm getting the fuck out of here. You help me, and you can do what you want after."

As we swung around, I saw Dinesso at the far end of the room, in an elevated box with high walls. Light glinted off the silver in his hair. And next to him was my angel, her face painted, her beautiful body wrapped in slinky black. Her throat was marked with bruises, and I could see a distinct handprint even from here.

My vision sheared again, and I was staring at myself from above. I was filled with desperate hope and desire. When I was back to myself, I saw her shiver. Dinesso put his hand on her leg, and she immediately lowered her head. He whispered in her ear, then fixed his attention on the pit. Her head remained down, but her eyes lifted to find me.

Tonight, I thought, hoping she could hear me.

She nodded, and I saw the tiniest smile on her face.

The human threw his head back and smacked my nose, then dropped his weight to slide out of my hold. We tussled in a flurry of punches and kicks. He was good, and not just for a human. Another of those shockwaves hit me, and suddenly he had his legs wrapped around my waist, both arms locked around mine to pin me. His mouth was on my ear. "You got a boat, mate?"

I wheezed, rocking us both over so I was on all fours. "Pretty little jump ship with clean papers. I'll take you anywhere Ilmarinen goes."

He threw another hard punch into my side. "Get me off this rock, and I'll help ya."

"You fuck me, I'll kill you," I said. I bit his arm, then threw him off. Lowering my shoulder, I plowed him into the steel pole at the perimeter.

The breath rushed out of him as I barred my arm across his throat and leaned in. His voice was choked, but he still smiled. "Same to you, horns. Got a deal?"

"Deal," I said.

"Boost me to the top," he ordered. The pit was covered in a fenced dome, at least twenty feet tall. I released him, took a hard kick to the gut, and knelt in the middle of the pit. The wiry man leaped onto my shoulders, and I surged to my feet, tossing him up toward the ceiling. Another powerful shockwave burst from him, and I flattened to the ground, breathless.

The whole cage rattled, and there was a wonderful scream of metal as he tore one panel of the fencing loose. It hung into the pit like a ladder, and I scaled it to follow him.

The crowd erupted into chaos, but I had eyes only for Vani. As I climbed out of the cage, she lunged for me, but Dinesso grabbed her neck and shoved her back to one of his subordinates. Luka shielded Dinesso, ushering him through a door at the top of the arena. People started scrambling over chairs and running for the exits.

Rico remained, fumbling the black box from his pocket. He jammed the button over and over. His face fell. I leaped over a row of folding chairs and grabbed a fistful of his coat. I wanted to make his death last hours, but they had my girl. Instead, I brought him close enough to smell his stale-alcohol breath.

"You should never have put your hands on her."

He was still jamming that stupid button when I twisted his head around backwards, leaving him dead and wide-eyed on the ground. Two more of Dinesso's men drew weapons and aimed. One trained his gun on my new human friend, so I tackled him to shield him. Gunshots rang out, and a dozen bullets pelted my back. It didn't feel great, but it clearly wasn't the result they expected.

"Thanks, mate," he said as I released him. He blurred past me and slammed one of them onto the floor. The air shimmered around him like a mirage. What the hell was he?

A woman's scream ripped through my head, nearly driving me to my knees.

They're taking me to the Dahlia! Havoc, you have to—

Her coherent thoughts faded into sheer terror. Then it was just my name, over and over, in a terrible scream. I could feel phantom hands on my throat. I tried to push it back, telling her *I'm coming, I'm coming. Just hold on. Trust me, angel, I'm coming.*

By now, the crowd had cleared out, and Dinesso's goons were either dead or following their boss. My new ally stripped two guns from the fallen gangsters, checking their pockets for ammunition. He zipped toward me, and the air shoved me back a step. He handed me a gun and a magazine. "Name's Kulikan," he said.

"Havoc," I said, slamming the magazine into the weapon. "Go to the Dahlia. Don't touch the women. Anyone else is fair game."

His grin was the nasty smile of an apex predator spotting prey. "Got it. I like how you think, big man."

Through our bond, I could only feel Vani's panic and pain. As I followed that magnetic tug, I felt my senses growing sharper. Every rock and crack in the asphalt beneath my feet. The air was thick with the stink of exhaust and spilled liquor. My blood roared in my ears. I felt a tug at my chest, like a rope was pulling me closer to her.

The Dahlia was a few blocks away, and I sprinted down the street amidst a chorus of shouts. I leaped off the hood of a stalled shuttle, leaving a dented hood in my wake. Kulikan blurred past me. He never even hit the doors, but they shattered in a rain of glass as he walked right through them. "Hullo, folks!" he greeted cheerfully before opening fire. "Good citizens, I suggest you fuck right off before my big friend comes in here."

People streamed out of the doors, and I dashed in behind him. Two women in glittering white lingerie were huddled on the stage, holding each other. At the sight of me, they didn't cringe, but looked at each other, then to me with a questioning look.

One of them jumped off the stage and ran to me. Up close, I could see she was barely more than a kid under the heavy, dark makeup and glossy red lips. This had to be Amira or Karysse. She released her tight blonde braid and shook it out. It wasn't for the sex appeal; as she combed her fingers through the waves, a folding knife fell to the ground with a clatter. She bent and retrieved it for me. "Naela said you were coming," she said in a wispy little voice. "I couldn't get anything bigger."

"Thanks," I said, tucking the little blade into my pocket. It would be completely useless, but I appreciated the thought and the resourcefulness of the petite dancer. The women of the Dahlia were a bunch of little mercenaries waiting to be turned loose. "Where's Vani?"

"Dinesso's office," she said, pointing to the bar. "Down the hall, then up the stairs. The code is 1134."

A gaggle of men in suits with a pair of girls in lingerie chasing them ran out of a side door with Kulikan on their heels, laughing like a maniac. "I just wanted to play a round!" he crowed as they tumbled out the door. He sighed. "That was fun." Then his eyes widened, and he lunged to grab someone behind the bar.

He recoiled, holding his nose, and Naela popped up from behind the bar with a broken bottle. "Fuckin' hell!" he swore. Blood streamed down his arm.

"Naela, it's all right," I said. "He's a friend. Or at least, an ally."

"Hello, beautiful," he said appreciatively. "I do love a redhead."

"Touch me and this goes in your balls," she hissed at him, brandishing the jagged bottle.

"Wouldn't dream of it, love," he said, taking a big step back.

"Naela, do you know where my ship is?" I asked.

She nodded. "It's at the Dockside. The owner owes Dinesso money so they wouldn't ask questions about where it came from."

"Kulikan, get them there. Naela." She approached me, and I pulled her in tight to whisper in her ear. "Tell Diana the override code. HSK 3947. Got it?" She nodded. "As soon as you get on the ship, go to the cockpit. There's a gun under the main seat. If he looks at you funny, you shoot him."

"I'll help you get Vani," she said.

I shook my head. "You take care of them. If Dinesso has backup coming, I can't be in two places to protect you. If I know the rest of you are safe, then I can focus on her. We both want that, right?"

That seemed to sink in. She nodded and patted my shoulder. "Be careful."

"Ladies, may I escort you?" Kulikan said, beckoning to them as he headed for the door.

With that, I stormed toward the door to retrieve my mate.

CHAPTER 26

Vani

Dmitri and Luka were poised at the door to Dinesso's office, both holding electrified prods. They were yelling about the Zathari being in the building, and the gunshots and screams downstairs told me he was here.

For me.

I barely dared to hope.

Jakob slammed me down into a chair and slapped a piece of tape over my mouth. He waited at the door, gun raised. Dinesso stood behind me, one hand digging into my shoulder. I wanted to fight, but my body hurt so badly; just walking and breathing hurt.

Downstairs, it had gone quiet, but I knew he was still there. I could feel his presence, like seeing a shadow out of the corner of my eye.

He'd called me his mate, and I knew somehow it was more

than just a polite term for *fuckbuddy*. It went beyond the sex, beyond the words we spoke, even beyond the promises we'd made. Something inexplicably powerful bound us together.

I reached for him, felt that big heart pounding against my own.

They're at the door. Don't come through right away.

A strange sensation prickled over my skin, like he was stroking my back. *How many?*

Three. Electric weapons.

Be safe, angel. I'm almost there. I've got you. This is almost over.

Feet thundered down the hall, and then the door flew open. Right on cue, Dmitri and Luka stabbed their weapons forward, but there was no Havoc. A gray hand blurred across the doorway and grabbed the weapon. It spun, and the electrified end was in Dmitri's belly. The stout bodyguard flew backward, convulsing violently. Seconds later, he went still.

Like the drunk idiot he was, Luka peeked out to see where Havoc was, and then he went down hard. I heard the squelching sound of joints tearing, and there was no more Luka. Jakob backed up, aiming his gun at the empty doorway.

Something cold pressed to my temple. Dread formed a lump of ice in my belly. I froze as Havoc stormed into the room. His violet eyes widened at the sight of me, then he glared at Dinesso. "You're a fucking coward," he seethed. "You send a girl to get my ship, and now you hide behind her."

"I didn't get where I am by being stupid," Dinesso said. "What you call cowardice, I call tactics."

"What do you want for her?" he asked. "You can keep the ship. Let me walk out of here with her."

I felt like my heart was going to burst.

Dinesso laughed. "I already have your ship. You're not very good at bargaining."

"Neither are you," Havoc said. "I already killed most of your bodyguards. I'm letting you decide if you share the same fate."

"Idiot beast," Dinesso snorted. "Put your hands behind your back. Jakob, cuff him. You move, and I blow her face off."

"You blow her face off, and you have nothing else I care about," Havoc said, calmly putting his hands behind his back. As he stared intently at me, I felt his mind tickling at mine.

I'm going to drop this one. You duck. I won't let him hurt you.

Wait. Keep him talking. I wasn't certain he heard me until he caught my eye and gave me a tiny nod. *Trust me.*

Jakob approached from behind, holding the gun warily on Havoc.

"You like beating up on women?" Havoc said, his voice taking on a sharp edge. "Picking up girls from the streets and roughing them up? Must make you feel like a big man. You ever fought anyone who could stand up to you?"

I shifted one foot, holding my breath to see if Dinesso responded. He was intent on Havoc. "Ah, lessons in morality from a horned beast," Dinesso said. "Tell me, did you search your soul before you fucked her? Was she good company? She's very good with her mouth, isn't she? I trained her well for you."

Havoc bristled, though his wicked smile never faltered. I carefully lifted my foot and found the smooth red button under his desk. He'd forced me onto my knees under this desk plenty of times, and I'd learn to avoid it. I pushed it with my stocking foot, and a red light flashed.

"Alarm system activated," a male voice announced.

The steel left my temple, and Havoc launched into action.

He was a blur as he leaped over the desk and tackled Dinesso. His gun clattered to the floor at my feet. I swept up the gun, aiming it at Jakob as he trained his own weapon on Havoc.

Something furious and primal clawed out of me, shoving aside all my hesitation and fear. Havoc was mine. Jakob was in my way.

I pulled the trigger without hesitation. Red bloomed on Jakob's white shirt, and he looked down in disbelief. My stomach tied in a knot as he staggered back.

Havoc hauled Dinesso up by his collar, then body-slammed him onto his own desk. Dinesso's hand fumbled toward the drawer where he kept a backup weapon. Havoc grabbed his wrist and snapped it like a twig. As Dinesso screamed, Havoc glanced at me. "Hi, angel," he said gently. "You okay?"

I held my breath and ripped the tape from my mouth. "I am now," I whispered, my voice scratchy from the rough treatment. Seeing Dinesso laid out on his desk, where he'd dished out his 'lessons' over the years, filled me with a fiery satisfaction. I handed Havoc the gun.

"You don't know what you're doing," Dinesso swore at him. "They'll hunt you to the ends of the galaxy."

"No, they won't," I said. "You're a big man on Earth. No one gives a shit about you anywhere else."

His beady eyes widened as he stared at me. "You mouthy little cunt."

Havoc palmed his face and slammed it back into the desk. "I want you to know, before you die, that you deserve far worse." He glanced at me. "Your call, angel. You want it fast or slow?"

Dinesso stared at me, his expression going soft. "Vani, sweet girl, you can't let him do this to me," he said. "Who took care of you for all these years? You gotta talk to him."

"Am I a mouthy little cunt or your sweet girl?" I asked calmly. "It's so hard to keep track."

He was actually shaking now. "You're not gonna let this monster kill your Nesso, are you?"

"Remember all those times I told you no, and you told me that I didn't get to tell you no? *No one tells Nesso no,*" I mocked. Then I shrugged. "Turns out no one tells Havoc no, either." I patted his arm. "Do it fast, please."

He nodded. "Turn away," he said gently. "Don't watch."

"Vani!" he begged as I turned my back and covered my face. "Baby, please—"

A single gunshot rang out, and then it was eerily quiet. The strength ran out of me, and I leaned heavily on the wall. Havoc ran to me, cupping my face. His big hands were too much at first, and I twisted away in pain. He shook his head and feathered the lightest touch across my brow. "I'm so sorry I let this happen to you."

"Don't be," I murmured. His hands trailed down to my chest, tracing the handprints Dinesso had left behind. "It's over now."

He nodded. "We've got to go, but I'm not taking another step before I tell you that I love you. I'm not entirely sure what that word even means, but I don't want to go anywhere without you ever again. You are my mate, and may the Wayfarers cast me aside if I ever fail you again."

Something roared to life in me. I grabbed his cheeks and pulled him down for a kiss. He was gentle, kissing the corners of my mouth to avoid the split lip. "I think you know exactly what that word means. I love you," I replied. "Mate."

He kissed my brow. "Your sisters are on the way to my ship, but we need to go before someone gets it in their heads to stop us. But on the way, I want you to think your filthiest thoughts about me and see how this starbonding thing works."

I imagined a rather lovely image of him in the captain's chair with me on my knees. A pulse of heat rippled through me.

"Fuck, you're a natural."

I laughed and took his hand as we left behind the wreckage of the Dahlia. There were shattered glasses everywhere, and the blaring electronic music still played even though Amira and Karysse were nowhere to be seen.

"Anything you need?" he asked.

I shook my head and squeezed his hand. "I've got what I need here."

There were lights and sirens in the streets, but Havoc was casual as we waited at the corner for a shuttle. Never mind that he was a towering juggernaut of stone-gray Zathari with blood splattered all over him and I was bruised and barefoot. Just another night in the Prospects.

We caught a shuttle, and I simply laid my head on his shoulder, basking in his warmth and the realization that he was everything I had never dared to hope for.

When we arrived in the hangar, Naela stood in the Nomad's shadow with a gun in her hand, while a man I didn't recognize held his hands up and protested, "Love, I was just trying to help."

"Naela," Havoc said in a calm voice. "What did he do?"

"Said he was going to tie me down," Naela growled.

I scowled at the strange man. "You did what?"

"I said I'd strap her in," the man protested. "To the seat. For a jump. Listen, love, you're absolutely smashing, but I'm not trying to put my cock in you five minutes after busting out of this shithole. It's safety, love."

"Don't call me love," she said.

"Naela, it's all right," Havoc said. "Let's put the gun away and get the hell out of here, yeah?"

She slowly lowered it, then drew her finger across her throat, her eyes still fixed on Kulikan. "I'm watching you."

The stranger shook his head, watching in wonder as she headed up the boarding ramp. Then he turned to me and grinned. "Must be Havoc's girl."

"That's me," I said suspiciously. "You are?"

"Kulikan," he said. "Havoc's new best friend."

"No, he's not," Havoc said as he brushed past me. Amira and Karysse were already inside, looking terrified as the Zathari male entered. He knelt in front of them, but he was still nearly as tall as they were. "When we leave here, we're probably not coming back. Vani cares for you, so you have my protection. I'll take you with me and find you somewhere safe if you want it. If you'd rather stay here, then you need to get off the ship."

Amira looked at me, eyebrows raised. I nodded to her. "Yes, sir," she murmured. "I want to leave with you."

Karysse had been brought to the Dahlia since I'd left, but we'd crossed paths at some of the other clubs where she served drinks. I smiled at her and asked, "Karysse, do you have anyone here? Do you want to stay?"

She shook her head. "I've wanted off this rock since I was old enough to know it was an option. Anywhere is better than here."

Havoc looked around. "Give me a few minutes, and we'll get you all ready for launch," he said.

"I'll help," I said.

He shook his head. "You sit and rest. Kulikan, make yourself useful."

Fifteen minutes later, the two men had unpacked folding seats and mounted them to the walls of the lounge. Havoc barely concealed a smile as he moved the spindly silver device that had been a source of so much entertainment, making room for another seat. "Captain, would you like me to find a place for that?" I asked innocently.

His violet gaze found mine, and I was inundated with an extraordinarily vivid image of myself sprawled out on it, completely naked and spread-eagled with his face between my legs. My body clenched and I shivered. I closed my eyes and instead imagined him in the same position while I rode him. His eyes widened, and his jaw dropped.

This was going to be fun.

Don't start a battle you can't win, his voice echoed in my head.

Who says I want to win?

He smirked as he guided the girls into their seats and gently buckled them in. Kulikan took his own, throwing Havoc a glare. "I'll take care of my own. Some service."

"I can still throw you out the back," Havoc said mildly.

"Nope," Kulikan said. "Deal's a deal, mate."

"Get ready for launch," Havoc said. He beckoned to me, and I followed him into the cockpit. Before I could sit, he closed the door behind him and pulled me into his lap. "Diana, begin launch sequence."

"Yes, Captain," she said. "Welcome aboard."

Instead of kissing me or sliding those strong hands under my dress, he just held me tight, murmuring silently against my throat. I rested my head atop his, stroking his sweat-damp hair. "If we didn't have a ship full of people, I'd spend the next twenty-four hours on my knees for you," he whispered.

"I'll hold you to that when we get where we're going," I said.

He chuckled. "I'm not kidding, angel."

"Neither am I, Captain."

He pulled away and stared up at me. "Will you stay with me? Go where I go?"

"As long as you'll have me at your side," I replied.

"Ain't that sweet!" Kulikan crowed from the lounge.

Havoc's eyes closed. "I'm going to kill that little fucker."

"Launch in thirty seconds," Diana announced.

I scrambled into my seat and buckled in. We clutched hands across the cockpit, and instead of the lustful thoughts, Havoc filled my head with reassurance and a tenderness I barely grasped. The windows were closed, but I knew that below me, Terra was falling away, receding into the darkness where I could pretend it had never existed.

CHAPTER 27

Havoc
Three Days Later

I wasn't sure which was better; watching Vani's eyes light up as we landed in the gleaming sprawl of Ir-Nassa, or the look of shock on her face when Mistral met us on the landing pad at the Silver Grove. He was a bit smaller than I was, but with upturned horns and a wicked burn scar from his left eye down to his chin.

Scratch that.

The best part of our landing was watching Mistral's face go from mild annoyance at my lateness to surprise at the sight of Vani on my arm to utter disbelief as three more women piled out after her, with Kulikan hot on our heels. "Havoc, I'm sure you'll understand my confusion when I ask what the fuck?" he asked calmly. "Did I misunderstand the trade? I thought we bought *alcamara*, not a harem."

Kulikan looked him over and thrust out his hand. "Any friend of Havoc's is a friend—"

"No," Mistral said bluntly, without even sparing a glance for the strange human. "Havoc?"

"Food and wine. I'll explain." Then I turned to Kulikan. "No offense, but our path stops here." He'd been annoying but clever about avoiding my questions, and the best I could figure was that he was a fugitive from the Dominion. Whatever he was, I wasn't risking our place here by letting him anywhere close.

"None taken," he said. "It was good of you to trust me on your boat." He patted Diana's hull, then said, "Oi, Diana?"

"Yes, Passenger Kulikan?" I bristled at the familiar treatment of my ship.

"Create a data file for Passenger Kulikan. Record code IILS-897-XR1," he said.

"File created," Diana said.

I tilted my head quizzically.

"You did me a solid," Kulikan said. "You ever find yourself in trouble, hail that code. Ask for the Ghost. I'll do what I can to help." He offered me a hand, and I clapped his arm. He turned to the women and bowed deeply. "Ladies, I regret that I must leave your presence. You ever need me, tell Captain Horns here to give me a ring, and I'll return to service you immediately."

Naela rolled her eyes, but Karysse bit her lip shyly. Then he walked out of the hangar like he knew exactly where he was going. Seconds later, he was gone amidst the afternoon traffic. Mistral watched him go, then gave me a questioning look. "Now, you explain."

Ninety minutes later, our refugee contingent was sprawled around the open sitting room in the shared apartment of the

Hellspawn. The apartment wasn't much, but it was in a secure building with air conditioning, which was obligatory in the sweltering humidity of Phade. Most of the cheap furniture concealed weapons cases, but we kept a proper Zathari dining space, with a low table and cushions to sit on for big family meals.

Huge plate glass windows overlooked a colorful bazaar. Our low table was covered in cartons of food from one of the Sahemnar stalls in the market, and the women were happily stuffing their faces with a grand improvement over the reconstituted food on the Nomad. We'd bought enough food for a family of ten, but I wasn't sure there would be any left after the girls finished. Once they were all settled, I kissed Vani's temple, glanced at Mistral and headed outside to the balcony.

He'd been remarkably patient, but he gave me less than a second after emerging from the apartment before he blurted, "What the fuck, Arumas?"

"It's a long story," I said. I pointed. "The one in the red dress drugged me, tried to steal the Nomad, and—"

"What?" he spluttered. "Back up. Start over."

And so I told him the story, though I left out some of the more explicit details, like how many times I'd pounded Vani into the bed and listened to her screaming my name to the stars.

"I didn't come back here to be a babysitter for your new pets," he snapped.

"Don't be a dick. The men on Terra were using these women," I said calmly. "Selling them. Violating them. I'm not asking you to be responsible for them all. But I would be unworthy of our name if I left them there."

His dark gaze held mine, and I knew exactly what he was thinking. I wasn't above manipulating him, though everything I'd said was true.

"The others won't like it," he said.

"I don't care what the others like. They can get over it," I said. "I'll figure something out for them for the long term, but this is the safest place for them right now."

Mistral sighed. "Anyone coming after them?"

"Doubtful. I killed their boss," I replied. "On the way here, I ran him through the Dominion databases and didn't find anything of note. Far as I can tell, he was just a big fish in a shitty little pond on Terra." I drew a deep breath, taking in the rich scents of food cooking from the marketplace below. "See the one in the red dress?"

"The one who got the jump on you?" he said archly.

"We're starbound," I said.

He scoffed. "Bullshit."

"I'm serious," I said. "It's like the stories old Zhafil used to tell us. We're connected."

"So the sex is good," he said. He shrugged. "You're the one who says human women love the horns. They're wired to like us. It doesn't mean anything."

I slammed my hand on the railing. "I'm not making it up. Watch. I'll bring her out." Without turning around, I gently prodded Vani with my mind.

Come out and speak to us.

The door slid open, and she waited expectantly. "Hi," she said quietly, still holding a little rice bun in one hand. "Do you need me?"

Always and forever.

Mistral stared at me. His disbelief was fading into something else. There was a vulnerability I'd never seen on his sharp features. I rested my hand on her back and said, "This is one of my brothers, Mistral."

She offered her free hand and smiled up at him. "I'm glad to meet you. Vani Adros. Formerly of Earth."

His lips curved ever so slightly. "And you willingly came along with this idiot?"

"He's stuck with me," she said with a mock sigh.

Mistral looked at her sternly, then back to me. Then his shoulders lifted. "If his personality hasn't scared you off, then you must be made of pure steel," he said. He finally took Vani's hand and shook it. "Welcome to our fucked-up little family."

I expected her to make a stinging retort, but she held his hand still. "I think your family is beautiful," she said earnestly.

He was startled, but he recovered. "Much better now that we have some lovely women. It's a big improvement over this," he said, gesturing broadly to me.

"I want you to stay with them until I get back from Irasyne. It'll be three days at most," I said to my brother. "You mind?"

"As much as I looked forward to a meeting with those pretentious fucks, I'll survive," Mistral said. "Fuck, no. You can have it." His gaze darkened. "But I'm ready to move out soon. Viper sent me some intel. He's been hearing rumors that someone's selling Zathari women through Vakarios. Obviously, I have a problem with that."

"Obviously," I said. "Tell me what you need."

"I will." Then he rubbed his belly. "I'm starving, and that tiny one with the yellow hair is about to eat the last of the sweet rice." He slid past me, bumping my shoulder as he hurried inside. There was a little gasp, then he said, "Care to share?"

Vani looked up at me hesitantly. "He seems nice."

I laughed. She was being exceedingly polite. "He is definitely not nice," I said. "But there's not a better man in the universe to protect those girls."

"Maybe you," she said.

I spared a smile. "Maybe me." I liked her confidence, but Mistral really was the one for it. After what he and his twin had witnessed in the ruins of Sonides, he was ferociously, homicidally protective of women. And he might be a dick about it, but he'd keep them from harm at any cost, both because I'd asked him to and because it was one of his few moral absolutes. "Do you want to stay or accompany me down to Irasyne? It'll be boring."

"Going somewhere with you will never be boring," she said.

"You say that—"

She leaned in and tucked herself under my arm. "Captain," she purred. "We just flew all the way from Earth with four other people in the ship. I am going to literally die if you don't get me in bed soon."

I squeezed her tight. "You are a delight."

"I know," she said with a sweet, devious smile. "You better eat up. You're going to need your energy."

That night was utter torture as I slept in one of the small bedrooms with her folded into my arms. With Mistral snoring in the front room and the other women split between the bedrooms, we had to behave ourselves. She was much too ener-getic and noisy in bed to try to sneak in a quickie, so I satisfied myself with whispering filthy promises into her ear. Even that had her giggling like a maniac, and I finally had to restrain myself before I embarrassed both of us.

The next day, after a quick supply run in the market, I took Vani to visit our doctor friend, Evhina, at her clinic. Half an hour with her top-of-the-line equipment had Vani on the mend, with just a few streaks of yellow bruising that echoed what had happened back on Earth. She also found and removed the tracker that Dinesso had implanted in Vani's arm, under the guise of a birth-control implant.

Once I was satisfied that she was no longer in pain, we headed to the hangar and launched for Irasyne. Though she assured me she was fine, I was careful with her. I silenced her protests by burying my face between her thighs until she was half-conscious.

My mood was dark as we closed in on the little blue planet. She had busied herself with making us both a cup of tea, and I was itching with the need to clear the air. When she handed me my cup, I blurted, "Vani, what do you want?"

"Huh? I didn't say anything."

I took a shaky breath. "From life. From me. I'm not a man who can give you a quiet life with a house full of babies."

She erupted into laughter. Then her face fell. "I'm sorry. You were being serious, weren't you?"

"I was."

She offered me her hand, and I took it tentatively. "Is there anything about me that makes you think I want a quiet life and a house full of babies?"

A reluctant smile pulled at my face. "To be fair, there was nothing about you that made me think you'd drug me and—"

"For the last time, I'm sorry."

"I know. I just mean to say that I'm not certain of what you want. I want to make you happy."

"Until we met, I never thought about a future," she said. "I just hoped for a time when there wouldn't be shitty men forcing me to do things I didn't want. I also didn't particularly care if something bad happened to me. If you'd just killed me in the desert, it would have been no big loss."

"Don't say that," I said, my chest tightening. The thought of never knowing this feeling was enough to turn my stomach out.

"But things are different now," she said. "I have you, and I have everything I need." I started to argue, but she shook her head. "As long as you don't get sick of me, I'm happy to sail the stars with you and Diana. This little ship is a better home than I've ever had because you're here. That's what I want. You make me happy by being yourself."

My eyes burned, and I pulled her in close so she didn't see the sting of tears. Even with days between us and Terra, I still feared that I was going to wake up from a fever dream to find that she was gone, just a figment of my imagination. "I love you," I said. "Mate."

She kissed the tip of my nose and sat on my lap. "I love you." I raised an eyebrow. "Mate. It's such a weird word, you know."

"Get used to it," I growled. She smirked at me. Then I picked her up and set her on the opposite couch. Her indignant look filled me with pride. "If you stay too close to me, I'm going to have to bend you over."

"Oh no," she said, flashing that wicked grin at me. "Whatever would I do?"

"If I'm balls deep in you while we land, it's going to be a bad time for both of us," I said.

She laughed. "After?"

"Most certainly," I said.

With a wicked smile, she ran one hand up my thigh, stopping just short of my cock, and flounced off to the cockpit. I was going to give her more than she bargained for if she kept that up.

My playful mood faltered as the landing pad at the small trading hub came into sight. A radio communique began, and I confirmed the ship's identification to the dispatcher. I had to take control manually, landing the ship on the big slab. Ours was the only ship in sight, and might be the only traffic they received here for days.

Huge growths of red rock loomed beyond the edge of the trading post. I headed to the cargo bay, where I met with a loading crew to transfer the cases into a hover vehicle. Vani waited in the ship, and I was just beginning to get impatient when she ran out with her hair tied back and a pair of goggles atop her head. "I almost forgot my glasses," she said breathlessly as she slipped them over her eyes. "Sorry."

I put on my own to fend off the sand and steered us toward the Zathari city of Eset. Despite my apprehension, it was a wonder to watch Vani as she gazed all around us. Even here on the outskirts of the desert, Irasyne was a beautiful, nearly untouched planet. Rich soil and good air grew jungles of towering trees that created a flowing canopy of green. Flocks of massive purple birds screamed overhead. The air itself smelled like growth and life. It was a good place for a fresh start for my people. Knowing I would never be welcome here made my heart ache.

It took half an hour in the zippy little craft to reach the crossroads, where I eased to a halt. Another few miles down the road was the strange patchwork of Eset. Rising from the tree-line were the curved silver hulls of long-defunct spacecraft and new walls built of the white marble they mined in the quarries. This was the largest community of Zathari anywhere in the universe, as far as we knew.

I waited patiently at the crossroads, and a trio of males in well-made leather armor approached. Their skin was lighter than mine, and their horns were slenderer. Something in the water, maybe. All three were armed with wickedly sharp spears. "Outcast," one of them greeted. All three had dark hair, much longer than mine, and braided intricately.

Vani leaned forward in her seat, and I felt her anger rolling off in waves. I put my hand on her thigh and squeezed firmly. "I have a delivery for Weaver Mozeyi," I said. "*Alcamara.*"

One of them nodded. "It is much appreciated, traveler," he said.

The leader, Jahass, glared back at him and then gestured. "We'll take it from here." He and I had crossed paths before. He'd been the one to tell us, in no uncertain terms, that the Hellspawn were not welcome in Eset now or ever. I could have dropped him with a single shot, but I accepted his decision, even if I hated it. Even if he was a raging asshole, I had a begrudging respect for how he protected the people here.

As the two lower-ranked warriors circled behind the vehi-cle, Vani's mind shoved into mine with a blistering, red-hot fury. She felt like lightning down my spine. *I'm going to tell them where they can put those spears.*

Her fury was a wondrous thing to behold. I knew that was love, just as much as when she whispered sweet and dirty things into my ears, just as when she woke me from a deep sleep with coffee in my hand and her mouth on my cock. I simply took her hand and kissed it, pushing back her anger.

I don't need them. I have you.

Her angry expression faltered for just a split second, but she fixed a stern glare on Jahass. He didn't speak, but he frowned slightly, as if he couldn't comprehend why this small, golden-skinned creature was giving him the glare of a hungry predator.

It took no more than ten minutes for them to unload the heavy crates. There was no exchange of money, not even a return of the last set of padded crates I'd brought. The three males loaded the containers onto the back of a hover vehicle, and rode it on the eastern road back to Eset.

When they were gone, a Zathari woman hesitantly approached with a fabric-wrapped bundle. I could smell the sweet bread even through the thick fabric. Her purple eyes were filled with sadness. "Your gifts are appreciated," she said.

"Thank you, cousin," I said. I hesitated and then took a handwritten note in a sealed envelope and a small box from my coat. "Can you see that this is taken to the city?"

She accepted it. "I will deliver it myself," she said solemnly. With the limited technology in Eset, it was hard to coordinate with my sister, but I liked to bring her gifts when I came.

"Thank you, cousin," I said again. "Be safe."

She raised a hand as I turned the vehicle. Vani waited until we were rolling over the desert again before she exploded.

"They can't talk to you like that! Not even a fucking thank you?" she spluttered.

"That's how it is," I said. I slid the warm bundle into her lap. "Sometimes they sneak us treats. Traditional things no one makes anywhere else. That smells like *khar fatiehr.* Spiced honey bread. You should try it."

"I don't want to eat their stupid snacks," she huffed. "I want to go back and punch that rude motherfucker in the face."

I laughed. "I love you for it."

"I'd do it," she fumed.

"I know you would. And that is why you are a wicked delight, Vani Adros."

CHAPTER 28

Vani

WATCHING THE WAY HAVOC JUST SAT AND LET THOSE JERKS TREAT him like trash made me unspeakably angry. Sure, they'd take the medicines he brought, but couldn't even give him the decency of welcoming him home. They were lucky to have someone like him.

I was angry enough for both of us, but he was quiet as we rode back to the ship. Humbled by his stoic silence, I tried to push it out of my mind. If he was determined to let it go, I wasn't going to keep rubbing his face in it. I had a surprise for him, and I had a feeling it was going to drastically improve his mood.

Instead of griping about his asshole cousins, I took in the untouched beauty of Irasyne. It reminded me of the glossy book I'd given Naela, full of pictures of Earth before the war with the Aengra Dominion.

Blanketed in dense green jungle beneath clear blue skies, Irasyne was breathtaking. And it was only one place. It was one place where Havoc wasn't welcome, but there were a thousand, maybe a million other places we could go. A million beautiful things I couldn't even conceive of. I had this beautiful, ferocious man and a whole universe to explore. And if he didn't have a home here, then I wanted to be home for him, wherever we were.

He was still pensive as we returned to the Nomad. The boarding ramp opened to let us in. "Ready?"

"Mm," I agreed. "Where are we going?"

"First, back to Ir-Nassa," he said as we walked up the ramp and into the Nomad. He let me go past, then grabbed my hips. "There's a boutique with delicate lacy things in every color of the rainbow."

"If you plan to tear them to shreds, you'd better buy me extra," I said.

"That won't be an issue. Bulk discount."

"And after that?" I asked.

"We'll see that your sisters are settled. Mistral is investigating something, and I'll back him if he finds a solid lead soon. Until then, I'll get in touch with my contacts for another job," he said as we settled into our seats in the cockpit. "If there's nothing interesting, we'll open the map, and you can pick the place that excites you most. And that's where we'll go."

The ship rumbled beneath me, and I held his hand tight as we launched, tearing through gravity's hold and breaking into the atmosphere. After Diana told us we had twenty hours to reach Phade, Havoc set course and gave me a knowing look. I barely got my harness unbuckled before he was on me, lifting me off my feet as we kissed and caressed our way back to the cabin.

My heart thrummed with anticipation as I watched him strip off his shirt to reveal that glorious, muscled chest. "I have something for you," I said. His head tilted. "Come and find it."

"I do love a good hunt," he said.

The twisting motion of his hands said he was about to shred something in his hurry to get me naked. I caught his wrists and backed away. "I like this dress. Take it off carefully."

"Are you giving me orders?"

"I certainly am, Captain," I said.

"You know that's not how this works, Lieutenant," he said. "I'll buy you another."

"No," I said. I held his hands tight as he frowned down at me. "This is the first thing you ever bought me, at the station on Inan Prime. It's special."

The tension on his face flowed away, leaving a soft smile that I tucked away in my mind like a hidden treasure. He kissed my forehead and carefully untied the closures down my side. His hands were gentle as he slid the dress off my shoulders, revealing the red lace beneath. Regardless of his claims to be in charge, he was becoming well-trained. I didn't want to tame him too much; his wildness was one of my favorite things about him.

"This is nice," he said, running his finger under my bra strap.

"That's not the surprise," I said.

I felt the sudden jolt of connection as he pushed at my mind. *Tell me!*

I laughed aloud. "It doesn't work that way," I said. He

growled and pushed me onto my back, pinning my wrists to either side of me as he kissed me roughly.

"I'll keep searching," he said. As he kissed me, his hips ground slowly against me, awakening the fire in my clit. Then he paused. "Are you sure you're up for this?" He kissed my collarbone, where the shadow of Dinesso's hands lingered. "It's not entirely healed."

There was still the faintest hint of an ache in my ribs, but it was barely noticeable. "I'm very ready for this," I said, pressing myself up into him. "You're not looking very hard. You must not want your surprise."

"Oh, I'm very hard," he said. And he was, that beautiful bulge straining at his snug pants.

Then he flipped me over, so I was astride him, and I unbuckled his pants to release his cock. I stroked him idly, watching as a flutter rippled through him from belly to throat. With the starbond growing between us each day, I could feel a tickle of warmth between my legs that was strange and unfamiliar. The line between his pleasure and mine blurred more and more, tangling us together into an unbreakable *we*.

"Is this my surprise?"

"Nope. But I'll put it on my checklist if you like." I pushed his head aside and raised my voice. "Diana?"

"Yes, Lieutenant Vani?" He'd taught Diana to address me as *Lieutenant* before leaving Phade, which delighted me to no end.

"Remind me to give the Captain a handjob before we get to Phade," I said.

"I will add it to your list of tasks," Diana said. "What priority?"

"Top priority," I said.

He looked chagrined. "Vani, you are a fiend. Misusing my ship for your depravity."

"She's very helpful," I said.

His full lips pursed, and he glanced up. "Diana? Please remind me to bend my co-pilot over a table and turn her ass pink. Medium priority."

"I will add it to your list of tasks, Captain," Diana said.

"One, I'm offended that you only put that at medium priority." He laughed. "Two, you somehow think that's going to make me behave."

He hooked his finger in the red lace between my breasts and pulled me down. Despite his protests about civility, he carefully unhooked it before he tossed it aside. He gripped my jaw gently. "Who the fuck said I want you to behave? I like you best when you misbehave."

I lowered myself for another kiss, rubbing myself along his hard body. His big hands slid down my back, cupping my ass. Then he jolted with a little *huh?*

I smirked as he slid his hand between my cheeks and tapped the hard plug there. "Surprise," I murmured. While he was checking cargo, I'd sprinted back into the ship, rooted through that drawer of kinky delights, and found a sparkling red plug as a treat for him. I'd told him I forgot my goggles to make him wait, and he was so focused on the delivery that he didn't question it. The plug was big enough that I was sure he'd notice me walking strangely, but I'd managed to hide it with my long, flowing dress. I hadn't planned on close to two hours on the damn hovercraft, but the discomfort was worth the look on his face.

Victory for Vani. His look of absolute adoration and

monstrous hunger was enough to make me melt. In a split second, he had lifted me to turn me onto my knees, and dragged my panties down, kissing my thighs as he did. "Fuck me," he groaned. "Did you do that for me?"

"No, I did it for Diana," I teased. "She watched and told me what a naughty girl I was."

"Such a smart mouth," he said.

"You love it."

His smile was incandescent. "I do." He cupped me, pressing the heel of his hand to the plug. I groaned at the rolling swell of sensation. His other hand tickled across my lips. "I can't wait to be inside you."

I wiggled my ass at him. "That's still not your surprise," I said. I sat back on my heels and grabbed his hands. "I'm ready for you. I'm yours. Every inch. Every bit of me."

His violet eyes widened. "Just to be clear—"

"You can put your cock in my ass," I said drily. "I'm not being coy."

He grinned and folded his arms over his broad chest. "Maybe I'm not ready."

I frowned at him. "No?" I'd been working up the nerve for days, and if he rejected me now, I was going to scream.

"No, because I need a snack first," he said. With a growl, he hooked my legs, dragged me to the edge of the bed, and went straight for his target. I squealed with delight. There was no working up to it, no teasing kisses up my thighs, just raw, desperate hunger as he feasted on me. One hand slid a finger inside me while the other gripped the plug, twisting and pushing slowly.

I was a boneless, quivering mess as I came, giggling wildly as he rose with his hair a mess and his lips dripping. "You stay there," he ordered.

"I don't think I can walk, anyway," I said with a laugh.

He rooted around in a drawer and returned with lube, then knelt next to me. "Are you sure?"

"I'm sure," I said dreamily. Despite my reassurance, I was nervous as he guided me onto my knees and gently pulled the plug out of me. I jolted, and he trickled the warm lubricant between my cheeks.

Two fingers slid into me, stretching gently. "I cannot believe that I found you. All the worlds in all the galaxies, and I found you," he said. As he had proved again and again, he was patient and thorough, covering my back and my thighs in soft kisses as his fingers spread me open, making way for him. "How does it feel?"

"Strange," I said. "But good. I always like you touching me." His head rested on the small of my back, and I glanced back to see him staring at me with sheer adoration. "I'm ready."

"Not yet," he said. "I don't want anything to hurt you." He continued to warm me up with his fingers, until my whole body felt loose and boneless.

Finally, he shifted, and I watched hungrily as he poured a generous handful of lube on his cock, stroking himself until that gorgeous rod gleamed like polished stone. My body tensed as he pressed himself against me. He was so big, I wondered if I had miscalculated. He gripped my hips gently and guided himself between my cheeks. "Push back. Just like before," he said, his head pressed to my entrance. "I'll go slow."

I exhaled and pushed against him. There was a hint of pain

and fear that rolled through me as my brain panicked. I tensed involuntarily and huffed a little. "Sorry," I said quietly.

He paused and said, "I'm not going to hurt you. Not ever. Tell me when you're ready. Remember, no is always acceptable."

His hands stroked big circles on my back, and I finally relaxed. "Try now."

I pushed back as he gently guided himself into me. It felt utterly impossible, but ever so slowly, he breached me with the head of his cock. With my body stretched to the brink around him, I felt like I had conquered the world. He groaned quietly. "Are you all right?"

"Yes," I breathed.

"Come to me when you're ready," he said. He was already breathing hard, but he didn't move, didn't force his way in. With a quiet sigh, I pushed further back against him, letting him deeper into me. As I did, he began to move in slow, shallow thrusts. My body went weak as a shudder of pleasure wracked me. The intensity of it was nearly overwhelming.

"You'll tell me if I hurt you," he said, the command crystal clear.

"I promise," I said.

Then he moved in slow strokes, nearly pulling out before sliding slowly back in. He was so big it felt like he would claim every inch of my body, like I would feel his cock against my throat if he kept going. "Every bit of you is mine."

"Yes," I agreed, barely able to speak as his thick, hard cock speared into me. It was so much, but I wanted it. I wanted him to have everything.

His pace quickened. "Do you like this?"

"Yes," I breathed. "I need you so much." He was so big I was just on the edge of pain, but I trusted him to love me, to care for me. I relaxed, pushing back against him as he fucked me. A wave of heat rolled through me, and that dividing line between us blurred once more. He hadn't pushed it, but I was ready for the rest of him. I wanted that magical warmth of his *dzirian* buried deep inside me. "All of it. I can take it."

"It'll hurt you," he said.

"But I don't want to hold anything back from you," I said softly.

"I know, angel," he said, his voice so tender and sweet I barely recognized it. He kissed my spine, giving me tiny thrusts. His fist was clamped around his shaft to keep from going too deep. "There's so much time for us. Let me take it slow this time."

Our mate bond flared to life, and I could feel the burning molten sensation gathering in his cock. I could feel his mindless euphoria, all surrounded in sweet, hot softness. In me. His mind was a beautiful red tangle of hunger and love and fiery devotion.

Until our orbits collided, I hadn't known what love really was. It wasn't only the affection and protectiveness I felt for Naela and the other girls. It was need and surrender and a desire to give him whatever I could to make him happy and whole, and knowing that whatever I gave I would get in return. It was trust. It was knowing that I mattered to him; not what I could do for him or how I could give him pleasure, but the intangible things that made me who I was.

Deep, almost painful tension gathered in my belly, tightening around my clit, and I reached one hand up to stroke myself. As if he felt me shifting, he slid his hand under mine, not allowing me to do the work.

"Mine," he growled. "All mine."

My legs shook as the pleasure mounted, tightening into some incomprehensible blur. I was losing control as my brain shut down, like I was going into emergency mode. Everything was fire and light and sheer sensation that drowned me.

My whole body twisted into a knot, yanked into a singularity around my clit. I trembled and gasped as something fiery burned through me, then exploded like a supernova. I couldn't make a sound. I was frozen in time, my pleasure crystallized in an endless moment that drowned everything out.

As I clenched tight around him, Havoc bellowed something in Zathari, his hips driving deep, cock jerking inside me. His arms tightened around me, until I could barely breathe. His thoughts overwhelmed me, just a jumble of emotion and mindless words.

love love need safe mine mine mine

"All yours," I murmured. I slumped under him, but he gently went to pull out. "No!" I protested. "Stay."

He chuckled against my neck, letting his hips rest against me as I pressed my head into the bed, my ass still claimed. The warm spill of his seed burned in me. His heavy, warm body lay against me, covering me entirely like a suit of armor. Without withdrawing, he kissed the back of my neck, my shoulders, my spine, as if to mark me even further as his.

"Are you all right?" he murmured.

"Mmhmm," I said, snuggling up toward him.

"You are mine, my angel," he said, looping his arms around my waist. "Your body."

"Yes."

"Your pleasure."

"Definitely."

"Your heart," he said. There was the faintest lilt to it, a question.

I turned my head so I could see his eyes. In his eyes was something I had rarely seen there. Fear. There was no need for fear in him. "Completely." His full lips spread in a smile, and he kissed my cheek. "And you, Captain Havoc, are mine."

"Obviously."

"Your body."

"Yes."

"Your cock," I said, barely suppressing a giggle.

He twitched his hips, sending a jolt through me. "Whenever you like."

"Careful of the promises you make, mate," I teased. His eyes widened at the word.

"I always keep my word, mate," he replied archly. "I'll be happy to show you." He kissed my cheek again, and I caught his lips, savoring that sweet promise.

Then I broke away. "And I lay claim to your heart and soul. You belong to me now."

"Forever."

The End

The Rogues of the Zathari continues with **Mistral.** When Mistral learns that Zathari women are being sold on the black market, he goes undercover to find the source and put an end to the trade. But when he stumbles on the lovely Helena and purchases her to get her away from a slave auction, he'll fight not only for justice, but to keep what's his.

Keep reading for a sneak peek!

And if you can't get enough of Vani and Havoc, I've got a little treat for you. Havoc always plays to win, but even he can't maintain a perfect winning streak. Find out what happens when Vani wins a bet and takes control of both the Nomad and its Captain for a night with a steamy bonus epilogue.

You can scan here and sign up to access the scene on BookFunnel!

MISTRAL: A SNEAK PEEK

Helena

ONCE UPON A TIME, I DREAMED OF BEING A PRETTY PRINCESS, like the rouged and ruffled girls in the yellowed books of my youth. Back in our grimy apartment on Earth, where the closest thing to a prince was the neighbor boy who brought me a sidewalk dandelion, that was quite a dream.

This was certainly not what eight-year-old Helena had in mind. Hurtling through space, a million miles from home, this was no pumpkin ride to a ball to meet my prince.

For one, my fairy godmother was a seven-foot-tall alien woman with muscles that would have made most human men cry. With one crimson-skinned hand, she gripped my jaw so tight I was worried she'd crush it to powder. She painted elaborate streaks of silver onto my eyelids and cheeks. Mumbling from amidst my squished cheeks, I asked, "Arna, can you lighten up?"

Her vivid orange eyes narrowed. "I am barely touching you, little piglet."

Ouch.

She applied black powder to my lashes, then tilted my face up firmly. I squeezed my eyes shut as she painted a chromed silver gloss onto my lips. Being pampered was one thing. Not that my life on Earth had been filled with luxury, but I could fantasize about it.

This wasn't it. I felt like a car being detailed, between Arna aggressively painting my face and her assistant Telah behind me, rubbing a glittery oil onto my chest and back so aggressively I was going to have a friction burn. With the vigorous motions, I could imagine the janitors back at my old hospital scrubbing the windows clean until they squeaked.

The cramped dressing room on the Basilisk was filled with half a dozen women and three men receiving the same treatment. Across from me, the other Terran woman, Milla, was already being dressed like a mannequin. Her eyes were closed as she lifted one foot, then the other for her glittering green shoes.

I had never liked being naked in front of people, but being snatched from Earth had forced me get used to a lot of things very quickly. I tried to look on the bright side; maybe I'd spent a very uncomfortable day with an alien woman wielding a laser in places only my gynecologist had seen, but I'd never have to shave again.

Without warning, Telah pulled the loose robe from my chest, baring me completely. "Up," she ordered.

Closing my eyes, I stood on a fluffy rug while the next team approached. I was no more than another piece on the assembly line. Hands grabbed my bottom like it was a piece of fruit in a market, while someone else strung an uncomfortable thong into place. I drifted away as brisk hands rigged silvery straps all over me. Cold spray blasted against my skin, adding another layer of sparkle that stung my skin. They were impersonal and efficient as they dressed and arranged me like a pretty little sex doll.

When they were done, Telah turned me around to a mirror. Painted in silver and wrapped in layers of silver straps and loops, the creature in the mirror was unrecognizable. Somehow, the brazen outfit made me look more naked than if I wasn't wearing clothes. Thin silver chains with dangling crystal drops draped over my hips and bare stomach. My long auburn hair was twisted up around a strange metal headpiece, set with dozens of shiny silver ornaments. I glittered like the old disco ball in Manny's back at home.

I missed my loose shapeless scrubs, and the way I could hide in the drab fabric. I never thought I would miss anything about Earth, but I would have given anything to be back in my tiny apartment, where the air always smelled like stale fry grease from the diner across the street, and I had to listen to my neighbors playing their creaky bedsprings at all hours of the day. I missed the people shouting and the bicycle bells ringing and the late night gunshots.

Maybe this was some sort of karmic punishment for all those times I dreamed of leaving Earth. Should have been more specific, I supposed.

Around the room, the others were dressed in similar outfits in different colors. Tonight, we were the Gems of the Galaxies, apparently. Boss Arandon had a real penchant for themes. His last sleazy soiree featured his stable of captives as a flock of flamingos. He was enchanted with telling his guests about the rare, long-extinct flamingo from Earth. I was still finding shreds of pink feathers in my nether regions, so this was an improvement even if I was going to have a wedgie for the next eight hours and glitter in my labia for the next eight days.

With a little shove from Telah, I joined Milla in the middle of the room. We'd both been snatched from Atlanta at the same time and became as close to friends as you could when you were captives on an alien ship hurtling through space a million miles from everything you'd ever known.

Milla's lithe frame was wrapped in a pretty green harness that accentuated her red hair. She squeezed my hand, spared a smile, and straightened up tall as Arandon's right hand and enforcer, Thenoch, walked into the room.

Wolfish yellow eyes gleamed against his cherry-red skin as he inspected us. Then he tipped his head, and we followed silently. My feet hurt already from the high heels, but I didn't dare complain. I'd learned the hard way that complaining got me nothing but more to complain about. "Piglet, drinks," he ordered. "Weasel, snacks."

"We have names," Milla said. Thenoch ignored us. *"Ashelo,"* she muttered.

Thenoch glanced back at us, tilting his head. The tentacle-like growths hanging from his temples flickered a warning orange. If his dead eyes and furrowed brow didn't give it away, that little bioluminescent signal was a sure sign of danger.

I bit my lips from inside to keep from laughing. In the months since we'd been stuck here, Milla and I had bonded over our common ground, lamenting the loss of the cheese

Danish at a corner bakery in Midtown. Like the rest of the ship's staff and Arandon's guests, we had translator chips hooked over our ears. They fed us almost real-time translations for hundreds of languages, letting us communicate with each other and with Arandon's never-ending stream of wealthy guests.

But the chip couldn't translate anything that wasn't a real language. Once we figured that out, we'd started developing our own slang. It was petty and childish, but some days, it was all that kept me from breaking down and crying.

"*Otherem kufer*," I murmured to her. Her eyes widened. *Mother fucker.*

"If you'd like to continue your games, I'll change your assignments to warm the lap of the Proxilar champion who just boarded," Thenoch snarled, the tips of his slender tentacles glowing red now.

I froze and shook my head. "No, sir."

"I didn't think so," he said. When he turned around, I tried to catch Milla's eye, but she was already drifting away, her face going pretty and blank. I desperately wished that I could get away like she did.

He led us into the bustling kitchen, where four staff members in uniform prepared real food, not the reconstituted mush that we ate most of the time. My stomach growled at the sight of tiny crackers topped with curious blue spreads, thin sliced cheeses, and something that looked like tiny octopuses sprinkled with chocolate shavings. One of the cooks shoved a silver tray loaded with shots of glowing blue liquor into my hands.

"Nice ass," one of the cooks crowed. There was a noisy guffaw.

I wanted to throw the tray of tiny octopi in his leering face, but instead I gave him a coquettish smile. "Thank you," I said sweetly, fanning my heavy eyelashes at him. As I walked out, I gave a swish of my hips.

Empty-headed and easy-going, that was me. That was the girl who survived.

The dining room of the Basilisk was dimmed to a hazy blue-purple glow. Floor-to-ceiling screens displayed the silhouettes of dancing figures, reminding me of the window dancers back in the Trench at home. Live musicians played on a trio of floating disks, high above the patrons. At a glance, I estimated three dozen guests gathered around the ornately decorated tables. There were a handful of humans, and a good number of Vaera, with their pretty new-penny copper skin and pointed ears. There were the odd, high-browed Il-Teatha with brilliant red skin like Thenoch and Arna, and a golden-skinned male with the peaks of bony wings rising from his back. I was fascinated with him, and the strangely cut garments he wore to accommodate those leathery wings.

With dread oozing into my belly, I noticed the huge Proxilar male in a corner with an Il-Teatha woman speaking quietly to him. I made a note to stay at arm's length from him. Just one of those big, bark-like hands would completely close around my neck and crush me like I was made of spun sugar. They had a reputation for breaking their toys quickly.

And in the back of the room, sitting at his elevated table like a damned king, was Vehr Arandon. He was handsome, with impeccably styled bronze hair and razor-sharp cheekbones.

Along the shaved sides of his head were ornate scars in spiraling patterns, clearly the work of an artist and not an accident. His ears were subtly pointed and adorned with tiny silver studs that complemented his tailored gray suit. He was coy about his origins, but Milla and I theorized he was part Vaera and part human. Whatever he was, he was one hundred percent shitbag, considering his swanky lifestyle was bankrolled on selling unwilling men and women to even worse men.

Watching him from the corner of my eye, I began my rounds of the dining room, offering the little shot glasses to the guests. "Compliments of Master Arandon," I purred to each one. It was an elaborate dance, sliding between chairs without bumping anyone or putting my bare ass directly into someone's face. As I plotted a course for my next table, a human male crooked his finger at me.

Dammit. I widened my smile. He smirked in response.

Playing along was the way to go. I'd always thought I would be tougher, like the fierce women in the dog-eared books I devoured. It was easy to imagine myself as one of those fiery heroines who spat in their captors' faces and somehow got the better of the beefy mercenaries that crossed them. I was no quitter, after all.

But when I woke up thousands of miles from home, surrounded by aliens examining my naked body like a tomato at the market, I'd had a rude and embarrassing awakening. I was not the fiery heroine. I was the quivering mess with runny mascara in the background that needed rescuing.

Not that I didn't try. At the beginning, I mouthed off a few times, even fought back when Thenoch manhandled me. I now knew all too well what it felt like to have fifty thousand volts of electricity lighting up my central nervous system, and I didn't care to do it again.

My life plan had changed. Now my plan was to behave, keep my head down, and pray that I'd figure it out eventually. The world had never been fair, but somehow, I magically arrived at the idiotic conclusion that things would turn around now. I'd develop some sort of brilliant instincts that would get me from this ship in unknown reaches of the galaxy back to my home on Earth.

By my best estimation, that was at least six months ago, and I was still on this stupid ship with skintight leather between my ass cheeks and glitter in places it certainly did not belong.

But it was better than being dead.

Wasn't it?

I sashayed over to the human male. A gnarly scar twisted across his cheek, pulling up one corner of his mouth in a gruesome smile that matched his cold, dark eyes. "Pretty little diamond," he growled. He slapped his lap. "Come and sit."

"Oh, I'd love to, sir," I said sweetly. "But I have to make sure everyone has drinks."

"I've got something you can drink," he said. He ran one hand up the back of my thigh, then palmed my bare ass. Revulsion twisted in my stomach. "Arandon's serving my favorite. Pretty Terrans."

"Oh, you're sweet," I cooed, sliding away from him to deliver glasses to his companions before making a hasty retreat. His touch still lingered, like a sticky stain on my skin.

My heart raced as I circled the room again. Milla was delivering little tarts filled with berries while the winged man gazed at her with raw lust in his glowing green eyes. What would it take to bribe him to fly us away from here?

As I returned to the kitchen to restock my tray with fresh drinks, Thenoch intercepted me. His warm hand closed on the back of my neck, uncomfortably hot. Someone really needed to tell him a simple *hey you* would suffice. "The human with the scar is looking at you."

"I noticed," I said mildly.

"Go entertain him a while," Thenoch said. He plunked a bottle of clear liquor onto my tray. "Boss wants him friendly."

"He's already gotten plenty friendly."

His grip on my neck tightened as one black-nailed finger dug painfully into a nerve. I buckled, trying not to whimper. "I misunderstood you, piglet."

"Yes, sir," I whimpered.

Tears pricked my eyes, but I hurried into the hall so he wouldn't see. Out in the short corridor, I leaned against the cool metal wall to catch my breath and compose myself.

Every time Boss Arandon held one of his parties, I hoped this would be the magical night when my luck would change. Whether it was a charming prince or a knight in shining armor with a boner for sleeping girls, I didn't care. I'd all but given up on my chances of escaping on my own.

After all, I only had to think about Nora to remember the foolishness of hope. Nora had been here a little while before I was taken, but she'd also been taken from Earth. And Nora was not one to play along or keep her head down. She'd planned an escape for weeks, even getting Milla and me in on it back before I realized it was a lost cause. Under Nora's guidance, we'd learned the security rotations and the ship's floor plan well enough to find the armory and make the most efficient path to the shuttle.

After weeks of planning, Nora went for it. After seeing Thenoch snap and beat one of the male captives, I'd lost my nerve and told her to wait. But Nora was determined, so Milla and I covered for her so she could slip away during a party. She'd managed to lift Thenoch's key from his jacket without him noticing. But when she infiltrated the armory, the security system locked her in. With all of that planning, we didn't even consider that there were cameras watching every inch of the ship. They'd left her there until the party was over, then dragged her into our sleeping quarters.

Thenoch beat her within an inch of her life. I'd never forget the way she screamed and cried, and then the way she just went silent and limp. Even worse, I'd never forget what a coward I'd been. When she cried *stop* for the first time, I was brave enough to step forward, directly into Thenoch's path.

"Enough. You're hurting her," I'd said, as if he didn't know it.

That was all I got out before Thenoch's massive hand swung out and knocked my frontal lobe into orbit. I was still seeing double when he leveled his harsh gaze on me and said, "Anything else?"

I wanted to be brave, but I was a coward. *He'll kill me,* I thought. And I couldn't do it.

All I could do was stare in horror as he broke her to little pieces. When he left her bloodied and barely conscious, I did my best to put her back together. The medical equipment on board was far superior to anything I had back on Earth, but I knew she'd still be scarred for life. Arandon had taken her on one of his auctions a few months later, and we never saw her again.

I tried not to think about it, but her face haunted me, watching over me through too many sleepless nights. And as much as I wanted to deny it, I knew that I would share her fate sooner rather than later.

Thenoch crept up behind me. "Go, piglet."

"Otherem kufer," I murmured.

Fixing a smile on my face, I returned to the hall and headed straight for the scarred human. I tried to remind myself that he couldn't hurt me too badly if he wanted to stay in Boss Arandon's good graces. His people would grope and pluck and manhandle us all day long to make us presentable for his parties, but I hadn't been used for sex. It certainly wasn't out of any respect for us, but rather that Arandon fetched higher prices at auction if we hadn't been passed around to his entire crew. That went double for his customers, who didn't get free samples. Mystery and anticipation drove prices higher, he said.

As I approached, the scarred man grabbed the tangle of straps across my back and pulled me to him. I lost my balance and stumbled right into his lap. My tray went flying, but his friend shot one hand out to catch the liquor bottle before it broke.

His breath was hot and wet on the back of my neck, reeking of the blue liquor we'd been serving. As far as I could tell, it was infused with something that made people extra aggressive and horny.

Fantastic.

The man stroked my shoulder, making my skin crawl. His

fingers came away sparkling with fine silver glitter. "What's your name, pretty little diamond?"

"Helena," I said sweetly. "What's yours?"

"Desmond," he said. "You from Earth?"

"Mmhmm," I said. "Are you?"

He grinned, drawing my eye to that oddly crooked smile. His features were handsome, but even without the scar, the cruelty in his eyes would have made him hideous. "I was. Now I'm from wherever the fuck I want to go."

"That sounds very exciting," I said. I started to rise, but he banded his arm around my waist. I stole a look across the room and caught Boss Arandon's gaze. His head dipped in a subtle nod. It was a sad state when your captor was the most comforting thing in the room. "Desmond, would you like a drink?"

I reached out to pour him a glass of liquor. Looping one arm around his thick neck, I slowly presented it to him. He skimmed his hand up my thigh, over my barely covered breast, where he lingered far too long, and finally took the glass in knife-scarred fingers. His bloodshot eyes leered at me over the edge of the glass.

"Pour us one, too," his quick-reflexed companion said.

I went to rise again, and Desmond yanked me back hard. "Pour your own, ya lazy fucks," he said. "She's got things to do."

My skin crawled as his rough hands gripped my thighs and spread them over his thick, muscular leg. *Keep your head down,* I reminded myself. *Just survive.*

He kept me there a while, as he and his buddies discussed stealing a shipment of medicines headed for a colony in a faraway galaxy. They laughed when they recounted the story of shooting some hapless Ilmarinen security officer in the belly, mocking the way he prayed to his gods as he bled out. I kept the liquor flowing and prayed that Thenoch would come and find something else for me to do.

"You're quiet," Desmond growled in my ear. His tongue slithered across my neck like a parasitic worm.

"Oh, it's just so interesting," I said. "I like listening to your stories."

His rough hand slipped up higher, cupping between my legs. I forced myself to remain still, like a possum playing dead. "I got something you'll find very interesting."

"And what's that?" I teased. Considering I was drier than the Sahara, I sincerely doubted he had anything I was going to enjoy. Unless he had a ticket back to Earth with my name on it wrapped around his dick.

"Unzip my pants and find out," he said.

"I'm sorry, I can't," I said.

His other hand wrapped around my throat. "You insulting me, little diamond?"

"No," I murmured. "My boss won't let me."

"I'll have a talk with your boss," he said. His thumb pressed slightly into my windpipe, just enough to hurt. "No one tells me no."

I entertained a delightful fantasy of breaking the liquor bottle over the table and ramming it into his leering face. I'd probably die an ugly death, but it might be worth it to be the first person to tell him *no*.

While I was still imagining which one of them would take me out, a warm red hand closed on my forearm. Thenoch glared down at me with those baleful yellow eyes.

No, not at me.

At Desmond. "Boss Arandon requests you not damage his merchandise," he growled. "Let go."

Desmond gave my throat another squeeze, then released me. Thenoch pulled me to my feet. As I stood there, frozen between two men who would gladly hurt me for blinking wrong, the man of the hour, Vehr Arandon, sauntered over. Gold lines were painted along his cheekbones and the bridge of his narrow nose. "Mr. Krix," he said warmly. "I see you've met my lovely Helena."

"A bit cold," Desmond griped. "Not much of an advertisement if you can't take it for a test drive."

Boss Arandon laughed. "I've heard such complaints before," he said. "I'll take it under advisement. I think having this little gem on your arm for the better part of an hour is quite a generous test drive. We'll be at the auction on Erebus in two weeks. You might bid on her then if you're interested."

My heart kicked against my ribs. Two weeks. Two weeks, and I would be off this ship and in the hands of someone who was willing to buy women.

Desmond's dark eyes skimmed over me. "Not sure your prices are worth it."

"My merchandise is well worth the price, I assure you," Arandon said. He offered me a hand, and I took it gratefully. From one monster to another. "Good evening, Mr. Krix." The crowd parted around him, and I followed. I could still feel Desmond's hands on me, his touch crawling like tiny insects.

When we returned to Boss Arandon's table, he glanced up at me, then tapped one shoulder lightly. I took my place behind him, gently rubbing his shoulders. He resumed his conversation as if he'd never left. A few of his guests spared me a fleeting glance, then carried on drinking their glowing cocktails and laughing at his jokes without a care in the universe. I was furniture, and nothing more.

Even if I was slightly safer now, he hadn't intervened for my benefit. It was a power move to put people like Desmond in their place, and to remind them all that Boss Arandon was in charge.

A dark thought crossed my mind. I'd behaved myself until now, hoping against hope that someone would come along and save me. That Arandon would cross the wrong person, or get himself arrested. But it had been months. No one was coming. And I had no illusions that I could get out of here in one piece.

But maybe I could escape another way. I wasn't going into the hands of someone like Desmond, or the monstrous Proxilar in the corner. Back on Earth, I'd been a trauma nurse. And I'd developed an unfortunately grim niche; I had a gentle hand and a strong constitution when it came to women who'd been brutalized. Sometimes by strangers, but more often by men who supposedly cared about them. I knew very well what people were capable of.

I also knew that Vehr Arandon was always armed. He often took me back to his quarters to keep him company as he undressed, then to rub his shoulders and his back until he was ready to sleep. There was always a stun-gun in a holster under his arm, and at least one knife strapped to his leg. That gun was within a foot of my hand right this second. He'd still be laughing and sipping his expensive cordial while I blew his brains out through his ear.

There was no way I'd survive such a brazen escape attempt.

And while I hadn't quite committed to it, hadn't accepted the morbid reality of it, that was the point. I had two weeks to think of something better, but I knew for damn sure that they weren't going to hand me over to someone like Desmond. I would make sure of it if it was the last thing I did.

You can find MISTRAL on Amazon in paperback and electronic format!

ABOUT THE AUTHOR

Despite dreams of the stars, Stella Frost lives on Earth, where she writes steamy, action-packed science fiction romance. She loves aliens with horns, smart mouths, checkered pasts, and golden hearts.

You can visit Stella online at her website!

She also has a serious TikTok problem, and you can catch up with her latest silliness by following her there.

For fun with Stella and several other amazing alien romance authors, check out the Facebook reader group, Interstellar Ever After!

ALSO BY STELLA FROST

Made in the USA
Middletown, DE
15 September 2024

60988398R00177